Praise for the National Bestselling Magical Cats Mysteries

Copycat Killing

"I've been a huge fan of this series from the very start, and I am delighted that this new book meets my expectations and then some. . . . Cats with magic powers, a library, good friends who look out for each other, and small-town coziness come together in perfect unison. If you are a fan of Miranda James's Cat in the Stacks Mysteries, you will want to read [this series]."
—MyShelf.com

"This is a really fun series, and I've read them all. Each book improves on the last one. Being a cat lover myself, I'm looking at my cat in a whole new light."
—Once Upon a Romance

"A fun whodunit. . . . Fans will appreciate this entertaining amateur sleuth." —Genre Go Round Reviews

"This charming series continues on a steady course as the intrepid Kathleen has two mysteries to snoop into. . . . Readers who are fans of cats and cozies will want to add this series to their must-read lists."
—*Romantic Times*

continued . . .

Also Available from Sofie Kelly

Curiosity Thrilled the Cat
Sleight of Paw
Copycat Killing

CAT TRICK

A MAGICAL CATS MYSTERY

SOFIE KELLY

AN OBSIDIAN MYSTERY

OBSIDIAN
Published by New American Library, a division of
Penguin Group (USA) Inc., 375 Hudson Street,
New York, New York 10014, USA
Penguin Group (Canada), 90 Eglinton Avenue East, Suite 700, Toronto,
Ontario M4P 2Y3, Canada (a division of Pearson Penguin Canada Inc.)
Penguin Books Ltd., 80 Strand, London WC2R 0RL, England
Penguin Ireland, 25 St. Stephen's Green, Dublin 2,
Ireland (a division of Penguin Books Ltd.)
Penguin Group (Australia), 250 Camberwell Road, Camberwell, Victoria 3124,
Australia (a division of Pearson Australia Group Pty. Ltd.)
Penguin Books India Pvt. Ltd., 11 Community Centre, Panchsheel Park,
New Delhi - 110 017, India
Penguin Group (NZ), 67 Apollo Drive, Rosedale, Auckland 0632,
New Zealand (a division of Pearson New Zealand Ltd.)
Penguin Books (South Africa) (Pty.) Ltd., 24 Sturdee Avenue,
Rosebank, Johannesburg 2196, South Africa

Penguin Books Ltd., Registered Offices:
80 Strand, London WC2R 0RL, England

First published by Obsidian, an imprint of New American Library,
a division of Penguin Group (USA) Inc.

First Printing, February 2013
10 9 8 7 6 5 4 3 2

PUBLISHER'S NOTE
This is a work of fiction. Names, characters, places, and incidents either are the
product of the author's imagination or are used fictitiously, and any resem-
blance to actual persons, living or dead, business establishments, events, or
locales is entirely coincidental.
    The publisher does not have any control over and does not assume any re-
sponsibility for author or third-party Web sites or their content.

ALWAYS LEARNING   PEARSON

ACKNOWLEDGMENTS

I am deeply grateful to everyone at my publisher, Penguin, for all the hard work they've put into each book in the Magical Cats series, especially my editor, Jessica Wade, and her assistant, Jesse Feldman, who can always find an answer to whatever question I've asked. Thank you as well to the staff at Bookends Literary Agency, especially my agent, Kim Lionetti, for her guidance and enthusiasm.

I'm indebted again to Police Chief Tim Sletten (Retired) of the Red Wing Minnesota Police Department for answering so many questions. Any errors in police procedure are because I've played with reality.

A big thank-you to fellow writers Laura Alden and Lynn Viehl for getting behind every story idea I have, no matter how outlandish it may be. And thanks to Judy Gorham and Susan Evans for being my cheering section.

Thank you to all the readers who have embraced Kathleen, Owen, Hercules, and everyone in Mayville Heights. I love hearing from you.

And lastly, thank you to Patrick and Lauren. I'm blessed every day to have you both.

1

For a second, I wasn't sure that I was seeing what I seemed to be seeing, which was a small, round sesame water cracker topped with half a sardine in Louisiana hot sauce and a slice of black olive making its way across Marcus Gordon's table seemingly under its own steam. I was tired. Was I just hallucinating? I pushed my bangs off my forehead, rubbed the space between my eyes with the heel of my hand and looked again. No, it was definitely moving, sliding across the speckled Formica tabletop like a slap shot from a hockey stick.

Or a swat from a cat's paw. An invisible cat's paw.

I leaned forward, snatching the cracker off the table as Marcus turned from the counter. It was too late to pretend I was just brushing away a few crumbs.

"I didn't think you'd like those," he said. There was a cute little furrow on the bridge of his nose, and a lock of dark wavy hair had fallen onto his forehead. I shook my head. This wasn't a good time to get distracted by how Detective Marcus Gordon looked when he frowned . . . or smiled . . . or walked across a room. I'd stopped by so he could check out a chair I'd gotten from my neighbor Rebecca—Marcus was certain he could fix it—and accepted his offer of a glass of lemonade and what was looking like a rather unique take on crackers and cheese.

"They, uh, just looked so good I thought I'd try one," I said. Okay, that wasn't exactly the truth. I liked the sesame crackers and the black olives, but I wasn't that crazy about the sardines in hot sauce. On the other hand, I couldn't put the cracker back on the plate and let Marcus eat it after it had been batted all over the table by a small gray tabby cat, invisible or otherwise.

"Are you sure?" he asked.

I nodded, trying not to inhale the combination of fish, spices and olives. "Cheers," I said, raising the cracker in a kind of toast. Then I stuffed the entire thing in my mouth, chewed rapidly and swallowed. And immediately began coughing.

Marcus started over to me, and I waved a hand to let him know I was all right. "I'm okay," I rasped. "It was just . . . spicier than I expected."

"Kinda sneaks up on you," he agreed. There was a hint of a smile in his blue eyes. "Would you rather have cheese?" He'd been about to slice a block of mozzarella.

"Please," I said, tucking a strand of hair that had come loose from my ponytail behind one ear. He turned back to the counter, and I reached for my glass of lemonade to rinse away some of the heat in my mouth. I glared in the general direction of where I figured my cat Owen was. I knew he was the culprit. He loved sardines. And he was the only cat I knew that could become, well, invisible. That cracker hadn't hopped down from the plate and gone sliding across the table under its own steam.

I pulled the plate closer in case he got the idea to try for another treat. And since Marcus had his back turned, I leaned forward and felt around, hoping that even though I couldn't see Owen, I could maybe get lucky and be able to grab him.

Not a chance. I couldn't see the cat, but he could see me, and all he had to do was jump out of the way of my sweeping hand. That was the problem with having a cat who could disappear at will. He did, generally when he wanted to do the opposite of whatever it was I wanted him to do—like horn in on my visit with Marcus instead of staying home. And how the heck was I going to get Owen back to the house again? He'd obviously snuck into my truck and then hopped out when I'd gotten here. Could I trust him to follow me when I was ready to leave? I needed something to use as incentive.

I took another drink and palmed one of the sardine-topped crackers, hoping Marcus hadn't counted exactly how many he'd put on the plate. Then I pushed my chair back and stood up, brushing a few stray cracker crumbs off my jeans. "I think I might have left my phone in the truck," I said. "I'm just going to check. I'll be right back." I kept the hand holding the cracker down by my leg, hoping it would be enough to entice

Owen. I knew he'd be tempted to just sit on the table and eat all the sardines from the plate. I was hoping he was smart enough not to try it.

"Owen," I stage-whispered, as soon as I was outside and around the side of the house. I looked around but I couldn't see him, of course. "You better be out here."

I opened the driver's door of the truck, set the cracker in the middle of the seat and waited. After a long moment, Owen appeared, gray head down, sniffing the food. I'm tall enough that when I leaned across the bench seat my face was inches from his. "You are in so much trouble," I hissed. He looked up at me, all innocent golden eyes. "How would I have explained things if Marcus had seen that cracker moving across the table all by itself, like it had little wheels on the bottom?"

The cat looked intently at me and it almost seemed as though he shrugged. Then he nosed the olive ring off the top of the sardine, bent down and ate it. I waited for him to spit it back out or at least make a face. All he did was lick his whiskers.

"Don't tell me you like olives, too," I said. "You know what Roma will say." Roma Davidson was one of my closest friends in Mayville Heights and also the town veterinarian.

Owen made a face and shook his furry tabby head at the sound of Roma's name. She wasn't one of his favorite people, although in the last several months it had seemed like he might be warming up to her. At least a little.

Roma had been very insistent that I was feeding

Owen and his brother, Hercules, way too much people food. And I probably would have agreed that she was right if they'd really been just everyday house cats, which they clearly weren't. Along with Owen's invisibility, Hercules had the ability to walk through walls . . . and doors and pretty much any other solid object that got in his way.

Of course, Roma didn't know about the cats' unique skills. No one did. It wasn't the kind of thing I could casually drop into a conversation without seeming more than a little . . . well . . . crazy.

Owen used his paw to nudge the chunk of sardine onto the seat. Then he sniffed it. He sniffed everything he ate. If I gave him four identical kitty treats, he'd sniff each one before it went in his mouth.

"You're not going to like that," I said, pointing at the bit of fish. "It's Louisiana hot sauce. *Hot. Sauce.*" I emphasized the last two words. Owen being Owen, he immediately gobbled up the fish. I waited for him to yowl and spit it back out again.

He didn't so much as gasp. His kitty eyes didn't water. He licked the last of the hot sauce from the top of the cracker and then pushed it at me.

"Thank you, but I don't think so," I said. "I'm going to go back inside now, and you're going to stay here."

He blinked and vanished.

"Okay," I said, straightening up. "I guess that means I'll have to stop at Harry Taylor's on the way home and give that bag of sardine crackers in the glove compartment to Boris. I can't give them to you if I can't see you, and I don't want them to get stale."

I knew Owen's tail had to be twitching in annoyance, even if I couldn't see it. Boris was Harry Taylor Junior's dog, a big, gentle German shepherd and Owen's mortal enemy—if a cat can have a mortal enemy. When all else failed, the threat of Boris getting the cats' treats was usually enough to convince them to see things my way.

I waited for Owen to reappear. He didn't. Was he trying to see if I was bluffing? Maybe I'd used Boris as a negotiating tool one time too many. Maybe I was giving the cat way too much credit. Maybe he hadn't understood a word I'd said. I was on the fence about how well Owen, and his brother, Hercules, could follow a conversation. On the other hand . . . I leaned along the seat again, opened the glove compartment and pulled out a small, plastic Ziploc bag about half-full of my homemade sardine-and-cheese cat treats. "I'll keep them with me so I don't forget to stop at Harry's," I said.

That did it. Owen yowled his objections. Maybe he did understand what I was saying. Silently, I counted to three and he appeared on the seat again.

I held up the bag. "You can have the whole bag if you stay here."

He glared at me, eyes narrowed.

"Your choice," I said.

I had started to back out of the truck when Marcus spoke behind me. "Did you find it?" He was wearing his usual citrus-scented aftershave—much nicer than Owen's sardine breath.

I shot the cat a look and made a small motion with one hand, both of which meant "Disappear, *now*."

One thing all cats know—whether or not they have superpowers—is when they have the upper hand. Owen sat up straighter, looked around me and gave a pitiful meow.

"Kathleen, is that Owen?" Marcus asked.

I sucked in a deep breath, blew it out slowly and twisted to look at him over my shoulder. "I guess he hid in the truck," I said. "He does that sometimes. I was just going to give him a few crackers, and then hopefully he'll take a nap." I turned back to look at the cat. He'd closed his eyes and hung his head. His shoulders were slumped. If they gave Academy Awards for cat acting, Owen would win. He looked pathetic.

"You can't leave him out here," Marcus said. "Bring him inside."

I could see the gleam of one golden eye as Owen watched to see what I'd do. "I don't think that's a good idea," I started.

"He can't hurt anything in the house."

I gave Marcus a half smile because I already knew I'd lost. I'd been bested by a small gray cat. And not for the first time.

Marcus put a hand on my back and leaned around me. "Do you want to come inside?" he asked.

Owen looked up all long-faced and meowed softly again.

"See?" Marcus said. "He doesn't want to stay out here by himself."

I reached over and picked up the little tabby, who immediately nuzzled my neck, a self-satisfied gleam in his eye.

I followed Marcus back around the side of the house. Watching his long legs move made up—a little—for the fact that I was now going to be sharing the rest of my visit with a devious, sardine-loving cat. "This is not over," I hissed at Owen as we stepped into the kitchen.

"It's okay," Marcus said. "You can put him down. I'm serious. He can't hurt anything in this house."

"You have no idea what he could do if he set his mind to it," I warned. I set the cat on the floor and whispered, "Behave yourself," in his ear, not that I really thought the warning would do any good.

Owen made a show of looking around as though he hadn't been in the room a few minutes earlier.

"You want some sardines?" Marcus asked the cat, who licked his whiskers again at the word "sardines."

I sat back down at the table. Marcus gave me a small plate with more crackers and some sliced mozzarella.

Owen waited patiently while Marcus got a bowl of the little fish ready and set it on the floor. He was careful not to touch the cat. Owen and Hercules had been feral kittens when I'd found them over a year and a half ago at Wisteria Hill, the abandoned Henderson estate. I'd come to town to be the new head librarian at the Mayville Heights Free Public Library and supervise its renovation. The cats happily draped themselves all over me, but it was hands-off with almost everyone else. Just last winter Owen had had a run-in with a police officer who had tried to pick him up. It hadn't gone well—for the officer. Luckily Marcus had been there to rescue the cat.

Owen did his suspicious sniffing routine; then he

picked up a chunk of one sardine, set it on the floor and started eating.

"Does he do that with everything?" Marcus asked, dropping into the chair opposite me.

"Ever since he was a kitten," I said. "You're probably going to want to wash that floor. He's not good at staying in one place." I could hear Owen nudging the bowl closer to the table, closer to us. He might not have liked to be touched, but he did like people.

Marcus rolled back the sleeves of his blue shirt. "I should be able to get at that chair tomorrow," he said, dipping his head toward the back door and reaching for a cracker at the same time.

The chair he was referring to actually looked more like a pile of firewood sitting on the floor. It was an old rocking chair—or would have been if it hadn't been in so many pieces. It had come from Wisteria Hill. Businessman Everett Henderson had sold the place to Roma at the start of the summer. Everett's fiancée—and my backyard neighbor—Rebecca, had been supervising clearing out the old house before the property officially became Roma's in a few days. I'd gone over to help a couple of times and rescued the old rocker from the discard pile.

"I'm not in a hurry," I said, picking a tiny clump of gray cat hair from the front of my tangerine-colored sweater. "I just hated to see it thrown away. The wood is beautiful. It's a good chair, or it would be if it hadn't come apart."

When I'd put the pieces of the rocking chair in the back of my truck I'd thought it would be easy to reassemble. And it had been. Except the rocker leaned about thirty degrees to the left. Marcus had heard me venting my frustration to my friend Maggie, and he'd offered to put the chair together for me. With Maggie grinning and poking me in the ribs with a finger, it had been impossible to turn down his offer.

Marcus looked from the pile of wooden pieces to me, and his eyebrows went up. "If you say so," he said, sounding like he wasn't exactly convinced.

I gave him a sheepish smile. "I like things that have a story."

He washed down another cracker with his lemonade. "This table probably has a story," he said, rapping on the top with his fingers.

"Where did you get it?" I glanced down at Owen, who was under my side of the table, enthusiastically licking hot sauce off the tail end of a sardine.

"Burtis Chapman."

I laughed. "If this table belonged to Burtis, it has more than one story." Burtis Chapman had a number of small businesses on the go in Mayville Heights. Some of them were even legal.

Marcus laughed, too. He had a great laugh. Maggie, who was my closest friend in town, had been trying to get Marcus and me together for the past year. She loved that we were "dating"—her word, not mine. I wasn't sure what we were doing. About a week after the library's centennial celebration, Marcus had made me dinner and let me prowl through his extensive book collection. Then he'd been gone on a computer forensics course for most of the summer.

I put another piece of mozzarella on top of a cracker and took a bite. That got Owen's attention. He shot me an inquiring look. "This is mine," I said. He wrinkled his nose and bent over his bowl again. I turned back to Marcus. "Burtis and a couple of his sons were starting to put up the tents down on the Riverwalk when I left the library."

"Are you going to the food tasting?" he asked, leaning sideways a little so he could see what Owen was doing.

I nodded. "I think so." I was about to ask if he'd like to go with me when Marcus knocked a cheese-topped cracker onto the floor and made a face. Owen's head came up again. The cat eyed the piece of cheese and then narrowed his gaze questioningly at Marcus.

"Okay if I let him have that?" Marcus asked. "It's already on the floor." He reached for my empty glass.

"Go ahead," I said, propping my feet on the blue vinyl seat of the chrome chair at the end of the table. "Although you do need to work on your whoops-I-knocked-the-cheese-on-the-floor routine."

He turned to look at me, lemonade pitcher in one hand. He looked guilty. Owen, waiting at my feet, was all wide-eyed innocence. He could give his coconspirator lessons. "Are you saying I dropped that cracker on purpose?"

"Are you saying you didn't?" I countered, struggling to keep the corners of my lips from twitching.

"Where's your evidence?"

The cat had scooted under the table while we were talking, grabbed the bit of mozzarella and retreated back to my side.

"Owen's eating it, Detective," I said.

Marcus held out both hands, palms up. "Sorry. Without the evidence you don't have a case."

I shook a warning finger at him. "If Roma gets after me about his cholesterol levels, I'm sending her to you."

His smile got wider, and he refilled my glass, his fingers brushing mine for a moment as he handed it to me.

Owen finished eating, took a couple of passes at his face with a paw and looked around. I knew what he really wanted to do was nose all over Marcus's house. I patted my legs. "C'mon up." He started washing his tail instead. "Owen," I said, a little more insistently.

"Kathleen, there's nothing he can hurt in this house," Marcus said, threading his fingers around his own glass. "Let him look around if he wants to."

"He sheds," I warned.

He ruffled his hair with one hand. "So do I."

I couldn't help laughing. "I'm serious."

"Sadly, so am I," he said with a grin. "Let him go."

Owen's golden eyes were fixed expectantly on me. "Stay out of trouble, and stay off the furniture," I told him sternly, shaking a finger for emphasis, "and come when I call you." I got a low *murp* for an answer, which might have meant he would. Or might have meant he wouldn't.

Marcus and I sat at the table for maybe another half an hour, talking about our respective jobs and what was going on around town. It reminded me of the first time we'd sat across a table from each other. I'd discovered the body of conductor Gregor Easton at the Stratton Theater the summer before this past one. Marcus was the investigating officer on the case. We'd gotten off on the wrong foot when he raised the possibility that maybe I'd been at the theater to meet the conductor—who was older than my father—for a romantic rendez-vous. I'd taken offense at what he'd been suggesting, and he'd taken offense at what he saw as me poking around in his case.

Gregor Easton's murder wasn't the first case of Marcus's that we'd butted heads on, but in the past few months we'd been trying not to do that. It helped that there hadn't been a major crime in Mayville Heights in a while.

I stretched my arms up over my head. I'd been stuck behind my desk at the library all day. "I should collect Owen and head home," I said.

"Have supper with me," Marcus said. Conversations with him sometimes veered off in unexpected directions. "We could go down to Eric's Place—that is, if you don't have plans."

"I don't," I said. "But I have to take Owen home first, assuming he hasn't decided he's going to live with you now." I got to my feet and called the cat. After a minute, he sauntered back into the kitchen. His fur was rumpled and there was a dust ball stuck to his tail. I picked him up and he licked the side of my face, clearly pleased with the way his visit had turned out.

"Thank Marcus for his hospitality," I said. Owen me-owed his appreciation.

Marcus nodded at the cat. "You're welcome." To me he said, "I'll follow you."

I grabbed my purse from the back of my chair and

carried Owen out. I didn't completely trust him to stay where I could see him, so to speak.

Once we were headed along the road toward home, I glanced over at him on the passenger seat. He was looking out the windshield.

"So did you have a good time?"

"Merow," he said. His gaze flicked to me and then he went back to staring straight ahead.

"Think of this little visit like it was two visits," I said darkly. "A first one and a last one." I didn't get so much as a whisker twitch for the rest of the ride.

I pulled into the driveway at home, and when I turned off the truck, Owen climbed onto my lap, put a paw on my shoulder and rubbed the side of his face against my cheek. "You're in big trouble," I warned, trying to sound mad but not really getting there. "Being cute is not going to save you."

He licked my chin.

"That would be a whole lot more adorable if you didn't have fish breath," I told him.

I carried Owen inside and left him in the kitchen. Hercules was nowhere to be seen. I ran upstairs, undid my ponytail, and ran a brush through my hair. I was still growing out my hair—with help from Rebecca, who used to be a hairdresser. I had layers with side-swept bangs, but I could finally pull it back off my face when I wanted to.

Owen was sitting by the refrigerator when I came down. "Nice try," I said. "You've already eaten. More than once." I made sure I could see him as I closed and locked the door behind me.

Marcus was waiting in the driveway. I climbed into the passenger side of his SUV.

"Is Owen okay?" he asked as he backed onto the street.

"Are you kidding?" I said. "He had sardines in hot sauce, a hunk of mozzarella cheese, and he got to poke his furry little nose into who knows what at your house. It was just about the perfect cat outing." I shifted sideways in my seat a little so I could watch him drive.

We started down Mountain Road, and Marcus glanced over at me. "So have you decided what you're going to do?" he said.

I didn't have to ask, "About what?" I knew he meant had I decided if I was going to accept the offer Everett Henderson had made to me on behalf of the library board and stay in Mayville Heights, or go back to Boston when my contract expired in about six months. I had until the end of the month to give the board my answer. I fiddled with the strap of my purse to buy a little time. "I'm not sure," I said finally.

His eyes stayed focused on the road ahead.

"I didn't think I'd miss my family so much." I cleared my throat. "One of the reasons I came here was to get some breathing room."

Marcus nodded without speaking.

"My mother and father, and Sara and Ethan, they sometimes tend to suck all the air out of the room."

My parents were both actors. My sister, Sara, was an aspiring filmmaker. Her twin, Ethan, was a musician. They were all dramatic people. I'd always been the practical, responsible one in the family. Moving to

Mayville Heights to supervise the refurbishment of the library had been the first impulsive thing I'd done in my life.

"When I went back to Boston to see everyone last month . . ." I let the end of the sentence trail away.

"It made the decision more complicated," Marcus finished.

"It did."

It had felt so good to be in the middle of my crazy, infuriating family again; to watch my mother and father rehearse, to see Ethan and his band play to an enthusiastic crowd in a little club in downtown Boston, and to play assistant to Sara as she worked out the details for a music video she was shooting for the group. But I couldn't imagine saying good-bye to Maggie and Roma and Rebecca. And Marcus. I couldn't see Owen and Hercules living in an apartment in Boston. But I couldn't leave them behind, either.

Marcus came to a stop at the bottom of the hill and waited for a couple of cars to go by. "I'd miss you," he said lightly, looking over at me as he made a right turn toward the diner.

"Really?" I said, giving him my Mr.-Spock-from-*Star-Trek* raised eyebrow.

He nodded. "Who would bring me coffee when I'm working on a case?"

"And who would you tell to stay out of your case?"

"That too," he said, scanning the street for somewhere to park.

A red pickup pulled out of a spot in front of the bookstore, and Marcus expertly backed into the space.

He turned to me as he pulled the key out of the ignition. "You should do what makes you happy," he said. "But I really would miss you."

I didn't know what to say. Marcus was already getting out of the SUV, so I did the same.

Eric's Place was about half-full, mostly of people I recognized, but a few tourists, too. Claire, my favorite waitress, showed us to a table by the window. Eric raised a hand in hello from behind the counter. His wife, Susan, worked at the library with me. They had twin boys, almost five, with genius level IQs. Susan's stories about their latest schemes always made me laugh. She claimed they were either going to become criminal masterminds or the first president/vice president twins.

Claire's eyes flicked over to Marcus as she handed me a menu, and she gave me a knowing smile. I knew that the two of us having dinner together would be all over town in no time. The Mayville Heights gossip grapevine could spread information faster than a fiber-optic Internet connection.

After we'd both ordered and Claire had headed back to the kitchen, I leaned sideways to look out the window.

"You won't be able to see the tents from here, but we can walk down after we eat," Marcus said.

I felt my cheeks get warm as I straightened in my chair. "I'm sorry," I said, realizing I'd been caught out with my attention away from my dinner companion. "That was rude."

He smiled. "No, it wasn't. And I'd like to see what's going on myself."

I put my napkin in my lap. "I was talking to Maggie when Burtis arrived. He started unloading the truck, and it made me think of one of those little cars at the circus that some implausible number of clowns gets out of. There was so much stuff. It looked as though he were going to set up something big enough to hold a circus."

"You think it'll work?"

"You mean the tents or the food tasting?" I asked.

"The food tasting," Marcus said, shifting in his chair so he could stretch out his jeans-clad legs. "I know Burtis will make the tents work. He's very . . . resourceful."

"That he is," I said with a grin. Among other things, Burtis Chapman was allegedly the town bootlegger. Allegedly, because it wasn't something he admitted to and he'd never been caught. "I don't know about the whole food tasting thing. I like the idea, but it's turned out to be a lot of work. And Maggie says Mike Glazer is"—I struggled for a moment to come up with the appropriate words—"challenging to work with."

"Challenging?" Marcus raised his eyebrows.

"Actually, she called him a festering boil. I was paraphrasing."

He was nodding like he agreed. "I probably wouldn't have called Glazer a festering boil," he said, "but from what I've heard, he has been challenging to work with."

Mike Glazer was a partner in Legacy Tours, a company out of Chicago that put together small, exclusive travel packages for its upscale clients. Several businesspeople in Mayville Heights were trying to entice Legacy to base a package around the town; the foliage was gorgeous in Minnesota in the fall, we had a thriving artists' community here—thanks to Maggie—and the food was terrific.

Mike had grown up in Mayville Heights, then moved away and eventually gone to law school. He hadn't been back in years, according to Maggie. He was in town for a few days now, listening to the pitch for the tour. Part of that pitch was a food tasting and small art show.

I was about to ask Marcus what he'd heard about the man when Claire came back with our food. We'd both ordered the same thing—Mediterranean fish stew— something Eric had just added to the café's menu. Claire set the steaming bowls in front of us and placed a basket of corn bread in the middle of the table. I breathed in the scent of tomatoes and onions and picked up my spoon.

I was down to the last spoonful of fragrant broth when Claire came back to the table. "Dessert?" she asked. "There's chocolate pudding cake in the kitchen."

"None for me," I said, wondering if there was a polite way to get the last bits of corn bread and cheese from the bottom of my bowl.

"I'll try some, please," Marcus said.

Claire smiled at him. "I'll be right back."

When she set the heavy stoneware bowl in front of Marcus, the scent of warm chocolate reached across the table like a finger beckoning me to lean over for a taste. He picked up the spoon and held it out to me without saying a word, but a smile pulled at his mouth and the corners of his eyes.

I thought about just shaking my head. After all, it

was his dessert, not mine. I thought about signaling to Claire for a dish of my own. I could see from the corner of my eye that she was watching us, even as she seemed to be giving directions to a tall man in jeans and a black and red jacket whom I remembered talking to earlier at the library. But I had a feeling from the smile that Marcus had been unable to stifle that sharing dessert had been his plan all along. So I smiled back at him and took the spoon. The man in the plaid jacket nodded at me as he passed us on his way out. "It's delicious," he said, gesturing at the bowl.

He was right. But I'd already known that.

"Who's that?" Marcus asked, giving the man an appraising look as he went out the door. Some small part of him was always in police officer mode.

"A tourist, I think," I said. "He came into the library this afternoon looking to use one of the public access computers and a printer. Then he asked me if I could recommend somewhere good for supper." I reached across the table and scooped up a spoonful of cake and warm chocolate sauce.

"And you said Eric's, of course."

I nodded. My mouth was too full of chocolate bliss to answer.

"Thank you for sharing," I said when we'd finished the pudding cake and our coffee refills.

"You're welcome." Marcus leaned one arm on the back of his chair. "Are you ready to walk up and take a look at the tents?"

I pushed back from the table. "Yes. I could use some exercise."

He got to his feet. "I have this," he said.

I opened my mouth to argue that I could pay for my dinner, but he was already halfway to the counter.

The sun was just going down and the sky over the river was streaked with red and gold when we stepped outside. I stopped on the sidewalk for a moment to take in the view.

" 'Red sky at night, sailor's delight. Red sky in morning, sailors take warning,' " Marcus said softly behind me.

I turned to look at him.

"My father used to say that," he said with a shrug. "Then he'd go into this long explanation about the light from the setting sun, dust particles and high-pressure systems."

"He wasn't wrong," I said as we started walking.

"Yeah, I know. But when you're ten and your friends are standing there, that kind of thing is embarrassing."

I waved my hand dismissively at him. "No, no, no, no. Embarrassing is your father doing the balcony scene from *Romeo and Juliet* on the fire escape. In tights. In January. Embarrassing is all your friends dressing up as tap-dancing raisins for Halloween because your father played one in a cereal commercial and became some kind of cultural icon slash cult hero."

"You're joking," Marcus said.

I sighed and shook my head. "No, sadly, I'm not."

"A tap-dancing raisin?" He still looked a little disbelieving.

"A shriveled, tap-dancing raisin that had no rhythm."

He nodded slowly. "You win. That definitely is more embarrassing."

I bumped his arm with my shoulder. "Someday I'll tell you about the time my mother picked me up at school after rehearsal for *Gypsy*."

"I look forward to it," he said, smiling down at me.

The street curved, following the shoreline, and ahead I could see that one of the tents was about three-quarters assembled. We crossed at the corner, and as we got closer to the boardwalk, I caught sight of Burtis Chapman and Mike Glazer.

Burtis was built like an offensive lineman, with wide shoulders and huge, muscled arms. His skin was weathered from working outdoors and his hair was snow-white in a Marine Corps brush cut. He was extremely well-read, I knew, but was happy to play the uneducated hick if it suited him.

Mike was about the same height, only leaner, with sandy blond hair cropped close and a couple days' stubble. In his black wool commando sweater and gray trousers, he looked like a city boy.

"I just think we'd be better served with something from this century," he was saying, pointing at the tent. He didn't look happy. "And a lighter fabric—a polyester or nylon."

I remembered Maggie rolling her eyes in exasperation as she'd described Mike as a festering boil on the backside of life. It was about as close to swearing as Mags got.

For all that Mike seemed to be arrogant and condescending, I knew he could be kind of personable as well. He'd spent some time in the library the previous morning, walking around looking at the large collage panels that told the history of the building.

"Could I help you?" I'd asked, walking over to the magazine section, where he'd stood.

He'd smiled and shaken his head. "Thanks, no. I was just taking a trip down memory lane. These photos are incredible."

"Take your time," I'd said. "There are more panels hanging in the computer room."

He'd checked his watch and frowned. "I wish I could, but I have to get going." He shrugged and looked around. He seemed a little sad. "Maybe Thomas Wolfe was right; you can't go home again."

"I prefer *The Wonderful Wizard of Oz*," I'd said.

Mike had frowned, not getting the reference.

"There's no place like home."

He'd nodded his head with just a hint of a smile at the corners of his mouth. "I'll try to remember that."

Burtis was standing silently, holding a sledgehammer in both of his large hands. His expression was unreadable, until I got close enough to see his eyes. There was a hint of menace in them. If the rumors I'd heard about Burtis were even partly true, I knew he wasn't a man to get on the bad side of.

"Well?" Mike said impatiently.

"My turn to talk now, is it?" Burtis said, looking at the younger man as though he were something Burtis had just scraped off his shoe. "First of all, boy, both these tents here are just a couple of years old. That canvas is water-repellent, mildew-resistant and flame-retardant. My tents don't sag when they're wet and they don't blow over. When my boys put a tent up, it stays up." There was a challenge in his body language and his tone.

Mike Glazer shook his head and made a dismissive gesture with one hand. "Forget it. I'll talk to Liam."

He walked away, heading for a group of people standing over by the retaining wall between the river and the boardwalk. Burtis caught sight of us. He nodded to Marcus and smiled at me. Whatever anger had been there just the moment before was gone.

"Hello, Kathleen," he said. "When are you comin' to have breakfast with me again? I don't have to wait for you to fall over another body, do I?"

We'd had a lot of rain early in the spring, and all that water had caused an embankment to let go out at Wisteria Hill while I was standing on top of it. The collapse had uncovered remains that had turned out to be those of Roma's long-lost father. Burtis had known the man. They'd both worked for Idris Blackthorne, who had been the town bootlegger back in the day. I'd had breakfast with Burtis early one morning, looking for any kind of information that would answer the questions Roma had about what had happened to her father.

"No, you don't," I said. I could feel Marcus's eyes watching me. "But does it have to be at six o'clock in the morning?"

"Now, don't be telling me you need your beauty sleep." Burtis grinned. "Because nobody's gonna believe that." He turned and, with one hand, swung the heavy sledgehammer up into the back of the one-ton truck parked at the curb. Then he looked at me again. "C'mon over to Fern's some morning. I'll tell you all about the good old days. Peggy makes some damn fine blueberry pancakes." His eyes darted over to Marcus for a moment. "Now, if you'll both excuse me, I got work to do." He headed for the half-finished tent.

For a moment neither Marcus nor I said anything. Then he cleared his throat. "You'll notice I'm not asking you why you were having breakfast with Burtis Chapman," he said.

"I appreciate that," I said. Before I could say anything else, Mary Lowe came around the side of the half-finished tent. Mary worked at the library when she wasn't baking the best apple pie I'd ever tasted or practicing her kickboxing. She was state champion in her age and weight class.

Her gray hair was disheveled and she looked exasperated, but she smiled as she drew level with us. "Hello, Kathleen, Marcus," she said. She made a sweeping gesture with one hand. "Welcome to the circus."

I knew she didn't mean the tent.

"Problems?" Marcus asked.

"Nothing that can't be fixed," she said, her gaze flicking over to where Mike Glazer was standing by the river wall. "Oh, and I'm probably going to drop-kick that boy's backside between those two light poles before we're done here," she said. "Just so you know."

2

"Should I go get my handcuffs?" Marcus asked. I could tell by the gleam in his eye that he wasn't serious.

Mary folded her arms over her chest. "Teaching that young man some manners would be a public service, not a crime," she said tartly. "But, no, I promise I'll behave." She gave me a cheeky grin. "Not that I couldn't take him on if I wanted to."

"I have no doubt about that," I said. And I didn't. I'd seen Mary compete. I'd also seen her dancing onstage in a feathered mask and corset to Bon Jovi's "You Give Love a Bad Name" during amateur night at the Brick, a club out on the highway, last winter, but I was trying to get that image out of my head.

"I need to go light a fire under Burtis," Mary said. "I'll see you tomorrow, Kathleen." She gave Marcus a little wave. "Good night, Detective."

"She wasn't serious, was she?" Marcus said, as Mary disappeared inside the tent.

I shook my head. "I don't think so. But trust me; Mary would be perfectly capable of drop-kicking Mike Glazer between those two light posts"—I pointed at the streetlights along the boardwalk—"if she felt like it. Just like a football through the middle of the uprights."

He opened his mouth as though he were going to say something, then closed it again and gave a little shake of his head.

"What?" I asked.

"I was just thinking that you know a lot of interesting people," he said, a hint of a smile on his face.

I was saved from having to answer because Maggie was cutting across the grass to us. Years of yoga and tai chi had given her excellent posture, and she moved with a smooth gracefulness, not unlike my cats.

"Hi, guys," she said. She looked from Marcus to me and she was almost grinning. "What are you two doing down here?" She was wearing the T-shirt I'd brought her back from Boston—*I ♥ Matt Lauer*. The black fabric looked good with her fair skin and short blond hair, but she would have worn the shirt even if it hadn't. Mags had a longtime crush on the morning-show host.

"We just came to see if the tents were up," I said.

She blew out a long breath. "We're getting there. Mike isn't sure this is the correct type of tent. He's been discussing it with Burtis."

That was probably the conversation Marcus and I had caught the end of.

"What about the art show?" Marcus asked. "Is it going to be in one of the tents?"

Maggie shook her head. "No. They're both for food. We're in the community center." She gestured over her shoulder to the building across the street. "There's more space and more light. Not to mention a roof. Liam thought it was a better idea. People can come back and forth."

Liam was Liam Stone, part-time bartender and full-time grad student in psychology. He was also the main organizer of the group that had put together the pitch to Legacy Tours. Maggie and I had met Liam the previous winter, when we'd been cruising the bars up on the highway, looking for information about who had run down former school principal Agatha Shepherd. (It was the same night I'd seen more of Mary than I had ever wanted to.)

Maggie had charmed Liam to the point that for a moment he'd struggled to make words into sentences. They'd been going out casually for months. She insisted it was nothing serious.

"Where is Liam?" I asked. I didn't see him anywhere. He was well over six feet tall, so he was hard to miss.

"He's just gone over to River Arts to get some backdrops to use with a few of the booths. Mike didn't think the ones Burtis brought were 'classy' enough." Maggie hunched her shoulders and stifled a yawn with one hand. "Sorry," she said. "I'm tired and I haven't had supper." She looked inquiringly at Marcus. "Have you two eaten yet?"

Maggie wasn't usually much for subtlety—getting

or using—but I knew by the gleam in her green eyes that her question was a fishing expedition. She was trying to find out if Marcus and I had had dinner together. Maybe she'd picked up some sneakiness from Owen. The cat's adoration for Maggie rivaled hers for Matt Lauer. I got a mental picture of Owen in an *I ♥ Maggie Adams* T-shirt and almost laughed.

"Yes," I said, sending her a slit-eyed glare. "And so has Marcus."

"I'll walk back to Eric's and get you something," he said. "What would you like?"

"You don't have to do that," Maggie said, running a hand through her curls.

"I want to." He smiled at us, and for a second I forgot what we were talking about. "Tea, right?" he asked. "And maybe some kind of sandwich?"

"Okay," Maggie agreed.

"I won't be very long," he said. He turned and headed back the way we'd come.

I watched him for a moment and turned back to Maggie. She smirked at me. "He's just as cute as a bug's ear," she said.

"'I haven't had supper. Have you two eaten yet?'" I said, mimicking her voice. "That was very creative of you."

"Thank you," she said, the smirk still firmly in place. "And don't think I don't know that the two of you had dinner together."

"Yes, we had dinner together. And yes, before you ask, it was fun. But don't push it. We're taking things very slowly."

She gave a snort of laughter. "Slowly? Fossils form faster than you two move, Kathleen."

I made a face. "I'm changing the subject now. Tell me how things are going here."

She sighed. "Remember when I called Mike a festering boil?"

I nodded.

Maggie glanced back over her shoulder for a moment. "I was too nice. I know that's mean, but he doesn't like the backdrops. He doesn't like the tents. He doesn't like the art show being across the street in the community center. He's even picking at who the vendors are for the food tasting." She took a step closer to me and lowered her voice. "Mike and Liam got into a shouting match a little while ago. They were standing over there by the wall, so I don't know what it was about. And then Mike started in on Burtis, and for a minute I thought Burtis was going to let him have it with a sledgehammer."

"I'm sorry," I said. "I know how much Liam wants this to work."

Maggie rubbed her hands on the front of her gray yoga pants. "If this all works out, it could bring a lot of money here every fall. Assuming somebody doesn't lose it with Mike. You know what I heard Burtis say when Mike was yelling at Liam?"

"What?"

"He said, 'Someday, somebody's gonna turn that boy into a license plate.'"

"That sounds like Burtis," I said.

She nodded. "I know. And I'm afraid that before

we're finished, Burtis—or someone else—is going to do it. Mike puts so much negative energy out into the world. Eventually it's all going to come back to him and more." She shook her head. "Okay, I'm done complaining. C'mon. I'll show you what the tents will look like when we're done."

Maggie walked me around, pointing out where the second tent was going to be set up and how the booths would be arranged. Marcus came back after a few more minutes with a huge turkey sandwich, a take-out container of soup, and tea for her supper. We walked across to the community center, where we found Ruby Blackthorne hanging one of her oversized abstract paintings.

Like Maggie, Ruby was an artist. She was also a lot more flamboyant. Her hair was currently red on one side of her head and blue on the other, and she was wearing a T-shirt that read *Ginger Did It Backward in High Heels*. She smiled at me but only nodded at Marcus. Last winter Marcus had arrested Ruby for the murder of Agatha Shepherd. Even though he'd kept working on the case and ultimately caught the real killer, Ruby was still a little cool with him.

"We're on for the morning?" Ruby asked as she pulled a couple of chairs over to a folding table pushed against the end wall of the long room. Maggie had offered to share her supper.

"Absolutely," I said. "Hercules is looking forward to it."

We said good-bye and headed back up the street to Marcus's SUV.

"What's Hercules looking forward to?" Marcus asked. "Is Ruby going to give him art lessons?"

I laughed. "No. He doesn't do anything that might get him wet or dirty. Although now I have a mental picture of him wearing a little beret with a paintbrush in his mouth." And standing next to his brother decked out in a Maggie T-shirt.

"Don't laugh," Marcus said, twisting his watch around his wrist. "I've seen video on the news of a beagle that paints with watercolors. And I think there was a story last winter about a cockatiel that did something artistic as well."

"I remember that. It sang opera," I said. "You have a better chance of getting Hercules to sing than you do getting him to paint. He does love Barry Manilow."

Marcus grinned down at me. "Barry Manilow? You can't be serious."

I stopped, hands on my hips in mock indignation. "Are you suggesting there's something wrong with loving Barry Manilow music?"

"No?" he said. "That is the right answer, isn't it?"

"Unless you're talking to Owen, yes," I said, as we started walking again.

"He's not a fan?"

"The fastest way to get Owen out of a room is to start playing 'Mandy' or 'Copacabana.'" I touched his arm. "You might want to remember that in case he ever decides to visit you again."

"Consider it filed away for future reference." He looked both ways and we crossed at the corner. "So if

Hercules isn't going to take painting lessons from Ruby, what is he doing tomorrow morning?"

"He's posing for her," I said. "Last spring, Ruby took some photos and then did a pop art painting of Hercules for a workshop she was teaching. He was lime green and Big Bird yellow. Maggie convinced her to hang the painting in the co-op store and someone bought it. For a lot of money. Now Ruby wants to do another painting of Hercules to donate to a fund-raiser for a cat rescue group. So she's taking more pictures tomorrow morning."

"That's really nice," he said.

"Ruby's a nice person."

There was a clunky silence. Then Marcus spoke. "I arrested Ruby based on the evidence."

"I know you did," I said. The SUV was just ahead.

He stepped in front of me and stopped. "Wait a second. You just agreed with me."

"I did."

"You aren't going to argue?"

I shook my head. "Nope."

He pulled his mouth to one side. "What am I missing?"

I held up my index finger. "Number one, I don't want to argue with you because I'm having a good time."

"So am I," he said.

I raised a second finger. "Number two, I know you have to look at facts and evidence. You can't make decisions based on emotion."

He opened his mouth to say something, and I raised my other hand in warning. "That doesn't mean I like it."

A hint of a smile flitted across his face.

I held up my ring finger with the other two. "Number three, if we argue, I'll have to stalk off just on principle and I'm tired. I don't want to walk all the way up the hill."

He looked expectantly at me. "What's number four?"

"I don't have a number four," I said.

"How about we can't argue because of Maggie?" He started walking backward down the sidewalk.

I followed. "Because of Maggie?"

Marcus held out both hands and almost backed into a garbage can. "She has been working awfully hard to get us together."

A rush of heat rose in my face. "You know?"

The hint of a smile turned into a full one. "Kathleen, Owen and Hercules probably know. Maggie hasn't exactly been subtle."

The cats did know, but I was pretty sure that had more to do with the fact that they weren't exactly typical house cats than it did with Maggie's lack of subtlety.

"I'm sorry," I said. "She played matchmaker with Roma and Eddie—indirectly—and I think now she wants everyone to have a happily ever after." The moment the words were out, I was sorry I'd said them. "I don't mean I think that you're some kind of prince on a white horse," I added. "Or even not on a horse. Or even a prince . . . not that you're not a great guy." I was babbling.

Marcus stopped walking so suddenly, I smacked into him, both of my hands landing flat on his chest. It was a very nice chest, broad and manly. I sucked in a deep breath. And he did smell good.

I gave myself a mental smack. What the heck was wrong with me?

Marcus put his hands on my shoulders. "It's okay," he said. "I know what you mean."

We stood there looking at each other like we were caught in a movie moment, the point where the hero gazes deeply into the heroine's eyes and then sweeps her into a passionate kiss, so passionate that one of her feet comes off the ground.

We didn't do that.

Marcus let go of my shoulders and I took my hands off his chest, trying not to act as flustered as I felt. We were standing next to the SUV. He unlocked the door for me and walked around to the driver's side.

On the way up the hill, we talked about all the efforts to bring more tourists to Mayville Heights in the traditional off-season. By the time Marcus pulled into my driveway, the awkwardness I'd felt on the sidewalk was gone. He walked me to the back door, and I thanked him for dinner. He smiled, told me he'd talk to me soon and walked back around the side of the house. No movie-moment kiss, not even a peck on the cheek. As I unlocked the porch door, I couldn't help thinking that Maggie was right: Fossils formed faster than the relationship between Marcus and me.

Hercules woke me before the alarm the next morning. I opened my eyes to see his black-and-white face next to mine as he gently batted me with one paw.

I yawned. "I'm awake," I said groggily, rolling over onto my back.

Hercules took a swipe at the blankets and meowed at me. Translation: "Get up now." If he could have figured out how to do it, I was sure he would have been pulling the blankets off of me. Did he somehow understand that we were going to see Ruby this morning?

I stretched and sat up. Hercules dropped back down to all fours. "Are you ready for your photo session?" I asked, pushing my hair off my face. He immediately took a pass at his own furry black-and-white face with one paw. Okay, maybe he did know where we were going.

Hercules was sitting in front of the refrigerator and Owen was under the table when I went down to the kitchen. I started the coffeemaker and then gave the cats their breakfast. Owen used one paw to push his dish across the floor so there was a good three feet of space between him and his brother.

Clearly he was in a mood about something. It was almost as if he were . . . jealous?

No. As special as both cats were, there was no way Owen understood that Hercules was posing for Ruby again this morning.

Owen took a bite of food from his bowl, set it on the floor and shot Herc a look. At the same time, he made a sound in the back of his throat that sounded an awful lot like a disgruntled *hmpft*.

I could accept that Owen had the ability to make himself disappear. Strangely, it was harder to believe that he was in a snit because Hercules was going to have his portrait painted.

I let him sulk while I had my own breakfast. As soon as Hercules was done eating, he began an elaborate face-washing routine. Even though Owen seemed to be ignoring Herc, I saw him sneak little peeks in his brother's direction. And in return, Hercules stretched a couple of times and casually eyed Owen.

I put my dishes in the sink and started putting together what Maggie called one of my clean-out-the-refrigerator salads.

"I could have gotten a gerbil," I said as I opened containers to see what I had for leftovers. "Gerbils are cute and furry. They don't shed on the furniture, and they never have sardine breath." The boys were too busy ignoring each other to pay any attention to me.

I was trying to figure out what else I could add to the bowl when I heard cat grumbling behind me. Swinging around, I saw Hercules and Owen, whisker-to-whisker, glaring at each other.

"Hey!" I said sharply, reaching for the kitchen tap sprayer. Two furry heads swiveled in my direction. "I know how to use this, and I will. At this distance, I could knock a sardine cracker crumb off either of your chins. Would you two like me to demonstrate?"

They looked at each other again; then, as though some unspoken signal had passed between them, both cats sat down.

"Wise choice." I let go of the tap, wiped my hands and walked around the table. "Owen," I said.

He looked up at me, for once not trying any of his I'm-so-cute tricks. "Ruby is going to do a painting of Hercules."

He made that grumbly sound again. I held up a finger, feeling slightly foolish. On the other hand, I was well aware that Owen in a snit was more than capable of strewing Fred the Funky Chicken parts all over the house.

"It's going to be auctioned off for charity—for cats that don't have any homes, or any catnip chickens to chew on." I tried to look serious and shook my head as I said the part about the chickens, grateful that no one without fur could hear me.

Owen seemed to be considering what I was saying. Or he could have been thinking about catnip chickens.

"And you." I pointed at Hercules. His green eyes focused on my face. "This is for charity. As talented as Ruby is, your portrait won't be going on exhibit in the Guggenheim Museum." I held up my thumb and index finger about half an inch apart. "Try just a little more humility."

I went back to my salad. After a minute, Owen came over and rubbed against my leg. "I love you, too," I said, as he headed for the living room.

A soft meow came from the direction of the refrigerator. "Yes, and you," I told Hercules.

Owen hadn't reappeared by the time we were ready to leave. I'd emptied the litter box, filled his water dish and left a little stack of sardine crackers beside it. I swung the cat carrier bag—which also doubled as a tote for my tai chi shoes—up onto my shoulder, locked the door and headed out to the truck.

Hercules poked his head out of the top of the bag as I drove down the hill, but he didn't bother climbing out. I parked in Maggie's slot in the small lot behind the River Arts building—she'd given me the okay. Hercules and I were a little early. Ruby's truck wasn't in her place.

I grabbed the cat, got out and locked the truck. Then I walked over to the side of the building and looked down the street toward the boardwalk. Both tents were up now, and I wondered if Burtis and Mike had come to some kind of agreement about the setup.

The carrier wiggled against my hip, and Hercules stuck his head out again. "Ruby should be here any minute," I said.

He looked around, then focused on the tents over on the grass, and his green eyes narrowed. He shifted in the bag, and before I realized what he was doing, he jumped out and started purposefully down the street along the side of the arts center.

"Hercules, get back here!" I shouted. I started after him, but he was already at the curb. He looked both ways, crossed to the other side and then continued down the hill, intent, it seemed, on checking out the tents.

I had to wait for two cars to pass before I could follow. By then, he'd made it to Main Street. Again he looked for cars and then trotted across the street. My heart was pounding like a Caribbean steel band in my chest. I ran, yelling for the cat, but he didn't even break stride.

When he reached the first tent, Hercules looked back over his shoulder at me, then walked right through the heavy canvas panel and disappeared inside. I was maybe half a minute behind him. I had to duck around the tent flap because I couldn't just pass through it.

"Hercules, wherever you are, get over here right now!" I called, waiting for my eyes to adjust to the darkness inside the canvas structure before I started looking for him.

Turns out I didn't need to look for the cat at all. He was sitting on the grass next to a plastic lawn chair. Mike Glazer was in the chair. Even in the dim light, I was almost positive that the man was dead.

3

Hercules looked over at me and meowed.

"Yes, I see him," I said. I let the bag slip from my shoulder onto the grass and made my way carefully over to where the body was slumped in the white resin chair. A square metal table sat maybe four feet or so away, a tangle of dark fabric piled on top.

Mike's eyes were closed, and his head sagged to one side. I knew he was gone even before I felt for his pulse, but I swallowed down the sour taste at the back of my throat and touched the side of his neck with two fingers just to be certain. His skin was cold and mottled and I couldn't feel the thrum of a heartbeat.

I closed my eyes for a moment and mentally wished his spirit safe passage, and then I straightened up and looked down at Hercules, who was sitting patiently at my feet. "We have to call the police," I told the little tuxedo cat.

Hercules picked his way carefully back across the

grass to where I'd dropped the carrier and climbed inside. I followed him, trying to stay in my original footprints on the grass. I grabbed the shoulder strap of the bag and stepped back outside.

Ruby was across the street on the sidewalk, looking up and down, probably wondering where I was. I pulled out my cell phone and dialed 911, and when she looked in my direction, raised a hand in recognition. She started over to me.

"Admiring Burtis's handiwork?" she asked with a smile as she reached the curb. Her red and blue hair was pulled back into a short braid, and she was wearing earrings only in the piercings in her left ear.

Something in my expression as I ended the call must have told her there was a problem. "Kathleen, is something wrong?" she asked, two frown lines appearing between her eyes.

I looked back over my shoulder at the tent. "Mike Glazer's . . . dead."

The color drained out of her face. "Good dog," she said softly, closing her eyes for a moment. "Have you called the police?" she asked when she opened them again.

I held up my phone. "I just did."

Ruby crossed one arm over her midsection. "Have you called Detective Gordon? I know the two of you are . . . friends."

I exhaled slowly. I had been planning to call Marcus.

"I think you should."

I punched in his number from memory, thinking I should program it into my phone.

He answered on the fourth ring. "Hi, Kathleen," he said. "I already know, and I'm on my way. Are you all right?"

"I'm fine," I said.

"Stay where you are. There's a cruiser on the way, and I'll be there in about five minutes." He ended the conversation, and I put my phone back in my pocket.

Ruby had been staring out at the water, but she looked back at me. "Ruby, could you take Hercules over to your studio?" I asked. I didn't want him getting out of the bag again, or even worse, demonstrating his walking through walls—or canvas tents—skills to the Mayville Heights police department.

I put my hand on the bag, and Hercules meowed from inside. "As long as you don't touch him, you'll be fine."

"Sure," she said.

I handed over the carrier and cat. Ruby headed back to River Arts, holding the bag out in front of her body by the strap as though it might spontaneously combust.

A couple of minutes later, a police car came down the street, lights flashing but siren silent. It stopped nose-in at the curb. Officer Derek Craig got out of the driver's side. According to gossip around town, the young policeman had applied to the University of Minnesota for winter admission. He'd been reading everything we had or had been able to request about the law and law school for months, so I suspected the rumors were true.

The other officer, Stephen Keller, was a little older than Derek. His serious expression and straight-backed posture made me think he'd been in the military before he'd become a police officer.

They both nodded at me.

"He's in that tent, in . . . in a chair," I said, gesturing behind me.

Officer Keller moved past me, to check on the body. Derek Craig took a couple of steps closer. "Good morning, Ms. Paulson," he said. "What happened? How did you find the body?"

Before I could answer, I saw Marcus's SUV at the corner. He pulled onto the street, swung around and slid in next to the cruiser. He got out from behind the wheel, and I was both relieved to see him and a little worried that he was going to give me a hard time. He came across the grass in a couple of long strides. He was wearing dark gray trousers and a black and gray tweedy sport coat over a white shirt and plum-colored tie. He looked good.

"Give me a second," he said.

I nodded.

He took a couple of steps away from me with Derek. The other police officer came out of the tent then and joined them. Marcus spoke briefly to the younger man, clearly giving him some kind of instructions, and then he followed Officer Keller back into the tent, pulling on a pair of latex gloves as he went.

I stayed where I was, hands in my pockets, staring out over the water until Marcus came back out and walked over to me.

"What happened?" he asked, peeling off the thin purple gloves.

"I came down to meet Ruby." I gestured across the street to the River Arts Center. "I was a bit early and she wasn't there."

He nodded, but didn't say anything.

"I had Hercules with me and, as we started for the building, he jumped out of the carrier."

"And?"

"And he ran down the hill and across both streets." I put my hand back in my jacket pocket.

Marcus exhaled softly. "Kathleen, don't tell me your cat discovered the body."

"I'm sorry," I said. "Cats have a highly evolved sense of smell—a lot more sensitive than ours."

His gaze automatically went to the studio building, one street up, before he focused again on me. "You think that Hercules knew there was a dead body over here a block and a half away?" Marcus's tone told me it wasn't what he thought.

"I know he did," I said. "He crossed two streets and came directly to the tent."

"What did you do?"

"I followed him. When I saw . . . the body, I checked for a pulse; then I called nine-one-one. Ruby had arrived by then. I gave her Hercules and called you. Then I just waited." The muscles in my shoulders were getting tighter, and I could hear an edge in my voice.

"Did Ruby go inside the tent?" Marcus asked. He wasn't writing any of our conversation down, but I knew he'd remember every word. Because of his dyslexia, he made fewer notes than most police officers.

I shook my head. "No. She didn't come any closer

than the curb. She didn't see anything. She didn't touch anything." I took a deep breath and slowly let it out. "I felt for a pulse at . . . Mike's neck. I didn't touch anything else." I held out my hands, palms down, and then rolled them over so he could see them. "I don't think Hercules touched anything, but I don't know for sure."

More vehicles were arriving. Marcus glanced past me, and then his gaze settled on my face again. "Where did Ruby go? Her studio?"

I nodded.

"Okay, wait for me there. I shouldn't be very long." His expression softened, just a little. "Please?" he added.

"All right," I said. I crossed the street, glancing back when I reached the sidewalk on the other side in time to see Marcus go back inside the tent.

Ruby had left the back door open. I climbed the stairs to her top-floor studio, stopping in the doorway to watch her take shots of Hercules. He was sitting on a long worktable in the middle of the room while Ruby snapped photos, giving the cat directions, complete with hand signals—which for the most part he seemed to be following.

It didn't really surprise me. Hercules couldn't spontaneously disappear the way Owen did. His "talent" was walking through walls—and doors. It didn't really seem that big of a stretch that he could strike a few poses for the camera. Or catch the scent of a dead body across the street.

I leaned against the doorframe and watched Ruby work until she straightened up and saw me. "Hey,

Kathleen," she said. "C'mon in." She set the camera on the table and massaged the back of her neck with one hand. "I went ahead and took some pictures. I don't mean to be insensitive, but the auction is just a few weeks away." She glanced at the windows overlooking the street. "I can't do anything for Mike Glazer," she said quietly, "but maybe I can help save some cats."

"It's not insensitive," I said. "It isn't going to help anyone if you don't do the painting for the auction."

Ruby bent down and reached for the fabric tote bag on the floor by her feet. Hercules didn't so much as flick an eyelash in my direction. All his attention was focused on Ruby.

She pulled a little brown and yellow box out of her bag, and he wrinkled his nose and sniffed. "They're organic cat treats," she said. "Roma said they'd be okay."

"Go ahead," I said.

Ruby poured a little pile of what looked like fish-shaped crackers on the table. Hercules meowed his thanks and dipped his head to eat. After the first cracker, he made a rumbly sigh of satisfaction deep in his throat.

I grinned at Ruby. "I think you're his new best friend."

She grinned back at me. "Fine with me." Then her expression grew serious. "Did Detective Gordon show up?"

I nodded and looked around for the cat carrier. "He's coming over in a few minutes. I'm going to take Hercules and go wait down by the door for him."

Hercules put one paw on top of the dwindling pile of cat treats and shot me a warning glare.

Which Ruby saw. "He's not going anywhere," she said. "And you don't have to either."

"I know Marcus isn't one of your favorite people . . ," I began.

"No, he isn't," Ruby said, folding her arms over her chest. "But you are, and I like the furry guy, too." She inclined her head in the cat's direction.

Herc gave her an adoring look and dropped his head over his food again.

Ruby shrugged. "And I figure it's not really good karma to keep on holding a grudge." She smiled then. "So help me choose which photo of Hercules to use."

We had the choice of photos narrowed down to three when Marcus knocked on the studio door.

Ruby got to her feet. "Come in, Detective," she said. Her voice was formal, but not unwelcoming.

Marcus came into the room as far as the center worktable. Hercules gave him a curious look and went back to washing his tail.

"I have a couple of questions, if you don't mind," Marcus said.

I wondered what he'd do if Ruby said she did mind.

But she didn't. "It's all right," she said, dropping back down onto the wooden stool where she'd been sitting before he knocked.

"Where was Kathleen when you got here?" he asked.

"Across the street, standing on the grass in front of the tents, talking on her cell phone."

Marcus gave an almost imperceptible nod. "What did you do?"

Ruby twisted the half-dozen narrow cord bracelets on her right arm around her wrist. "I walked over to her. When I got close, I could tell by her expression that something was wrong. She told me she'd found Mike Glazer's body in the tent and she'd already called nine-one-one."

"Did you go see the body for yourself?"

She shook her head. "No. Kathleen's not the kind of person who would make something like that up. I got the cat carrier from her and brought Hercules over here."

At the sound of his name, Herc looked over at Marcus and meowed.

I thought I saw something close to a smile cross Marcus's face. He looked at me. "Kathleen, I need to look at his paws," he said.

"Sure," I said, getting to my feet. "What are you looking for? He's already washed the front two."

"Does Hercules need a lawyer?" Ruby asked. Her expression was serious except for the gleam in her eyes.

Before Marcus could answer, the cat looked at him and meowed loudly again.

"I think he just waived his right to counsel, at least for now," I said.

"I just want to make sure he didn't pick up anything on a paw that might be evidence," Marcus explained.

I held up Hercules's paws one at a time, and Marcus looked each one over carefully while the cat, in turn, seemed to be intently studying the detective's face.

"Thank you," Marcus said when he was finished, and it almost seemed as though he were directing the words more to Hercules than to me.

"Do you need anything else?" I asked. I'd almost asked if he had any questions for the cat.

He shook his head. "That's it for now." He leaned sideways to look around me. "Thank you," he said to Ruby.

"You're welcome," she said.

"I'll talk to you later," Marcus said softly to me.

I nodded, and he left. I spent a few more minutes with Ruby, and then I nudged Hercules back into the bag. I had just enough time to get back up the hill and get dressed for work before it was time to open the library.

As soon as I pulled out of the parking lot, Herc poked his black-and-white head out of the bag, followed by one paw and then the other.

"How did you know Mike Glazer's body was in the tent?" I asked when we got to the stop sign at the corner.

The cat wrinkled his nose and his whiskers twitched.

"That's what I thought," I said, flicking on my turn signal and heading up Mountain Road. "Did you see anything—or anyone?" I shot a quick glance to the right just in time to see him put a paw over his face and duck his head. I had no idea what he meant—or if he'd even understood the question. Between their unique, magical talents and their ability to listen intently, it was easy to forget that Hercules and Owen were still just cats.

On the other hand, every time I'd gotten mixed up in one of Marcus's cases, they seemed to as well. Each time, the boys had found something that had helped me figure out the killer's identity. Maybe it was all a coincidence. Maybe.

There was no sign of Owen when we got home. I changed, grabbed the lunch I'd made earlier and drove down to the library. Susan was coming up the street as I pulled into the parking lot, and she waited for me at the bottom of the library steps. She was wearing her black cat's-eye glasses, and her hair was in its usual Pebbles Flintstone updo, secured with a small cocktail fork. Sometimes I wondered if the twins did her hair every morning.

"Good morning," she said, a huge smile lighting up her face.

I smiled back. "Good morning." I went ahead of her up the stairs, opened the doors and disarmed the alarm system.

Susan moved past me to snap on the lights. "So how was your night?" Her knowing tone told me she already had the answer to the question.

I shook my head at her as I relocked the main door. "I know that you know I had dinner with Marcus Gordon last night."

The smile turned into a grin. "Eric told me," she said. She clasped her hands behind her back and pushed her glasses up her nose. "So, did he sweep you into those strong, manly arms for a good-night kiss? And when are you going to see him again?"

"Number one, none of your business. And number

two, I've already seen Marcus this morning—and not because last night stretched into this morning."

It took a moment, but then Susan's face grew serious as she made the connection. She'd obviously already heard what had happened to Mike. "Don't tell me you found Mike Glazer's body."

I shifted my leather briefcase from one hand to the other. "Technically, it was Hercules who found the body," I said.

"Hercules?" Susan's eyes darted from side to side in confusion. "What was your cat doing down on the Riverwalk?"

"We were at the studio building. Ruby wants to do another cat painting. Remember the one Maggie sold this summer?"

She nodded.

"We were a few minutes early. I didn't have the zipper closed all the way on the carrier . . ." I gestured with my free hand.

"And the cat's out of the bag."

I nodded. "Pretty much."

"Do you think Hercules sensed . . . something?"

"Maybe," I said. "Cats have a much better sense of smell than we do." I didn't add that both Hercules and Owen had an uncanny ability for poking their furry noses into things they shouldn't. Marcus would probably say the same thing about me.

"I guess this is the end of the pitch to Legacy Tours," Susan said as we headed for the stairs to the second floor.

"Probably," I agreed.

"Well, not to speak ill of the dead, but from what I heard, Mike Glazer was pretty much impossible to please, so I don't think the idea had much of a chance anyway. I'm sorry to hear he's dead, though."

Behind us, someone tapped on the front door. "That'll be Mary," I said.

"I'll go," Susan said. She hurried over to the entrance and let the older woman in.

"Hi, Kathleen," Mary said, hustling into the library as though she were being pushed by a sudden gust of wind. "I'm sorry I'm running late." She was a little out of breath, and I noticed that her jacket was buttoned wrong.

"How did swimming lessons go?" she asked Susan. The boys had gone for their first swim class in the pool at the St. James Hotel.

"Wet," Susan said with a grimace. "Very, very wet. On the other hand, we haven't been banned from the hotel property, so I take that as a positive sign."

"I really didn't mean to be late," Mary said, turning to me.

"You're not late," I said. "We don't open for another five minutes."

"Oh, good." She patted her gray curls, which looked as though they'd been lacquered into place with about half a can of extra-strength hair spray. "I swear this whole tour thing is turning out to be way more trouble than it's worth. Heaven help me for saying it, but there are moments I think Burtis is right; someone ought to smack a little sense into that Glazer boy."

Susan and I exchanged awkward glances.

Mary saw the look that passed between us. "What?" she asked, blue eyes narrowing. "Something's up. What is it?"

I exhaled slowly. "Mary," I began, "Mike is . . . dead."

"Lord love a duck," she said softly.

4

I told Mary about discovering the body in the tent. She sighed and shook her head. "He hasn't been home in years, and now this happens—as if that family hasn't already been through enough."

"What do you mean?" I asked as we headed up to the second-floor staff room.

Mary gave me a half smile. "That's right. You weren't here when it happened." Her forehead furrowed in thought. "Let me see. It must be close to ten years ago now. The Glazers lost a son—Michael's older brother, Gavin—in a car accident."

"That's horrible," I said.

"It gets worse," Mary said. "His parents were away for the weekend. Gavin hit a guardrail and rolled his car down an embankment. He died in the hospital, and they didn't make it back in time to say good-bye."

Susan nodded in silent confirmation.

"That's why Mike has no family here anymore." I fished the keys to my office out of my pocket.

Mary slipped her bag down off her shoulder. "He left for Chicago maybe a month or so after the accident. His mother and father eventually moved as well, just to get a little space from their memories, I think." She shook her head. "No one deserves this."

I touched her arm. "If you'd like to take the day, Susan and I can handle things here and I can call Abigail to come in."

Mary gave me a small smile. "Thank you, Kathleen. That's very thoughtful, but I'm fine."

Susan patted her canvas tote. "I have a piece of lemon-blueberry coffee cake. Want to split it?"

"Oh, that does sound good," Mary said. She might have claimed she was fine, but there were tight lines around her eyes and mouth.

"It is," Susan said, pushing her glasses up onto the bridge of her nose with one hand and linking her other arm through Mary's. "But I keep telling Eric that I'm not sure so he'll keep trying the recipe."

They started down the hall to the staff room. I unlocked my office door, put my things away and then went back downstairs to officially open the building for the day.

It was about ten thirty and I was at the checkout desk, looking at a picture book that Susan had discovered in the book drop with every page covered in glitter glue, when Wren Magnusson came in. She looked around, almost as though she wasn't sure if she was in the right place, and then she walked over to us.

I didn't know Wren very well. She'd been away at university, living with her older brother in Minneapolis. Her mother had died suddenly about six months ago, and Wren had taken the fall term off to sort through the things in her mother's house and spend some time back in Mayville Heights.

Wren was tiny, with white-blond hair and fair skin that seemed even paler this morning. She was twisting her left thumb tightly with her other hand, although she didn't seem to really be aware of it.

"Excuse me?" she asked in her soft voice. "Is Mary Lowe here?"

"She is," I said. "I'll get her for you."

"Thank you," she said.

Mary was shelving books at the far end of the non-fiction section. While her hands were working, her thoughts were clearly somewhere else, and she jumped when I came around the end of the metal shelving unit and spoke her name.

"I'm sorry," I said. "I didn't mean to scare you."

"Don't apologize," Mary said. "I was woolgathering when I should have been paying more attention to what I'm doing."

"Wren Magnusson is at the checkout desk, looking for you."

Mary made a face and pressed a hand to her forehead. "I forgot all about the child being back in town. How could I do that? She must have heard what happened."

Clearly the fact that I had no idea what she was talking about was showing on my face.

"Wren knows"—she shook her head—"knew Mike.

She was close to all the Glazers when she was a kid. It's . . . complicated."

A lot of the relationships in Mayville Heights were, I'd come to learn. So was my own background, for that matter. My mother and father had married each other twice, with my brother and sister, Sara and Ethan, front and center with my mother, so to speak, at the second ceremony.

"Go talk to her," I said. "Take half an hour. It's not busy. Susan and I will be fine."

"Thank you, Kathleen," Mary said. She patted my arm as she squeezed past me. "You have a good heart."

I followed Mary as far as the children's reading area and watched her fold Wren Magnusson into her arms. Mary was the one with the good heart.

She pulled out of the hug, keeping her hands on Wren's shoulders as she studied the young woman's face. After a moment Mary hooked her arm through Wren's and they headed for the library entrance.

I walked over to Susan. She looked up at me. "That poor kid."

"She knew Mike," I said.

She nodded. "She was almost part of that family."

I frowned at her. "What do you mean 'almost'?"

Susan pushed the seafood fork a little more tightly into her topknot. "You know that older brother of Mike's Mary was telling you about?"

I nodded. "Uh-huh."

"Wren's mother was going to marry him."

I blew out a breath. "So Gavin Glazer was going to be Wren's stepfather," I said.

Susan traced a finger around the outside edge of the heavy hardcover book she was holding. "The Glazers already treated them as though they were family. Wren's mother never really got over what happened. She cut off all contact with the family even before they moved away. I think it was just too painful for her." She sighed. "But it had to be hell for Wren. She didn't just lose Gavin. She lost that entire family." She set the book on the counter.

"Sometimes life isn't very fair," I said.

"You got that right," Susan agreed.

"I'm going to finish shelving that cart Mary was working on," I said. "Yell if you need me."

I was putting back issues of *Scientific American* into their cubby when Mary returned about twenty minutes later. She walked over to me, and I got to my feet, brushing my hands on my black pants.

"How's Wren?" I asked.

"A little shaky, but all right, considering," Mary said. "If her brother wasn't up in Alaska until the end of the month, I would have suggested she go back to Minneapolis."

"Susan told me about Wren's connection to the Glazers."

"She was so happy to get the chance to reconnect with Mike. She'd been going to see him today. She was even talking about getting to see his mother." She tucked her hands into the pockets of her peach-colored cardigan. "Kathleen, do you have any idea how Mike died?"

I hesitated, unsure how to answer.

Before I could say anything, Mary held up a hand and gave her head a little shake. "I'm sorry. How could you know that?" She sighed softly. "It doesn't make any difference how he died," she said. "It doesn't make him any less dead. I just thought maybe it would help Wren if I could tell her that he didn't suffer." She shook her head again as if to clear it. "Not a very nice way to go, alone in that big old tent of Burtis's."

"Is there a good way to die?" I asked, picking up another book from the cart.

"Well, I darn sure know how I plan on going," Mary said, a saucy gleam suddenly lighting up her eyes.

I put one hand on my hip and looked skeptically at her, happy to have the subject changed. "I don't think that's something you can really plan, but that doesn't mean I don't want to hear what those plans of yours are."

She pulled herself up straight to her full height, which wasn't actually that tall. "I plan to live to be one hundred and be shot in bed by the jealous girlfriend of a much, much younger man." She smiled at me. "And since I'm nowhere near the century mark right now, I'm going to go wash my hands and then come back and finish those books."

I watched her head for the stairs. She was in excellent shape. If anyone was likely to make it to a hundred, it was Mary. And even though she was very happily married, I'd seen her get admiring looks from men a lot younger. Those long, strong legs of hers tended to turn men of any age into mush.

I went back over to the desk to see if Susan needed

anything, and when she didn't, I headed upstairs to my office. I dropped into my chair and swung around to look out the window.

How had Mike Glazer died? That question had been rolling around in my mind since I'd stepped into the tent and caught sight of his body slumped in that plastic lawn chair. There had been no blood, no signs of a fight. The body had been cold and stiff.

But when I'd felt for a pulse, my fingers had brushed over something—a small bump, a little smaller than an egg, on the back of Mike Glazer's head, behind his left ear.

I wasn't sure that even mattered. Not compared to what I'd noticed on his face. Tiny red marks barely bigger than a needle prick—petechial hemorrhages was the medical term for them—and I knew they were a sign of suffocation, among other things. Which meant Mike Glazer's death probably wasn't an accident.

I pressed the heel of my hand to my forehead. A headache was starting to throb behind my eyes. I knew it was possible that I was wrong. But I was pretty sure I wasn't.

5

The library got busier as the day went on, and I over-heard more than one person speculating on what was going to happen to Mayville Height's pitch to Legacy Tours. At lunchtime I tried calling Maggie, but all I got was her voice mail. I left a message telling her I knew what had happened and I'd see her later at tai chi class.

Both cats were waiting by the kitchen table when I got home. They seemed to have put their differences from the morning aside. I hung up my coat and bent down to pet them both. Owen had the slightly loopy look that told me he'd been into his Fred the Funky Chicken stash. Rebecca, whose house backed up to mine, kept him in the neon-yellow catnip chickens, using any excuse to buy him one, including Hug Your Cat Day and the summer solstice.

"How was your day?" I said to Hercules. He held up one front paw. There was a jet-black feather stuck between two toes on his right paw. I bent over to pull it loose. "Did you and that grackle get into it again?" I asked. Hercules had been having a war for months with what seemed to be one bird that liked to dive-bomb his head when he was in the backyard. I had nicknamed him Professor Moriarty because he was an arch-nemesis if a cat ever had one. He and Herc had had a couple of run-ins, one of which had ended with Hercules as the proud possessor of another large black wing feather. The bird had disappeared for a while after that. I was guessing he was back.

I pointed to his paw. "Do I want to know what happened?"

He immediately put his left paw on top of his right and looked at me, blinking his big green eyes.

"That's fine with me," I said. "Whatever happens in the backyard stays in the backyard."

I turned to Owen. "And how was your day?" I asked, reaching over to scratch under his chin. He gave me a blissful if slightly stoned-looking smile, and leaned in to my hand.

After I'd gotten some cat love, I went upstairs, changed into my tai chi clothes and came back down to get supper. I made a grocery list while I ate, making sure I put sardines on the list so I could make the cats' favorite stinky crackers on the weekend.

When the dishes were done, I realized I had enough time to walk down to tai chi class. I put my shoes and a towel in my bag—after picking out a little clump of black fur—pulled on a sweater and called good-bye to the boys. They had disappeared as soon as I'd started the dishes.

Roma was coming up the sidewalk from the other direction as I got close to the artist's co-op store. She waited for me by the door. "Hi," she said. "I heard about this morning. Are you okay?"

"I'm fine," I said. "And, technically, it was Hercules who discovered Mike Glazer's body." We went inside and started up the steps to the second-floor tai chi studio.

"Ruby told me she's doing another painting of Hercules," Roma said, running her hand through her sleek, dark bob. "I hope it brings in as much as the last one. Cat People needs the money."

Cat People was a rescue group that worked with feral cats in this area. The fund-raiser Ruby was donating the painting to was for them.

At the top of the stairs, Roma dropped onto the bench near the coat hooks to change her shoes. I pulled off my sweater and draped it over a hook.

"How did Hercules end up over by the tents in the first place?" Roma asked, tucking her sleek brown hair behind one ear. She slid to the right and I sat down beside her.

"I didn't have the zipper on the cat carrier closed all the way." I felt my cheeks getting warm. "He hustled down the street, looked both ways at the curb and made a beeline for the tent."

"At least he knew to watch for cars," she said with a smile.

"Roma, do you think he really could have smelled . . . something at that distance?" I asked, swapping one running shoe for one of the purple canvas pull-ons I wore for class.

"It's possible. A cat's sense of smell is vastly superior to ours."

"I know," I said. "I swear Owen can sniff out a catnip chicken all the way across the backyard at Rebecca's house."

"And Owen and Hercules aren't exactly typical cats either, Kathleen," she said.

My stomach gave a little lurch. Did Roma know more about my cats' abilities than she'd let on? "What do you mean?" I asked, as she stood up to pull her sweatshirt over her head.

"Well, they were feral, or at the very least, abandoned as young kittens." Her voice was muffled a little by the fabric. She pulled the shirt off the rest of the way and shook her head. Her hair fell back into its shiny bob. Even with Rebecca's expert scissors styling my hair these days, it never quite behaved like that. "And they definitely don't have a typical house cat's digestive system," she added with an eyebrows-raised, sideways glance.

I felt myself relax. Roma didn't know that Owen could disappear like a rabbit from a magician's hat or that Hercules hadn't just walked into Burtis's tent; he'd walked through it.

"By the way, what was the last treat you gave Hercules?" Roma asked, still eyeing me.

"One of those stinky sardine crackers I make," I said. "And Ruby gave him a few organic fish-shaped treats this morning, which she said you okayed."

"Good," she said, putting her sweatshirt over one of the coat hooks.

We walked into the studio space. Maggie was standing in the center of the room with Ruby and fifteen-year-old Taylor King. Ruby was showing them something on her cell phone. Taylor was the newest student in the class. The teenager smiled when she saw Roma.

The Kings had bought an old horse for their daughter, and Roma had spent a lot of time nursing Horton back to health. Now Taylor was interested in becoming a veterinarian.

"Hi," Ruby said, holding up the phone. "Want to see which photo I finally decided on?"

"Yes," I said, leaning in for a look.

"Me too," Roma added.

Hercules was looking directly at the camera in the photograph. He was standing on Roma's worktable with his head turned just a bit to the left with what I recognized as his "serious" expression on his black-and-white face.

"That's perfect," Roma said, smiling at Ruby. "I can't wait to see the finished painting."

"I like it," I agreed.

"I love your cat," Taylor said shyly. "Ruby said he came from Wisteria Hill."

I nodded. "That's right. So did his brother, Owen."

"Do they like people?" she asked.

Roma rolled her eyes. "They think they are people," she said.

Both Maggie and Ruby laughed. "Roma's right," I said with a smile. "They do sometimes act like they think they're people. They just don't like to be touched for the most part, by anyone other than me. But, yes, both Hercules and Owen like people." I elbowed Maggie. "Especially Owen. He loves Maggie."

Mags wrinkled her nose at me. "Which just goes to prove how smart that cat is."

Everyone laughed at that.

I turned to Roma. "Maybe Taylor could help feed the cats out at Wisteria Hill sometime."

The teenager's eyes lit up. "Could I?" she asked.

"That's a good idea," Roma said. "We can always use another volunteer." She pointed to Ruby's cell phone. "Do you still have a picture of Lucy?" Lucy was the matriarch of the feral cats that lived on the Wisteria Hill estate.

"I think so," Ruby said, bending her red and blue pigtailed head over the screen. "Let me see if I can find it."

Maggie narrowed her gaze at me. "Excuse us a second, please," she said. "I need Kathleen for just a minute and then we're going to get started." She caught my arm and all but dragged me over to the small table where she kept a kettle and a selection of herbal teas. "You didn't tell me you were the one who found Mike's body," she said, frowning and propping one hand on her hip.

"It didn't seem like the kind of thing to share in a phone message," I said, "and, technically, Hercules found the body." I smiled at her. "I'm fine, Mags."

She pulled her free hand through her short blond curls. "You know I didn't like Mike, but this is awful."

"What's going to happen to the pitch for the tour?" I asked.

"I don't know. Liam's having a meeting"—she glanced at the clock over the door—"right now with the other people on the committee." She exhaled, lifting her bangs off her forehead. "They're hoping that either Alex or Chris Scott—they're Mike's partners— will come, but I doubt it. I think they'll probably go ahead with the food tasting and the art show anyway. There's been so much work put into it all."

"If I can do anything . . ," I said.

Maggie smiled. "I know. Thanks." She held both arms out a bit from her body and shook them. Then she started for the middle of the room. "Circle, everyone," she called.

Mags took her usual place with her back to the wall, facing the door. Ruby slid in beside her as everyone else spread out. Taylor stopped to pull an elastic from her pocket and pull her red hair up into a high ponytail. Roma smiled at me and patted the air to her left. I took the empty space next to her.

Rebecca was already hurrying across the floor. She joined the circle beside me. "Hi, Kathleen," she whispered.

"Hi," I whispered back as Maggie started the warm-up.

"Have you gotten the rocking chair back together yet?" Rebecca asked. Her arms were swinging forward and back and the light sparkled off the diamond ring on her left hand.

I was happy that Rebecca and Everett were getting their happily ever after, even though it had taken close to fifty years for it to happen. And I had a permanent little bubble of warmth in my chest knowing that the cats and I had played a very tiny role in helping the two of them find their way back to each other, though I couldn't imagine that it wouldn't have happened anyway. As Ruby liked to say, "What's meant to be will always find a way." I wasn't a big believer in fate, but in the case of those two, I was willing to make an exception.

Before I could answer Rebecca's question, Maggie called across the circle to me, "Kathleen, bend your knees."

I gave a melodramatic sigh and everyone laughed. It was a running joke in the class. I thought I was bending my knees. I was trying to bend my knees. It just seemed that my knees didn't know that.

I got down a little lower to the ground and Rebecca gave me a sympathetic smile, the way she always did. "To answer your questions, yes and no," I said, keeping my voice low.

"I'm sorry," she said, not the slightest bit out of breath even though she was twice my age. "I'm not following you."

I was already a tiny bit winded. I made a mental resolution to leave the truck at home more often and walk to the library. "I got the rocking chair all together okay, but it had a decided list to one side," I said.

"Oh, dear," Rebecca said, two frown lines appearing between her blue eyes. "Maybe Oren could help you."

Oren Kenyon was a jack-of-all-trades. He'd duplicated the old trim for the library restoration and created the beautiful carved wooden sun that was over the entrance. If Marcus couldn't fix the chair, maybe I would ask Oren.

"Marcus is going to try to put it together for me," I said.

Rebecca beamed at me. "He's a very nice young man," she said, with a gleam in her eye that even with her gray hair made her look about as old as Taylor King. "I'm glad the two of you have become friends."

"You're as bad as Maggie," I said.

Rebecca gave me a look that was all innocence. She was much better at it than either Owen or Hercules.

Marcus had figured out that Maggie had been trying to get the two of us together. I wondered if he knew that it seemed as though everyone else in town was trying to do the same thing.

Maggie worked us hard. By the time we did the entire form at the end of class, the neck of my T-shirt was wet with sweat. Some of my movements still needed more practice, especially Cloud Hands, but I could go all the way through all one hundred and eight movements of the form.

I walked over to Roma and Taylor, who were standing by the table while Roma made herself a cup of tea that smelled like cranberries and cinnamon. "I'm never going to be able to do that," Taylor was saying as she shook her hair out of its ponytail.

"If you mean the entire form, yes, you will," Maggie said, joining us. She'd peeled off her T-shirt to uncover the red and purple tie-dye tank she had on underneath. I was pretty sure Ruby had made it. "Everyone was where you are when they first started. You just take it a movement at a time."

Taylor shook her head. She didn't look convinced.

"It's just like eating an elephant," Ruby said, walking over to us as she pulled the elastics off her pigtails.

Roma frowned at her over the top of her teacup. "I don't get what you mean," she said. "How do you eat an elephant?"

Ruby grinned. "A bite at a time."

Everyone groaned, and Ruby made a face at us. Then she turned to Taylor. "If you keep at it and you practice, you'll get it all. Anytime you want to come over to my studio and practice with me, you can."

"Really?" Taylor said. "Because I know my right hand isn't, well, right when I do White Crane Spreads Wings."

"Show me," Ruby said, draping the towel around her neck. She looked at Maggie. "You don't mind?"

Mags made a sweeping movement with one hand. "Go ahead."

Taylor followed Ruby over to a spot near the middle of the studio.

Roma took another sip of her tea and turned to Maggie. "Do you have any idea what's going to happen with the food tasting and the art show now that Mike Glazer is dead?"

Maggie shook her head. "I was telling Kathleen earlier that Liam was having a meeting with the others on the committee while we were doing class." She glanced over at the clock above the door. "They've probably decided what to do by now."

"You think they'll go ahead?" Roma asked.

"With the show and the tasting?" Maggie said, grabbing a cup to make herself some tea. "I think they might as well. We were only a few days from it all coming together. I hate to see everyone's hard work go to waste. As far as the pitch to the tour company, I think that's done." She reached for the box of chocolate-spice tea bags. "I don't think it was going to work anyway, even if Mike hadn't had a heart attack or whatever it was."

For a moment I could almost feel the man's cold skin under my fingers. I swallowed as my stomach tightened. "Why do you say that?" I asked.

Maggie dropped a tea bag into her cup and added hot water. The tea smelled delicious—like cloves and chocolate. "I hope Mike was welcomed by the light," she said, "and I don't like to be critical of someone who isn't here to defend himself anymore, but most of the time, he acted like he thought we were all a bunch of small-town hicks."

I thought about Burtis fingering the sledgehammer while Mike ranted at him and about Mary saying she was going to kick Mike's backside between two light posts like a placekicker going for three points. Given what I suspected about how Mike Glazer had died, I didn't like knowing how many people had disliked working with the man.

"I noticed that last night," I said carefully.

"But maybe it was just that he knew what kinds of things his customers were looking for in a getaway," Roma offered.

Maggie shook her head. "It was more than having high standards. I don't have a problem with that. I have very high standards for how my art is displayed." She sighed. "I got the feeling Mike thought we didn't know how to do things properly, let alone well."

Roma drank the last of her tea and set the cup on the table. "It sounds as though he'd forgotten where he came from."

"Maybe he didn't want to remember," I said quietly.

Maggie and Roma both looked at me. "What do you mean?" Maggie asked.

"Wren Magnusson came into the library looking for Mary," I said. "Susan told me about Mike's brother."

Maggie laced her fingers around her cup of tea. "I'd forgotten about that," she said. She turned to Roma. "You were gone when Gavin Glazer was killed in that car accident, weren't you?"

Roma nodded. "But I remember reading about it. His car went off the road. It was up on the bluff, wasn't it?"

Maggie sighed again. "He was on his way into town. Celia"—she looked at me—"that was Wren's mother—was a different person after the accident, colder, closed off. She . . . she didn't want to have anything to do with Gavin's family."

"I can't fault her for that," Roma said, twisting the silver ring she wore around her index finger. "When Luke died, it was hard for me to be around his family at first; all I saw was reminders of what I'd lost. We'd been married such a short time. More than once I'd catch sight of his brother—at the counter in the kitchen, or coming down the stairs—and I'd think, 'Here's

Luke,' and for a split second it was as though the accident hadn't happened. And then I'd remember that it had." She exhaled slowly. "But they were Olivia's family—her grandparents, her aunts and uncle. Over time it got"—she shrugged— "not exactly easier, just not so raw. I'm sorry Celia was never able to get to that place."

"Mary said that Mike left Mayville Heights not long after his brother died," I said.

Maggie nodded. "This was literally his first visit back."

"And his last," Roma added softly.

I wondered what it had been like for Mike to come back to the place where he'd grown up after almost ten years, to see people he hadn't seen in all that time. I'd had an aching attack of homesickness when my plane had landed in Boston, and I'd been away for only a little more than a year. When I caught sight of my mother and father and Ethan and Sara waiting for me, I'd almost burst into tears.

Roma touched my arm. "Would you like a drive up the hill?" she asked.

"I should walk," I said.

She shrugged. "I didn't ask you if you thought you should walk. I asked if you'd like a drive."

I nodded. "Please." Suddenly I was tired. All I wanted to do was go home, hug Owen and Hercules—assuming they felt like coming when I called them—and then pick up the phone and call my parents.

Roma and I changed our shoes out on the landing. She pulled on her sweatshirt. I stuffed my sweater in my bag. Maggie leaned against the doorframe. "Don't forget lunch tomorrow," she said to me. She looked at Roma. "Can you come?"

Roma shook her head, and it seemed to me she was trying to stifle a smile. "Sorry. I can't." Then the smile got loose. "I'm getting the keys to Wisteria Hill tomorrow." She was moving in once renovations to the old house were done. Given how much work it needed, that might be a while.

Maggie's eyes lit up and she did her little happy dance, which looked pretty much like a two-year-old having a tantrum.

I threw my arms around Roma. "That's wonderful," I said.

"We're going to be at my studio," Maggie said. "Stop by for a minute if you can, so we can toast your new home."

"Okay," Roma said, dropping her shoes in her bag. "I'll try."

I leaned around Mags to wave good-bye to Ruby and Taylor, and then Roma and I headed down to her SUV.

Roma didn't say a word as she pulled out of her parking spot and started down the street, but I saw her eyes dart in my direction a couple of times. There was something on her mind. Something she hadn't wanted to say in front of Maggie—or anyone else.

"What is it?" I finally asked. The fact that she didn't immediately ask me what the heck I was talking about told me my hunch was right.

Her mouth moved for a moment before any words

came out. She shot me another look before speaking. "I may regret asking you this, but . . . what do you know about Mike Glazer's death that the rest of us don't?" She held up one hand for a second to head off what she probably figured would be my objections before putting it back on the steering wheel. "And don't say 'nothing,' because I saw your face when Maggie made her comment about him having a heart attack."

I looked out the windshield for a minute before answering. "It's not that I 'know' anything," I began.

"Okay, you suspect something."

I shrugged. "Suspect might even be too strong a word. It's just . . ." I folded my arms over my chest, suddenly wishing I had put on my sweater. "I told you it was Hercules who found the body."

Roma nodded but remained silent, her eyes on the road.

"Mike was sitting in one of those white plastic lawn chairs and there was just something about the way—I knew he was dead, but I felt for a pulse at his neck, just to be sure." I took a deep breath and let it out. "There wasn't one. His face was blotchy, mottled. His skin was cold."

"And?" she prompted softly.

"There were tiny red spots on his face." I touched the side of my face.

"Petechiae?" she asked.

"Yes."

Roma slowed down, flicked on her turn signal and pulled into my driveway. She put the SUV in park and shifted in her seat to look directly at me. "Kathleen, I know you've seen more than your share of dead bodies since you came to Mayville Heights," she said. "And none of them were from natural causes."

"But," I said.

"But not every death is something suspicious," she said with a half smile. "Lots of things can cause pete-chiae: a violent coughing jag, vomiting, certain medica-tions, a blood disorder. By themselves, petechiae don't necessarily mean Mike Glazer was murdered."

"I didn't realize that," I said. "Thanks." I smiled and held up a hand with my first and second fingers crossed. "Good luck tomorrow."

Her smile got wider. "I'll stop by Maggie's studio if I can."

I got out of the SUV and waved as she backed out of the driveway. Then I walked around the side of the house and let myself into the porch. Not only was Roma a very good vet; she also had first aid training. So I believed what she'd said about there being lots of rea-sons for those red pinpoints on Mike Glazer's face.

I toed off my sneakers and unlocked the kitchen door. Those marks didn't mean that someone killed him, I told myself firmly. But I couldn't stop the thought that it didn't mean someone hadn't, either.

6

Hercules was sitting next to the kitchen table like a statue of the Egyptian god Bast. "Hi, Fuzz Face," I said. I hung my bag on the hook by the back door, and he trailed me into the living room.

I sank into the wing chair and propped my feet on the footstool. Hercules jumped into my lap. His nose twitched and he narrowed his green eyes.

"Hey, I was at tai chi class," I said. I dropped my head and sniffed, feeling a little foolish because I was checking to see if I was offensive based on Hercules's cranky face. All I got was the scent of line-dried T-shirt and baby-powder-scented deodorant. "I don't smell bad," I told him.

He put a white-tipped paw over his nose. "Yes, I know," I said. "Cat's noses." Satisfied that he'd made his point, he stretched across my chest, resting his furry head just below the hollow of my throat.

Owen came down the stairs then, jumped up and

sprawled sideways across my legs so his head was just below my knee and his back paws and tail were mostly on the footstool.

"Everyone comfortable?" I asked.

Owen meowed, rolling partway on to his back. Hercules rubbed the side of his face against my T-shirt and began to purr. The warmth from their two furry bodies somehow chased away that lingering pinch of homesickness I'd felt back in Maggie's studio. I decided I wouldn't call Boston after all. Instead, I pulled the phone closer and punched in Marcus's number.

I got his voice mail. "Hi, Marcus," I said. "It's Kathleen. Call me when you have time. Please." I recited my number in case he hadn't memorized it, the way I somehow seemed to have done with his.

Both cats were staring at me when I hung up the phone. In Owen's case, he was looking at me upside down. "I'm not trying to get information," I said.

Neither one of them so much as blinked.

"I like Marcus," I said. "I think he likes me. I don't want this case—if it even is a case—to mess that up before I at least get a chance to kiss him. Plus I didn't tell him about that bump on Mike Glazer's head—and why am I explaining all of this to the two of you?"

Hercules lifted his head and cocked it to one side, almost as though he were wondering the same thing. Owen stayed sprawled over my legs, golden eyes fixed on mine, and I would have sworn from the expression on his upside-down face that he was laughing at me.

Marcus didn't call me until the next morning. I was sitting at the table with a bowl of yogurt, homemade granola, and an apple—the one breakfast neither cat would try to mooch off me—when the phone rang. I left the dish on the table, confident that there was no way it would "accidentally" end up on the floor the way a plate of scrambled eggs and toast would.

"Hi, Kathleen. It's Marcus," he said when I answered. "I got your message, but it was too late to call you back last night."

"Hi," I said. How was I going to say this?

Suddenly I could hear my mother's voice in my head. "Katydid, if you have to dance with a bear, put on your best high heels and tango." It was her colorful way of saying get on with it. So I did.

"I forgot to tell you yesterday that when I checked Mike Glazer's body for a pulse, I noticed a bump—at least I think that's what it was—at the back of his head, behind his ear."

"I saw it," he said, "but thanks for calling me."

I didn't want him to hang up before I'd said everything I wanted to say. It was time to tango. "And I wanted you to know that I'll stay out of your case, assuming there even is one."

"I appreciate that," he said. There was silence for a moment; then he added, "Does that mean you're not going to bring me coffee?"

I laughed. "Not necessarily."

"Kathleen, I know this is short notice, but would you like to have supper with me tomorrow night?"

Two furry faces were watching me around the kitchen doorframe.

"I would," I said.

"Full disclosure: I'm cooking."

"As long as you're not planning on making something with sardines in hot sauce, I think I'll be okay," I said.

It was Marcus's turn to laugh. "So does that mean that there won't be any cats joining us?"

"Yes, it definitely does." I glanced over at the doorway again. Owen and Hercules had disappeared.

"About six thirty?"

"I'll see you then," I said. "Have a good day."

"You too, Kathleen," he said, and he was gone.

I went back to finish my breakfast. Owen and Hercules were sitting beside my chair like two adorable, well-behaved cats.

"I'm not fooled," I said, picking up my spoon. "I know you heard enough to figure out that Marcus invited me for dinner, and I'm not taking either one of you."

"Rrrow," Hercules said. It seemed he wasn't happy that Owen had been to Marcus's house and he hadn't. Or he might have been trying to point out the piece of yogurt-covered apple that had just fallen off my spoon onto the floor.

"Nice try," I mumbled around a mouthful of granola. "But it's not as though your brother had a five-course meal when he was visiting Marcus." I glanced down at Owen, who was still in well-behaved mode. "And it's not like he'll be visiting again anytime soon. Emphasis on soon."

Hercules poked the chunk of apple with a paw and then made a cranky face when he ended up with yogurt on his fur. He held up the sticky paw and glared at me, a sour expression on his face.

"It's only a bit of yogurt," I said. "From soy milk. Look." I held up my spoon and licked the back of the bowl. "Lick it off your foot. You might like it. Abigail made it."

He looked uncertainly at his paw, glanced over at the sink and then focused on me.

I shook my head. "No," I said. "I'm not washing your feet again."

He made annoyed noises in his throat. I figured he was probably muttering "Bite me" in cat. Then tentatively, he licked his paw. Then he licked it again. Then he looked up at me and made a hacking sound, like he was about to bring up a fur ball—or that tiny dab of yogurt.

"Oh, for heaven's sake," I said in exasperation. I stood up, went over to the cupboard and got the container of stinky crackers. "Here. Maybe this will get rid of the taste."

Owen meowed, reminding me—as if I could forget—that he was here, too. "Yes, you can have one, too," I said, leaning over to set the sardine cracker on the floor in front of him.

I went back to my breakfast, and it occurred to me that if I could keep Owen and Hercules from popping up—literally—somewhere they weren't supposed to be and outing themselves and their talents to the world, I should be able to keep a police investigation from coming between Marcus and me.

Usually on Fridays I didn't go down to the library

until noon, but I'd changed shifts with Mary because of the upcoming food tasting, and since she hadn't called, I was assuming she still wanted the time.

Eric dropped off Susan just as I was unlocking the library doors. "Hi, Kathleen," the twins yelled, waving from the backseat. I waved back as Susan hurried up the stairs.

"Did you hear?" she asked.

"Hear what?" I said as I keyed in the code on the alarm pad.

"If you have to ask, then you didn't." She smiled. "The pitch to Legacy is still a go. One of the Scott brothers is coming for the tasting and the art show."

"That's good news," I said.

"Yeah, it is," Susan said, unzipping her jacket as she followed me inside. "Most of the work is already done. What's the worst that can happen?"

Given that Mike Glazer's body had been found in one of the tents that was going to be used as part of the presentation to Legacy Tours, I was pretty confident that the worst had already happened. "I forgot to ask you," I said, switching on the downstairs lights. "What's Eric making for the tasting?"

Susan grinned at me. "Three kinds of pudding cake—chocolate, apple spice, and lemon—and little mini muffins—cheddar and spinach, cinnamon streusel, blueberry, and ham and Swiss."

I groaned. "You're making me hungry."

"Eric said you'd say that." Susan held up her fabric tote. "That's why he sent a little care package." She held the top of the bag open, and I looked inside. It was actually a big care package, assuming all the food was staying at the library.

"Your husband is wonderful," I said.

"Yeah, he is pretty great," she agreed as we headed for the stairs. "He snores, but I kick, so it all works out."

I dropped my things in my office while she headed for the staff room. The coffee was started, and Susan was putting a selection of muffins on a glass plate when I got there. There was a metal crochet hook skewered through her updo.

"Susan, why do you have a crochet hook in your hair?" I asked.

She pushed her dark-framed glasses up on her nose and put two mugs on the table. "I couldn't exactly leave it lying around the house," she said. "The boys would put someone's eye out with it."

She was right about that. The twins were scary smart. Literally. They generally used their smarts to do something involving heights and electrical appliances.

"I didn't know you crocheted," I said.

Susan gave a snort of laughter. "I don't. Abigail is trying to teach me how to make a scarf, but let's just say it's not going well and leave it at that."

I looked at her, eyebrows raised. She sighed and inclined her head toward her bag, hanging on the back of a chair at the end of the table. "Take a look," she said.

I set the bag on the table, reached inside and pulled out a tangle of soft, cranberry-colored yarn that filled both my hands. "It's not that bad," I said. "All you need to do is wind this into a ball and you can start your scarf."

She turned from the counter, coffeepot in her hand. "Kathleen, that is the scarf."

My cheeks reddened. "Oh. Well, it's soft."

Susan filled my mug and pushed it toward me. "It's a mess."

"It's not that bad," I said, turning the clump of wool over in my hands. "It's just kind of twisty."

She filled her own cup and put the pot back. "It's supposed to be that way. It's one of those spiral scarves—you know, with a ruffled edge." She made a circular motion with one finger.

"Well, at least you got that part right," I said.

Susan started to laugh. "Honestly, Kathleen, I appreciate the fact that you always say something nice, but that is not a spiral scarf. It's not any kind of scarf. It's a tangle of yarn that might make a good bird's nest, but that's about it."

I handed the scarf back to her and she stuffed it back in her bag. "Maybe you'd be better at knitting," I suggested, eyeing the muffins, wondering which one I should try first.

"Maybe I'd be better at buying a scarf," she said. She pointed at the plate. "Try that one. It's ham and Swiss. I think you'll like it."

I bit into the muffin and made a little moan of happiness. "Could we just keep the doors locked and maybe stay here and eat muffins all morning?"

Susan shook her head. "We have a ninth-grade English class coming for a tour at nine thirty. You have five minutes to eat as many muffins as you can, and then it's time to get this show on the road."

It turned out I could eat three of the tiny muffins in five minutes. Then Susan and I went downstairs to open the building for the day.

It was a busy morning. It seemed like half of Mayville Heights had run out of reading and viewing material, and the ninth-grade class had dozens of questions about the reference section. I was glad I'd asked Abigail to come in early. Things finally eased off about twelve thirty.

I found Abigail still in the reference section, reshelving some books. "You were great with that class," I said. "Thank you."

She smiled. "It was fun. They asked some great questions."

I smiled back at her. "They were trying to stump you."

"I know." Her hair, red-gold shot with streaks of silver, was in its usual braid, and she flipped it over her shoulder. "That's exactly the kind of thing I used to do when I was that age, so I can pretty much guess what the questions will be."

"Susan told me you're trying to teach her how to crochet."

Abigail laughed. "You've heard the expression 'all thumbs'?" she asked.

"I have," I said, reaching down to line up the spines of three dictionaries on a lower shelf.

"If we could get to that point, I'd be happy."

"She showed me the scarf," I said.

Abigail shook her head. "I have no idea what the problem is. She's working at it and I'm watching every stitch. I glance away for a second or two, and it goes from a scarf to something that looks like Medusa's head." She brushed lint off the front of her sweater. "That doesn't mean I'm giving up, though."

"I didn't think you would," I said. Out of the corner of my eye, I saw a woman coming toward us.

Abigail caught sight of her and smiled. "I'm glad you're here," she said to me. "I want you to meet my friend Georgia."

Georgia Tepper was about my height, with jet-black hair cut shorter than Maggie's. She had long, strong fingers, I noticed as Abigail introduced us and we shook hands.

"Georgia is one of the vendors for the food tasting," Abigail said.

"You're Sweet Things," I said, realizing I'd heard Maggie mention her name—and rave about the maple cream cupcakes she'd made for the reception after the final concert of the Wild Rose Summer Music Festival. I'd been in Boston and missed the festival.

Georgia smiled. "Yes, I am."

Abigail nudged me with her shoulder. "And she's doing some of the baking at Fern's, too." Fern's was the fifties diner where I'd had breakfast with Burtis Chapman. "You'll love her devil's food cupcakes." She knew about my penchant for anything chocolate. "With dark-chocolate frosting and bittersweet shavings," she added with a sly grin.

"You'll be my first stop," I promised Georgia.

"Wait a minute," Abigail said. "Does that mean the food tasting is still on?"

Georgia and I both nodded.

"That's great," Abigail said. Her gaze shifted to Georgia. "So you're not dropping out?"

"No, I'm not," she said. She flushed and gave me an embarrassed look. "I was thinking about not doing the tasting, but I'm a new business and this is a great opportunity for me."

"And now that Mike Glazer is . . . well, gone, things should run a little more smoothly," Abigail said. She shrugged her shoulders and looked from Georgia to me. "I mean no disrespect, but from what I heard, he was making everything—the food tasting and the art show—difficult."

"I know," I said, nodding slowly. "I heard that he was . . . challenging to work with."

Georgia's cheeks got pinker. "Mr. Glazer had some very strong ideas about how things should be done. He said that chocolate was so last year. He wanted me to make something trendy like peanut butter jalapeño cupcakes."

Abigail made a face. "Peanut butter and jalapeño cupcakes. For that fiery sensation that sticks to the roof of your mouth? I don't think so. Trendy isn't what people are looking for when they come here."

"What are people looking for when they come to Mayville Heights?" I asked.

"Clean air, gorgeous scenery and charming eccentrics like me," she retorted. Her stomach growled before I could answer. "And good food," she added, patting her middle.

"Go have lunch," I said. "Everything's under control here." I smiled at Georgia. "I'm glad we met."

"Me too," she said. "I'll see you at the tasting. I'll save you a chocolate cupcake."

I headed for the checkout desk, where Susan was answering the phone.

Mary was just coming in. "Hi," she said, walking over to me. "You can go for lunch anytime."

"Thanks," I said. "How was your morning?"

She set her quilted bag on the counter. "Very good. Burtis made some adjustments to the tents, and we have more than half the stalls set up in the second one." She laced her fingers together on top of the bag. "Go have some lunch, Kathleen," she said. "Susan and I have things under control."

Susan leaned over, resting her head against Mary's arm, and they gave me the same kind of faux-innocent look that Owen and Hercules sometimes used. It didn't fill me with any more confidence than I had when the cats did it.

"That's what scares me just a little," I said, holding up my right thumb and forefinger about an inch apart.

They both smirked at me.

"I'm going upstairs to get my purse and my sweater," I said. "I'll be at Maggie's studio if you need me." I started for the stairs. "Don't do anything *outlandish* to my library while I'm gone," I warned. I was only half joking.

"Would we do that?" Mary asked. I knew she was pretending to talk to Susan even though she'd raised her voice a little so I'd hear her.

"Yes," I answered, not bothering to turn around.

"Well, not on purpose," Susan called after me.

I let that one go.

The sun was shining and there were just a few fluffy clouds, looking like puffs of cotton, floating in the blue sky overhead. I walked over to River Arts, glad to have the time to stretch my legs. Maggie was waiting for me at the back door. "Hi," she said. "Roma called. She can't make it. She has to do emergency surgery on a golden retriever. But she did get the keys to Wisteria Hill."

"That's good," I said. "I'm so glad the place isn't going to be turned into a subdivision."

Maggie nodded. "Me too. So how was your morning?"

"Busy," I said. "I think half of Mayville Heights was looking for something to read."

"Good," she said as we headed up the stairs to her top-floor studio. "That means the user numbers will be up, and Everett and the board will be so impressed, they'll offer you whatever you want to sign a new contract and stay."

Maggie was waging an unapologetic campaign to convince me to stay in Mayville Heights. Truth be told, it made me feel good that she cared so much.

"How was your morning?" I asked.

"Also busy," she said, glancing back over her shoulder at me. "You must have heard by now everything's a go."

"I did."

"Liam had to change the date to a week from this coming Monday instead of Sunday, but otherwise we're still on schedule."

"So Liam saved the day."

"He really did," she said.

We came out into the top hallway and started down to Maggie's studio.

"And will he be appropriately rewarded?" I asked.

Maggie rolled her eyes at me. "Maybe by the town council, but not by me. I told you, there's nothing serious between us. We're mostly just friends."

I stopped and put both hands on my hips. "Oh, c'mon, Mags," I said. "Liam is funny, he's smart, he's working on a PhD and this proposal for Legacy Tours, he's still tending bar and he's majorly cute."

"Majorly cute?"

"We had a ninth-grade class in this morning for a tour," I said. "I picked up a few phrases to expand my vocabulary."

She pulled her keys out of her pocket. "Yes, Liam is smart, and he makes me laugh, and he is, as you put it, 'majorly cute,' but we're just friends. You're wasting your time if you're trying to play matchmaker." She opened the studio door and I followed her inside.

"Why is it that all the times I told you that you were wasting your time playing matchmaker with Marcus and me, you just ignored me?"

The high worktable in the center of the room was set with two place mats and cutlery. I pulled out a stool and sat down while Maggie plugged in the kettle and started taking food out of her little refrigerator. "That's different," she said, moving between the table and the fridge.

I leaned an elbow on the paint-spattered tabletop and propped my head on my hand. "Why? Because it's you?"

"No," she said. "Well, yes, at least partly." Her expression turned serious. "I'm good at this kind of thing. I got Roma and Eddie together."

"That was an accident," I protested. "People saw Roma with the mannequin you made and thought she was dating the real Eddie. He never would have gotten in touch with her if it hadn't been for that."

Maggie set a large bowl on the table between our plates. She'd made her pasta salad with sun-dried tomatoes. It was one of my favorites. "Exactly," she said. "Roma ended up with the real Eddie because of the Eddie I made. The universe was working through me."

I would have laughed at that, but I knew she was serious. "You said 'partly,'" I said. "What's the other part?"

"You and Marcus are perfect for each other. You're yin and yang." She added hot water to her teacup and brought it over to the table.

I groaned. "Oh, please don't say we're soul mates. I don't want to lose my appetite before I've even had one bite."

Maggie slipped onto the stool opposite me. "I'm not saying that," she said.

I knew that didn't mean she wasn't thinking it. "I'm officially changing the subject," I said. "Let's talk about the art show or the food tasting or the *Gotta Dance* reunion tour. They've added three more stops to the schedule."

I glanced over at the Matt Lauer doll perched on a chair by the windows. I'd found the eight-inch-high knitted doll wearing a dark blue suit and a gray fedora in the same store where I'd bought the *I ♥ Matt Lauer* T-shirt. It seemed as though the *Today Show* host had a lot of fans in Boston.

"There are rumors that as a former *Gotta Dance* champion, Matt's going to join the others for a few dates to show off his moves," I said.

"I know." Maggie made a face. "But they aren't coming anywhere close to here, and so far Matt hasn't said for sure that he is going to be part of the tour."

"Maybe that's for the best," I said.

"You're just saying that because the beefcake didn't win the crystal trophy."

The "beefcake" was Kevin Sorbo, aka Hercules from the syndicated TV show *Hercules: The Legendary Journeys*, and *Gotta Dance* runner-up to Matt Lauer. I shook my head. "No, I'm saying it because I'm pretty sure if we went to see Matt Lauer in person, you would rush the stage and end up in jail, and I'd have to call my so-called soul mate to pull some strings to get you out."

"You say that like it's a bad thing," Maggie said. Then she laughed.

I grinned at her across the table. "Okay, let's talk about the art show and the food tasting. Things really are going okay?"

She set down her fork, and a shadow slid across her face. "Uh-huh. They're just better overall. I'm sorry to say it, but Mike rubbed people the wrong way. Now Liam's basically in charge. Alex isn't going to have his fingers all over everything the way Mike did." She shrugged. "Liam says it's far from a done deal, though."

"I'll keep my fingers crossed," I said. I speared another corkscrew of pasta. "I met Georgia Tepper this morning."

"You're going to love her cupcakes," Maggie said, taking a sip of her tea.

"She said Mike told her chocolate was 'last year,'" I said. I waved my fork at her. "This is good, by the way."

Maggie smiled. "I'm glad you like it." She frowned at her tea, got up and rummaged in the old pie safe until she found a small container of honey. "Yeah, Mike wanted Georgia to make some kind of 'in' cupcake with chili peppers or jalapeños. He told Mary white tablecloths were a throwback to the fifties, and I don't know what the heck he said to Burtis to aggravate him."

"Burtis is not someone you want to be on the bad side of," I commented.

"True," Mags said, drizzling a little honey into her tea. "But it was Georgia who almost took a swing at Mike with a serving tray."

"You're kidding," I said.

She twisted her mouth to one side. "I'm not."

Before I could ask her for more details, there was a knock on the half-open door and Ruby poked her head in. "Hi," she said. "Got a minute?" She was looking directly at me when she asked the question.

"Sure," I said, setting my fork down again.

"Could I paint Owen?"

"You mean the same way you're doing with Hercules?"

"That's what I was thinking."

"That's a great idea," Maggie said, putting a little more pasta salad in her bowl. "Are you thinking of letting them go to auction as a set, or as two individual paintings?"

Ruby wrinkled her nose in thought. "I'm leaning toward listing them separately just because I think that'll bring in more money for Cat People. What do you think?"

"Oh, definitely," Mags said, waving her fork like a flag. "Are you going to do a frame?"

I leaned sideways so I was a little more in Ruby's line of vision. "You can paint Owen. It's fine with me."

Ruby nodded and waved her hand absently at me. "I went with metal the last time, but I'm thinking about a black floater frame."

Okay, so she wasn't talking to me.

Maggie frowned. "What about charcoal instead of black?"

Neither was Maggie.

Ruby nodded slowly. "That might work. I don't want a frame that screams 'Look at me!'"

I leaned a little farther sideways and waved my arms in the air, kind of like I was a flag person on a highway construction crew. "Hello," I said.

They both looked at me then. "Do you need something?" Maggie asked.

"Yes," I said, sinking back on my stool. "I need to tell Ruby that she can paint Owen."

Ruby and Mags exchanged glances. "I did get that," Ruby said. "Thank you."

"Anything else?" Maggie said. I might have been imagining the tiny hint of impatience in her voice.

"I could bring Owen down first thing tomorrow morning before the library opens, if that works," I added.

"That'll work," Ruby said.

I turned to Maggie and made a move-along gesture with one hand. "I'm done."

"Thank you," she said. No, that wasn't impatience I was hearing; it was a tiny bit of sarcasm.

Mags and Ruby went back to discussing possibilities for framing the cat portraits, and I went back to my pasta salad. By the time they had settled on a charcoal frame, I was done eating. I stretched my arms up over my head, which caught Maggie's attention.

"Do you have room for a cup of hot chocolate?" she asked. "I have more of those homemade marshmallows you like."

I glanced at my watch. "Okay," I said. It was chocolate. I didn't need much persuading.

She looked at Ruby. "Rube? Hot chocolate? With marshmallows from the farmers' market?"

Ruby smiled. "Mmm, that sounds good."

Maggie got up to put the kettle back on and get out the mugs and cocoa.

"How's the setup going for the art show?" I asked Ruby.

"Better," she said, leaning her elbows on the table.

"Let me guess," I said. "You had problems with Mike Glazer as well." There seemed to be no shortage of people who did.

Ruby slid her bracelets along her arm and sighed. "Kathleen, I think everyone had problems with Mike. If he hadn't died when he did, I swear someone would have smacked him with a two-by-four by now." She shrugged. "Maybe me. Or Burtis. Wednesday night, Burtis was pounding in tent pegs with a sledgehammer and there was a moment when I actually thought he was going to take a swing at Mike."

"It's sad," Maggie said. "He spent the last days of his life arguing with people."

I thought about Wren Magnusson's face when she came into the library. She seemed to be the only person who really felt bad about Mike Glazer's death. "What was Mike like when he was younger?" I asked.

Ruby smiled a thank-you as Mags set a steaming mug in front of her. "I don't know. He was older and we didn't have any of the same friends."

Maggie handed me a cup and sat down holding her own hot chocolate. I snapped the lid of the marshmallow container open and held it out to Ruby, snagging a couple for myself. They smelled like spun sugar and vanilla.

"He was the kind of guy everyone liked, pretty much," Maggie said. "Popular, smart enough to do well in school without having to work very hard." She reached for the marshmallows, popped one in her cup and after a second's thought dropped in two more.

I leaned my forearms on the table and laced my fingers around my mug. "So when he came back a few days ago, he was different?" I said.

She nodded. "It was like he had something to prove."

"Maybe he did," I said.

"Small-town boy makes good?" Ruby asked. "You really think it was that old cliché?"

I shrugged. "Things become clichés for a reason: because they happen a lot."

"So you don't think he'd been taken over by a malevolent entity or replaced by an evil twin?" Ruby asked, eyes twinkling.

"Probably not," I said.

Ruby told me a little more about some of the artwork that was going to be on display and then available for sale online. I really hoped everything worked out.

I finished the last of my hot chocolate and stood up. "Thank you. Lunch was delicious," I told Maggie. "But I need to get back to the library."

She wrapped me in a hug. "Anytime," she said. "I wish Roma could have made it."

"Maybe we could have dinner sometime next week."

"Good idea."

I tugged on my sweater and slipped my purse over my shoulder. "I'll see you in the morning," I said to Ruby.

She smiled. "Thanks for letting me paint the cats. Tell Owen I have fish crackers."

I grinned back. "And Maggie right across the hall. Two of Owen's favorite things in the same place. You might never get rid of him."

I gave them both a little wave and headed out. As I

came level with the tents set up by the Riverwalk, I felt a chill, like a cold finger trailing up my spine. What was going to happen when everyone found out Mike Glazer's death hadn't been an accident? Because no matter what Roma said, I couldn't shake the feeling it hadn't been.

7

O wen woke me the next morning by sticking his face about an inch away from mine, and when I opened my eyes, the first thing I saw were his golden ones. He meowed at me, so I got a blast of kitty morning breath, too.

"What have you been eating?" I asked, rolling on to my back and stretching.

He was already at the bedroom door. He stopped long enough to glance back over his shoulder. "Merow!" he said. Then he kept on going. I knew cat for "Get up" when I heard it.

I yawned and sat up. Another meow, louder and more insistent, came from the hallway. Translation: "Now!"

When I got down to the kitchen, Hercules was sitting by the cats' food bowls. I bent down to pet the top of his head. "Good morning," I said. Owen was sitting next to the table, carefully washing his face.

He knew. I'd explained everything over supper last night, and I was certain that somehow he understood Ruby was going to take pictures of him and use them to paint his portrait. Now he was meticulously getting ready for that. It wasn't something I'd ever be able to explain to someone who wasn't a cat person.

"Why don't you wait until you've eaten to do that?" I said as I got the cats' breakfast.

He hesitated with a paw in midair and seemed to consider my words. Then he went back to washing the right side of his face. Apparently, having one's portrait painted required a lot of grooming.

Owen ate breakfast with even more care than he usually exhibited. Then the face-washing routine began all over again. Hercules watched his brother with what seemed to be amusement. The first problem came when it was time to leave. Owen refused to get in the cat carrier. He shook his furry gray head, marched over to the back door and sat down in front of it.

"No," I said emphatically. "You go in the bag or you don't go."

He disappeared, his default play when he couldn't get his own way.

"Fine," I said. I hung the carrier back on its hook, kicked off my shoes and sat down at the table again. I leaned forward, forearms on my knees, and smiled at Hercules, who still had that slightly amused expression on his black-and-white face.

He looked from me to approximately where I figured Owen was and then back to me again. Probably wondering who was going to blink first.

"So, what do you have planned for this morning?" I asked. "Sitting on the sunporch? A nap? Maybe some grackle stalking?"

He meowed enthusiastically at my last suggestion.

"I have to work on the staff schedule for next month." I brushed a bit of lint off the bottom of my pants. "And decide what we're going to do for Halloween programs. What do you think about a puppet show?"

He bobbed his head up and down. It might have been a yes or it might have been that he was following a dust mite drifting near the floor.

"Did you hear the phone ring last night?" I asked. "That was Roma. She invited me to have lunch out at Wisteria Hill next week."

He put a paw on my leg and looked over at the carrier bag. "I'm sure Roma wouldn't mind you going out for a look around sometime," I said.

Owen winked into view then. He stalked over to where the bag was hanging, tail flicking like a whip, and sat down underneath it.

I gave Hercules a scratch on the top of his nose. "Have a good morning," I whispered.

I got up, went over to where Owen was standing, his back to me, and set the cat tote on the floor. He got in without looking at me while I stepped into my shoes. I put the bag over my shoulder, grabbed my keys and briefcase and headed for the truck.

I set the carrier on the passenger side and unzipped the top so Owen could at least poke his head out. He took riding shotgun very seriously. We were halfway down Mountain Road before one ear emerged out of the zippered opening. After a moment, the rest of the cat followed. He sat on the seat with the bag between us and stared out of the windshield for the rest of the ride.

When we got to the River Arts Center, I pulled into Maggie's parking spot, the way I had the last time. "Bag," I said to Owen.

He climbed inside with a twitch of his ears and a flick of his tail. I made sure the zipper was done up all the way before I got out of the truck.

Ruby was waiting by the back door. "Good morning," she said, holding it open for me.

"Hi," I said.

She bent over and peeked at Owen through the front mesh panel of the carrier. "Hi, Owen," she said.

"Murp," he said in return.

Ruby laughed. "I love your cats," she said. "They're like little people in fur suits."

"You have that right," I said, following her up the stairs. "Owen definitely thinks he's a person and should have all the same rights and privileges."

Another meow came from the bag.

"See?" I said.

Ruby laughed again.

Once we were in Ruby's studio, it didn't take long for the "photo shoot" to begin. Ruby had cleared her workspace, and her camera was ready. I opened the bag and lifted Owen out. He blinked, shook himself and took a couple of passes at his face with one paw.

"You look fabulous," Ruby told him, and he immediately sat up straighter and held his head up a little higher.

"Oh, for heaven's sake!" I muttered.

Only the twitch of one ear told me that Owen had heard what I said, but since I was still on "ignore," he didn't even bother to so much as glance in my direction.

I stood over by the windows, out of the way, while Ruby took photos, posing the cat with both instructions and hand signals. I didn't think I had ever seen Owen be so compliant. When she was finished, she pulled the bag of organic fish crackers out of her tote bag and dumped a generous pile in front of Owen. He gave her a cat smile and started his sniff-and-eat routine. Ruby came over to me, scrolling through the pictures she'd just taken.

"Did you get what you needed?" I asked.

"I did. Thanks," she said, holding out the camera so I could look at the images. "That cat is so photogenic."

Owen lifted his head for a moment to look over at me. I had no idea how he knew what "photogenic" meant, but I knew cat smug when I saw it.

Ruby and I talked about her plans for the two paintings while Owen ate and did a far less meticulous washing of his face and paws than he had earlier.

"Okay, Fuzz Face," I said, setting the carrier on the table. "Time to go."

"Thank you, Owen," Ruby said.

He tilted his head to one side and meowed softly, and then he climbed into the bag.

"And thank you, Kathleen," Ruby said, giving me a

one-armed hug. "I'll let you know when both paintings are done, if you'd like to see them."

"I'd love to see them," I said. There was a loud yowl from inside the bag. I patted the side. "Apparently, so would Owen."

I put the strap of the cat carrier over my shoulder and headed for the stairs, double-checking to make sure the zipper was closed before I started down them. At the bottom, I pushed the back door open with one hip, feeling in my pants pocket for my keys.

They weren't there. Where had I put them? I felt the pockets of my coat sweater. The keys to the truck were deep in the left pocket, the ring snagged on the cranberry-colored wool.

"Crap on toast!" I muttered.

I slipped the carrier off my shoulder and set it on the pavement so I could use both hands to get the keys free without making a hole in my favorite sweater. Which means I didn't see a small gray paw figure out how to slide a zipper open from the inside.

The first thing I did see as I worked the key ring free of my sweater pocket was two gray paws and a tabby head poke out of the top of the carrier.

"No!" I said sharply. Like that ever did any good. Owen was out of the bag faster than Houdini from a straitjacket. I lunged for him, but being a cat, he could move faster. And did. Along the side of the building, straight for the tent across the street.

Not again.

"Owen! No!" I shouted. One ear twitched, but he kept going, like Hercules, pausing both times at the curb to look each way before darting across the street. I ran after him, skidding to a stop on the sidewalk to let an SUV and a half-ton truck go by before I could cross Main Street. That meant by the time I made it to the other side, Owen was already at the end flap to the tent.

"Owen! Stop!" I yelled, knowing I was wasting my breath. He poked his head around the canvas and disappeared, both inside the tent and out of sight.

I stopped outside the yellow crime scene tape that still roped off the tent. Should I duck under and go after Owen, or call Marcus? Without an officer standing guard, the area wasn't exactly secured. It wasn't a good enough excuse to ignore the yellow tape, though.

"Owen, get your furry little cat behind out here," I called.

I waited. Nothing. I looked around to see if anyone was watching and then, feeling kind of silly, I stuck one arm under the crime scene tape and moved my hand through the air, just in case the cat was sitting there, invisible, watching me make a fool of myself.

If he was, he wasn't anywhere I could get my hands on him.

I pulled out my phone and keyed in Marcus's number, mentally crossing my fingers that I got him and not his voice mail. This wasn't something I wanted to explain in a message.

"Hi, Kathleen," he said, answering after just a couple of rings.

"Hi, Marcus," I said, wondering, for a moment, how to start explaining what had happened. "I, uh, kind of have a problem."

His voice rumbled through the phone against my ear. "What is it? Did one of your cats find another dead body?"

I pulled my free hand down over my neck and one shoulder, wishing that Owen would come out of the tent and I could just scoop him up and head home. He didn't, of course.

"No," I said slowly. "But Owen's . . . in the tent."

For a moment there was silence. "Which tent?" Marcus finally asked, his tone cautious.

"The one that's surrounded by crime scene tape," I said, cringing as the words came out.

I heard him sigh on the other end of the phone, and I could picture the tight line of his jaw.

"Why? How?" He paused for a second. "Never mind. I'm on my way. Don't move." He stressed the last two words.

"I won't," I promised, but he was already gone.

I stood on the grass, hands in the pockets of my sweater, jingling the keys that had started this whole mess. I kept one eye on the flap of the tent just in case Owen decided to grace Riverwalk with his presence. I knew he'd come out when it suited him and not a moment before.

Marcus pulled up about five minutes later. "I don't suppose Owen decided to come out by himself," he said as he came around the front of his SUV.

"I haven't seen even a whisker," I said. At least that was true. If Owen wasn't in the tent anymore, then he was likely sitting somewhere close, watching us, hiding in his own personal Cloak of Invisibility.

Marcus started for the yellow tape. "Do I want to know how this happened?" I'd expected him to be a lot more, well, annoyed—mad—about what Owen had done. There was a time he would have been. Of course, there was a time I never would have imagined Marcus cooking dinner for me.

"I think you do," I said, "being someone who likes to stick to the facts."

He almost smiled. Then he ducked under the plastic tape and beckoned to me with one finger. "So tell me the facts."

"You want me to come with you?" I said.

He nodded and I got a small smile as well. "I saw what happened when somebody other than you tried to pick up that cat. Remember?"

I did. Owen and I had almost been killed when a couple of propane tanks exploded. I'd ended up in the back of an ambulance, suffering from hypothermia. Despite Marcus's warning to everyone not to touch the cat, a police officer had tried to move him out of the paramedic's way. The officer had ended up needing his own paramedic.

Marcus held up the heavy canvas flap, and I followed him into the tent, pausing a couple of steps inside to let my eyes adjust to the dimmer light. Everything looked pretty much the same as the last time, except, of course, that the body and the white resin chair were gone. And there was a gray tabby cat, digging at the ground by the long side wall of the tent.

"Owen," I said sharply. "What are you doing?"

The cat looked from me to Marcus. Then, with his

golden eyes locked on the detective's face, he scratched at a spot on the grass where about two inches of the tent wall made a lip on the ground and meowed loudly.

I walked over and crouched down beside him so I could get a closer look at where he'd been digging. Something seemed to be stuck in the damp earth. "Marcus, you better look at this," I said. "I think Owen found something."

Marcus came to stand beside me, leaning over to see where I was pointing.

"I think it's a button," I said. It looked as though it had fallen on the grass and then been stepped on, pushing it down into the ground. It was metal, and at first glance, it looked to be vintage. Handmade, maybe.

He bent down for a better look. He didn't say anything, but I caught an almost imperceptible nod of his head. Then he straightened and felt for his phone.

I reached for Owen. "Good job on the button or whatever it is," I whispered. "Don't think you're not in trouble, though." He rubbed the side of his face against my neck and shifted in my arms so he could watch Marcus.

Once Marcus had finished his call, he looked at me. "You can take him outside," he said, inclining his head toward the cat while his eyes were already drifting back to the tent wall.

I pointed at the small patch of torn-up grass and earth. "Do you think that button belongs to the person who killed Mike Glazer?"

That got me all of his attention. "I didn't say anyone killed Mike Glazer," he said. He hadn't, but I knew him well enough to hear the tiniest edge in his voice, and I knew that just because he hadn't said it didn't mean I wasn't right.

"No, you didn't," I said. "Owen and I are just going to wait out there for you." I'd said I was going to stay out of his case and I was, even though it seemed as though the cats were on a mission to drag me into it.

I used my shoulder to nudge the tent flap out of the way, and then I ducked under the yellow tape and stood on the grass next to the sidewalk. Owen twisted in my arms.

"If you're thinking what I think you're thinking, don't," I warned, but all he did was shift around until his paws were on my shoulder and he could watch the tent.

Marcus came out in a minute or two. He stood next to me, feet apart, hands in his pockets. "Start from the beginning. Tell me what happened."

I did, starting from when I'd stepped out of the River Arts building. Marcus's eyebrows rose when I explained how Owen had figured out how to slide the zipper pull from the inside of the bag. The cat, in turn, seemed to pull himself up a little straighter in my arms, as if he were proud of his ingenuity—which he probably was.

"You can go, Kathleen," Marcus said when I finished. "If I need to know anything else, I'll call you. You'll be at the library?"

I glanced at my watch. There wasn't time to take Owen home. "Yes," I said.

He reached out and touched my arm as I started for

the curb. "Thanks for calling me. You could have just gone in and grabbed Owen."

I made a face and shook my head. "No, I couldn't."

I got a smile for that. "I'll see you tonight, if I don't talk to you before then," he said.

A police van pulled in behind Marcus's SUV.

"Okay," I said. I made sure I had a secure grip on Owen, nodded to the two officers who had gotten out of the van and crossed the street.

The cat carrier was still sitting on the pavement by the back door of the studio building. I bent down and snagged the strap with one finger. Once we were next to the truck, I set it down again, got out my keys and unlocked the driver's side. Then I put Owen on the seat. He walked across to the passenger side and sat, the picture of a well-behaved cat. I set the bag beside him and got in. "Why did you do that?" I asked

He meowed and scraped a paw on the seat cover.

"Yes, I know you might have found a clue," I said. "You also trespassed on a crime scene."

Two wide eyes stared blankly at me. Either he didn't understand what I'd just said to him, or he didn't care.

I was betting on the latter.

8

At the library, I took Owen straight up to my office. He climbed out of the bag onto my desk, shook himself and gave me a pointed look. I knew what he was looking for.

"Ruby already gave you a treat," I said, trying to keep my tone stern. "And after what you did, you should be on bread and water."

Defiantly, he pawed at the top of my desk. So he was going to try righteous indignation instead of cute and adorable.

"Just because you might, *might* have found some kind of clue doesn't mean you weren't wrong," I said, lowering my voice because I didn't want Mary or Susan to come in and hear me arguing with a cat.

Owen stared at me. I glared back at him. "You drive me crazy sometimes," I said after a couple of minutes of the eyeball-to-eyeball routine. I sat on the edge of the desk, and he came and put his front paws on my lap. I stroked the top of his head. "I'm serious," I said. "What if someone had seen you disappear? How would I have explained that to Marcus?"

Owen lifted a paw and swatted one of the buttons on my sweater.

"That did look like it could have been a button you dug up," I said. "Doesn't mean it was dropped by whoever killed Mike Glazer."

Owen made a low murp. "I know," I said, scratching behind his right ear. "Doesn't mean it wasn't, either." I leaned over so my face was inches from Owen's soft gray one. "You're making it really hard to stay out of Marcus's case, you know."

I gave Owen some water, a couple of sardine crackers and an emphatic warning not to leave my office. Then I locked the door for good measure. I was back downstairs just as Susan and Mary arrived. I let them in and followed them up to the staff room. "Oh, before I forget, Owen is in my office," I said.

Susan pushed her glasses up her nose. "Because?" she prompted.

"Because he was over posing for Ruby. She's going to paint him. It's for the Cat People fund-raiser."

"I thought she was painting Hercules," Mary said, pouring water into the coffeemaker.

"She's doing both of them." I got the coffee out of the cupboard and handed it to her.

"That's really nice," Susan said, shrugging off her jacket and pulling on a cropped black cardigan. She stopped with one arm half in a sleeve. "I have chicken salad, if he's hungry. He probably wouldn't like the arugula or the black olives, but the chicken isn't too spicy."

"Thanks," I said. "Owen's fine. Ruby had some organic fish crackers for him." I didn't bother telling her I'd just recently learned that Owen apparently loved black olives.

Susan and I spent most of the morning unpacking two boxes of books that had been donated to the library—a mix of children's picture books, graphic novels and reference books, including a huge atlas and a book of star charts—and entering them into our system. I called Abigail at home to talk about plans for a Halloween puppet show and installed a new math game on the two computers we kept reserved for kids.

As far as I could tell, Owen spent the morning napping in the sunshine on my desk chair. That's where I found him after we'd closed down the library at one o'clock. I knew that didn't mean he hadn't nosed all over my office, just that he hadn't left any obvious evidence. There was a good chance that sometime next week I'd find a clump of hair behind a book or in one of my desk drawers. I was glad that we closed early on Saturday. How much mischief would he have been able to get into if he'd spent the whole day alone in my office?

Hercules was waiting in the porch when we got home. He looked from me to Owen, wondering, maybe, if we'd been off somewhere having fun while he was stuck at home.

"If you're wondering why I didn't bring your brother back earlier, it's because he decided it was a better idea to go digging around in a crime scene," I said.

Herc murped at Owen, who murped back. I wondered what they were talking about. Were they discussing the button or whatever it was Owen had uncovered? Or were they plotting how to get me to open a can of sardines?

For lunch, I heated the last of the chicken soup I'd made earlier in the week with my Crock-Pot. Hercules trailed me, making little rumbles and meows from time to time. Every once in a while, he'd stop and look expectantly at me and I'd say, "Really?" or "I understand."

I spent the afternoon doing laundry and cleaning the house. Hercules and I had recently discovered Nickelback. It turned out Owen didn't like Chad Kroeger any more than he liked Barry Manilow. We didn't even get to the chorus of "Never Gonna Be Alone" before Owen streaked through the kitchen like Boris the dog was on his tail, vaulting the mop in his haste to get to the porch door and the backyard.

It took me a ridiculously long time to get dressed and do my hair for supper with Marcus. I stood in front of the closet door with Owen on one side and Hercules on the other, pulling out things and putting them back on the rod. Finally, I settled on jeans and a lavender shirt my sister, Sara, had convinced me to buy when I was back in Boston. Neither cat yowled or hid under the bed, so I figured I looked okay.

I double-checked to make sure there was fresh water in the boys' dishes and a clean litter box downstairs. "I'm leaving," I called as I pulled on my jacket. Hercules poked his head around the living room doorway. "Don't wait up," I told him, waggling my eyebrows. That got no reaction.

After a moment, Owen's gray tabby head appeared on the other side of the doorway. "Stay off the footstool," I reminded him. I knew he wouldn't.

It was a beautiful evening, with just a bit of a chill in the air, a reminder that fall was here. The leaves were starting to turn and I could see splashes of gold and red in the trees around Marcus's little house.

I knocked on the back door, and after a moment he called, "Come in, Kathleen."

I stepped into the kitchen and immediately smelled chocolate. That was a good sign. I breathed in deeply. I could also catch the scent of oranges and something spicy as well. Marcus was at the counter, slicing a zucchini.

"Hi." He smiled at me over his shoulder. He was wearing a denim shirt and jeans. The hair at the nape of his neck was just a little damp.

"Hi," I said, suddenly feeling a little awkward. "It smells wonderful in here."

He set down the knife. "That's probably Eric's pudding cake."

I took off my jacket and hung it over the back of one of the kitchen chairs. "You made Eric's chocolate pudding cake?" I asked.

Marcus shook his head. "No. Eric made Eric's chocolate pudding cake. I just brought it home and stuck it in the oven." He reached for the knife again. "Are you hungry? I can start cooking in about five minutes."

I nodded. "Great. Is there anything I can do to help?"

"I have it all under control," he said, turning back to the counter. "Have a seat."

I pulled out a chair and sat down while he made short work of the rest of the zucchini. "Marcus, could we talk about this morning and get that out of the way?" I asked. It wasn't exactly the Sword of Damocles, but I didn't want Owen's sleuthing hanging over us all evening.

"Sure," he said, wiping his hands and turning around.

"I'm sorry that Owen trespassed on your crime scene."

Marcus leaned back against the edge of the counter, braced his hands on either side of his body and smiled at me. "Kathleen, I do know you didn't send Owen into the tent on purpose."

No, I hadn't sent Owen across the street, but I was certain he'd headed for the tent deliberately. Just the same way that he'd prowled through a pile of recycling when Gregor Easton had been killed. And discovered a puzzle box and a piece of paper—hidden in a stack of cartons at River Arts—that turned out to be the key to the scam that artist Jaeger Merrill had been running. Both Owen and Hercules seemed to have a nose for sleuthing.

"Maybe I could teach Owen to at least bring you a cup of coffee if he's going to stick his whiskers in your case," I said, trying to keep my tone light.

"I think I'd rather have coffee with you," Marcus said.

His deep blue eyes met mine, and for a moment what I'd been going to say next fell right out of my head. If the timer on his stove hadn't started buzzing just then, I think I would have just kept staring at him.

"I have to check dessert," Marcus said, gesturing in the direction of the oven with his eyes still glued to my face.

Was it my imagination, or was he flustered, too?

I waited while he looked at Eric's pudding cake and adjusted the oven temperature before I said anything else. I liked watching him move, and it took me that long to get my train of thought back on the rails.

"Do you think that button Owen found had anything to do with Mike Glazer's killer?" I asked finally. "And yes, I know it doesn't sound like I'm staying out of things."

"No, it doesn't," he said, turning the heat on under the wok that was sitting on one of the stove's front burners.

"Would you believe I'm only asking because Owen wants to know?"

"Given that Owen isn't like any other cat I've ever been around . . ." He shook his head and laughed. Then his expression grew serious. "What makes you think someone killed Mike Glazer?"

"The petechiae—those pinpoints of bleeding under his skin. I saw them when I checked to see if he was still alive. I think he was asphyxiated somehow."

"You're really observant."

Maybe we really had changed our past pattern. I frowned at him. "No, you see, that wasn't your line.

You were supposed to say, 'Stay out of my case, Kathleen.'" I made my voice low and gruff and my expression stern.

"I do not look like that, and I don't sound like that, either." He frowned. I wasn't sure if the expression was meant for me or the wok.

I leaned back in the chair and laced my fingers over my middle. "Yes, you do," I said.

He dumped a plate of chicken into the wok. It sizzled as it hit the hot oil. I waited.

Finally, he nodded. "We're not going to be able to keep it quiet much longer. You're right. It doesn't look like Mike Glazer's death was an accident. For now we're just calling it suspicious."

"Does that mean the whole pitch to Legacy will be off again?"

"I don't know," he said. "Maybe. Maybe not."

I watched him cook for a couple of minutes. I knew how hard Liam and Maggie and a lot of other people in town had worked to make the food tasting and art show come together. If Legacy did decide to base a fall tour package around Mayville Heights, it could be very good for the local economy. But would they really want to bring their clients to a place where one of their partners had been murdered? I didn't think so.

"I don't suppose you could figure out who killed Mike Glazer and prove that it was no one from Mayville Heights in, say, the next forty-eight hours?" I asked.

He shot me an amused look. "Sorry," he said, pouring a small dish of sauce over the chicken and vegetables in the wok. "It doesn't quite work that way. The investigation's just getting started."

"Owen already found a clue for you," I teased. "That button."

"I didn't say that was a clue," he countered. "I didn't even say it was a button."

"But it was." The conversation was beginning to feel a little like a volleyball match. Every time I spiked, Marcus managed a return.

"Okay, let's say it was a button your cat found—for the sake of argument. That doesn't mean it came from something the killer was wearing. Half the town has been down on the Riverwalk in the past few days, including both of us." He drained a pot of noodles with one smooth, fast motion and used a long pair of chopsticks to divide them between two blue china bowls before moving back to the stove.

"I didn't lose a button," I said. "You're welcome to check my jacket. And there's a pretty good chance the one Owen found is either vintage or handmade. It definitely wasn't mass-produced plastic."

Marcus's eyebrows went up. "Owen told you that?"

Orange and spices tickled my nose as he set one of the blue bowls in front of me. I picked up the set of black lacquer chopsticks at my place. "Didn't you know? I speak cat."

He slid into the chair opposite me and reached for his own chopsticks. "You know, I half believe you," he said. "I've always wondered why you seem to be able to communicate with Lucy. She has some kind of rapport with you that she doesn't have with any of the other volunteers who feed the cats out there."

"Out there" was Wisteria Hill. There was a colony of feral cats that called the old carriage house on the estate home. Lucy, a little calico, was the undisputed leader of the group, and we did have some kind of connection I couldn't explain. When I'd asked Roma what she thought the reason was, she'd just shrugged and said simply, "She likes you."

"That rapport might just be because she thinks I smell like sardines," I said. "I do make a lot of stinky crackers for the boys."

"Somehow, I don't think it's the sardines," Marcus said.

I didn't think it was the sardines, either. I couldn't say it to Marcus or Roma, but I sometimes wondered if Lucy, like Herc and Owen, had some kind of "unique" ability that I just hadn't seen yet and that was why she responded to me. I'd always felt that the boys had chosen me, not the other way around, and like Lucy, they were Wisteria Hill cats. Maybe I was some kind of magnet for cats with paranormal abilities.

Okay, that definitely wasn't the kind of thought I could share with Roma or Marcus. "This is good," I said, gesturing to my dish.

"Thank you," he said.

Dang, he was cute when he smiled. Plus he could cook and fix rocking chairs and he had his own mini library in the spare bedroom. All of a sudden I couldn't remember any of the reasons I'd always insisted to

Maggie and Roma that Marcus and I were completely wrong for each other.

This was either a very good thing or a very bad one.

"You didn't answer my question," he said, his tone just a tad too casual. "Why do you think that button is either old or was handmade?"

I shook my head and refocused my attention. "The hypothetical button?" I asked.

A bit of color flushed his cheeks. "Okay, you got me," he said. "It was a button Owen found, but that stays between us."

I nodded and scooped more noodles from my bowl. "I only got a quick look at it, but from what I saw, it didn't look like a plastic button. I think it might have been metal, probably brass, which suggests something old or at least something not mass-produced. And the design—square center and sloped sides—is very old-style."

Marcus looked at me, clearly skeptical. "You got all that from a 'quick look'?"

I felt my own face warming now. "You said I was observant. I guess I am. It probably comes from living with two actors. My mother and father notice everything, every detail, every nuance about people and situations. That's why they've both always been good at creating characters and it's probably why my mother is developing a reputation as an excellent director." I didn't add that my parents' keen powers of observation meant that at any given time they might be "living" their characters as well.

I snared a half-moon of zucchini with my chopsticks.

"And I know a little about a lot of things. That's just part of being a librarian."

"Why did you decide to be a librarian and not an actor?" Marcus asked. "Or something else artistic? Your brother's a musician, right?"

I nodded. "Uh-huh, and Sara is a filmmaker and a makeup artist. She's shooting and directing Ethan's band's first video."

"So why aren't you on stage or behind a camera?"

"Short answer: I have no talent."

He slowly shook his head. "I don't think so. What's the long answer?"

The conversation had taken a sharp detour away from the Glazer case, but that was okay. There wasn't anything else I wanted to know. At least, right now there wasn't.

"The long answer." I frowned at the ceiling, trying to find the right words to explain. "Well, I didn't exactly have the white-picket-fence childhood. My mother and father performed in theaters all up and down the East Coast when I was a kid and even for a while when Ethan and Sara were little. Big elaborate theaters with live orchestras and balcony boxes and little rinky-dink places that seated only fifty people above a bakery where everyone went for sticky buns during intermission."

"You're kidding."

I laughed. "No, I'm not. And I'm not saying it was a terrible childhood, because it wasn't, but it sure wasn't conventional."

Marcus pushed his empty bowl away and leaned

back in his chair. "So you wanted 'conventional'?" he said.

"I wanted normal. Or what I thought of as normal."

"Mayville Heights is your idea of normal?" he said, a smile crinkling the corners of his eyes.

"Compared to how I grew up? Oh, yeah." I twisted the last three noodles in my dish around one chopstick and ate them. "Except for the fifteen months my parents were divorced, I always had both of them in the same house. But sometimes I was living with Lady Macbeth and Banquo, and sometimes it was Adelaide and Nathan Detroit. I wanted parents who went to the office and came home and made meat loaf and mashed potatoes for dinner, not a mother and father who staged Act One of *Les Misérables* in the dining room." I gave a half shrug. "The acoustics were better than the living room."

"Of course," he said as he got up and collected our dishes.

"Everywhere we lived, I always managed to find a library and my favorite books. When I found out I could actually work in one, well, I never thought of doing anything else." I tucked one leg up under me as Marcus took the pudding cake out of the oven. "And there probably was a little rebelliousness in the decision."

"Instead of running off to join the circus, you ran off to join the library."

"Pretty much." I watched him spoon dessert into two more blue bowls. He set one in front of me, and I closed my eyes for a moment and inhaled the rich chocolate scent. When I opened them again, he was watching me and smiling.

"So what about you?" I asked, picking up my spoon.

"What do you mean?"

I had to make a little moan of pleasure at the taste of the first mouthful before I could answer. "Why did you become a police officer?" I waved my spoon at him. "And I want to hear the long answer."

He pulled a hand back through his dark hair. "I don't know if there is a long answer. A police officer is what I always wanted to be except for the summer I was five when I wanted to drive the ice cream truck."

"Who wouldn't?" I mumbled around a mouthful of cake and sauce.

"I have been told I have an overdeveloped sense of right and wrong," he said. "Maybe that's part of it."

"I don't think I used the word 'overdeveloped,'" I said.

"It was implied," he said dryly.

We ate in silence for another minute or so. Then Marcus spoke again. "Probably my father had something to do with it as well."

"Was your father a police officer?"

He shook his head. "No. But he was a very black-and-white kind of person." He made a chopping motion in the air with one hand to emphasize the words. "And very focused on the facts. Not really a people person."

"You're a people person," I said, trying to decide if it would be rude to lick sauce off the back of my spoon.

Marcus was already on his feet to get me a second

helping, which I thought about turning down for maybe a millisecond. "You're just saying that so you can have seconds," he said.

"No, I'm not," I said, smiling a thank-you at him. "Yes, I sometimes think you get too caught up in the facts and forget about the feelings involved, but people like you. Maggie, Roma, Rebecca, Oren—they like you and they respect what you do." I ate another bite of pudding. "And the cats like you—not just my two; look at Desmond over at Roma's clinic. Even Lucy will come closer to you than she does to anyone else besides me."

He grinned. "Kathleen, cats are not people."

"I wouldn't say that out loud around Owen or Hercules," I warned. "They think they're people."

His grin just got wider.

He pointed in the direction of the living room then. "Don't let me forget. I have something I want to show you."

"Do I get a hint?" I asked.

He shook his head. "No."

I couldn't coax even the tiniest clue out of him. He sat there with just the ghost of a smile on his face, slowly—on purpose, I was certain—finishing his dessert and sipping his coffee.

Finally, he pushed his chair back and stood up. "Are you finished?" he asked.

I nodded. "Yes."

He led me down to the living room. A small cardboard box was sitting on the coffee table.

"Go ahead," he urged. "Take a look."

I lifted one flap of the carton and peeked inside.

Then I turned my head to grin at him. "Where did you get these?" The box was about two-thirds filled with vintage Batman comic books from the early 1970s.

"One of the guys at the station found them in the attic of the house he just bought. He was going to toss them."

I shook my head. "These are pop culture. These are art. I'm so glad you saved them." I pointed to the comic on top of the pile. "That's *Wail of the Ghost Bride*, and it looks to be in decent shape. Who knows what else is in there?"

"Why don't you go through them and find out?"

"You don't mind?"

He was sitting on the edge of the blue corduroy sofa, leaning forward with his elbows resting on his knees. "Kathleen, they're yours."

For a moment I'm sure my mouth gaped like a fish that had jumped too high and to its surprise ended up on the shoreline instead of in the water again. "Mine?" I finally said.

"You're the Batman fan," he said.

I was. In fact, Owen and I had been watching episodes of the old TV show online. I'd discovered Batman comics—it was still hard for me to think of them as graphic novels—the summer I was twelve and my parents were performing in a partially converted theater in New Hampshire. Emphasis on "partially."

One of the stagehands had found a pile of Batman comic books mixed in with a stash of old *National Geographics* and some girlie magazines. In its previous incarnations, the theater had been a dentist's office and a funeral parlor, and sometimes I wondered just whose waiting room the magazines had come from.

"I can't take these," I said, putting one hand on the top of the box. "Some of these issues could be worth money."

"I told Kevin that, but he didn't care, probably because he was getting the barbecue."

I waved a hand in his face. "Wait a second. What barbecue?"

"The barbecue I got from Eric," he said. "It was one of the ones he used at the party to celebrate the library's centennial. Remember?"

I sank down onto the opposite end of the couch from where Marcus was sitting. "No," I said. I shook my head. "I mean, yes, I remember the party, but I didn't know you ended up with a barbecue."

Marcus nodded. "Uh-huh. Eric wanted a utility trailer that he could tow with his van, so we traded."

"But there's a barbecue out on your deck," I said, gesturing in the direction of the backyard.

"I know."

We were already way off track, but I couldn't seem to stop myself from asking. "Why did you trade for a barbecue with Eric when you didn't need a barbecue?"

He shrugged. "I didn't need a utility trailer, either."

I knew where this was going. "Because you already had one."

"Right."

Since I was already deeply confused, I decided to go for broke. "How did you end up with two utility trailers?"

"I had one that I'd built. The second one came from Burtis. It was smaller."

I pushed a stray piece of hair off my face. "And Burtis got?"

"The blue bench that I got from you."

The blue bench was something I'd trash picked and painted. And then discovered it was an inch too long for the space under the coat hooks in the kitchen.

Marcus gestured at the box. "So Batman is all yours."

It was *Let's Make a Deal*, Mayville Heights style.

I reached over and gave his arm a squeeze. "Thank you," I said. "I can't believe you did this. I can't believe you even remembered that I'd told you I was a Batman fan." I reached over and took the top comic out of the carton. "I haven't read any of these vintage Batman in . . . in a long time. They take me back to my geeky girl days."

He leaned back against the cushions and crossed his arms over his chest. "I can't picture you as ever having been geeky," he said

"You'll just have to use your imagination," I told him, pulling the comic books a little closer.

"I can do that," he said.

I ducked my head over the open box. I wasn't sure I was ready to hear exactly what he might be imagining.

I spent maybe another five or ten minutes exclaiming over the stack of comics, holding up issues and giving Marcus a summary of their story lines. Then he poured us each another cup of coffee, and we went out onto the deck in the fading light. He sat in a slat-back wooden chair and propped his feet up on the railing while I took the swing, kicking off my shoes so I could curl my feet underneath me.

"This is so beautiful," I said, looking out over the backyard, rimmed with trees. The leaves were already turning, and even in the half-light of dusk I could still see colors from amber to scarlet. "How long have you been here?"

"Three years this winter," he said. "I liked the place the moment I saw it." He sank a little lower in his chair. "You know, it's kind of because of Desmond that I'm here."

"Roma's Desmond?" I asked.

"Uh-huh."

Desmond was another Wisteria Hill cat. Marcus had found the cat, injured, by the side of the road and taken him to Roma's clinic. She'd ended up having to treat both of them. Desmond wasn't exactly social.

Curious, Roma had done a little exploring at the old estate and found the feral cat colony. Marcus had been her first volunteer, although I wasn't sure if he'd actually volunteered or if he'd been conscripted. Oddly, the cat seemed to like the clinic, so Roma had kept him. Desmond was long and lean with sleek black fur and there was something just a little intimidating about his presence. He was missing one eye and half an ear, which only made him seem more imposing.

I made a hurry-up motion with one hand. "Tell me," I said.

"There isn't that much to tell," he said, setting his mug up on the railing. "I found Desmond. I took him to the clinic, and that's when I met Roma for the first time. I knew she'd taken over the practice when Joe Ross retired. A couple of days later, I went back to see how Desmond was doing and we started talking. She told me that Joe had bought a sailboat and was planning to sail around the world so he was selling his house. I drove past on my way home and made him an offer in the morning."

He reached over and patted one of the railing's wooden spindles. "Most of the work has been outside so far. The yard was kind of overgrown. The end wall of the garage had a tilt that had to be fixed. And I built the deck."

"You built this?"

He nodded. "With a lot of help from Harry Taylor." He laughed. "Don't worry. Harry put the swing together, so you're safe."

"I wasn't worried," I said, folding my hands around my cup. He could cook. He could build things. He smelled good. I took a sip of my coffee. I needed to think about something else.

"So what's next?" I asked to distract myself from thinking about how great Marcus smelled.

"The attic," he said at once. "There are boxes up there from whoever owned the house before Joe bought it. I have no idea what's in them or who they might belong to."

"A mystery," I said. "I like those."

"I've noticed that," he said with a laugh.

We talked about his plans for the house for a while. I set my mug down on the wide deck boards and rubbed my left arm.

"Your wrist hurts," Marcus said, dropping his feet and straightening up in the chair.

"A little bit," I said. "I think we're going to get some rain." I'd broken my left wrist just over a year ago, and since then I'd become pretty good at predicting the weather based on how it felt.

I stretched and slid my feet back into my shoes. "I should get going. Owen could have Fred the Funky Chicken parts all over the kitchen by now."

Marcus got the box of comic books and carried it out to the truck for me. "Thank you for those," I said, tipping my head toward the carton on the passenger seat. "And for dinner. Will you come and have dinner with me—and the fur balls? Maybe next week?"

"I'd like that," he said. "I'll check my schedule and let you know."

He smiled, and I thought about standing on my tip-toes, grabbing the collar of his shirt and pulling him down for a kiss. While I was thinking about it—and having a little internal debate with myself—he leaned down and kissed me.

His mouth was warm, his lips were soft and for a second—which was about how long the kiss lasted—I forgot how to breathe. Aside from kissing my dad on the cheek and Ethan on the top of his head—mostly because it bugged the heck out of him—I hadn't kissed a man since Andrew. Andrew whom I'd thought I'd marry until we had a fight and he went on a two-week fishing trip and came back married to someone else.

I'd forgotten how much I liked kissing.

Marcus trailed one hand along my shoulder and then he took a step backward. "Good night, Kathleen," he said.

"Good night, Marcus," I said.

I got in the truck, started it and concentrated on backing slowly and carefully out of the driveway. Marcus raised a hand, and I did the same as I drove away. I didn't think at all about backing him up against the door of the truck and kissing him until he was the one who couldn't breathe.

No, I didn't.

Hercules and Owen were sitting by the back door when I stepped into the kitchen, almost as though they'd been waiting for me to come home.

"Hello. How was your evening?" I said.

They exchanged glances and then looked at me, cocking their heads to the left at the same time, like the movement had been choreographed. They trailed me as I hung up my jacket and carried the box of comic books into the living room. I sat down in the big chair and set the comics on the footstool.

Herc narrowed his green eyes and studied the cardboard carton. I patted my lap. "Come up," I said. "You know you want to." He jumped up onto my lap and stepped carefully onto the end of the footstool. Then he stood on his back legs so he could poke his nose inside the box.

"Batman," I said.

The furry black-and-white face surfaced, and it looked like he was frowning. "No," I said. "Batman, not bat like the one who chased you across the backyard." He made a small sound and his head disappeared back under the cardboard flap.

Owen had run out of patience by then. He didn't wait for an invitation. He launched himself onto my lap, then leaned over and gave the carton a poke with one paw. Hercules meowed his annoyance, his head still inside.

"Stop that," I said sternly to Owen.

He gave a snippy meow of his own; then he turned around, settled himself and stared at me.

"What do you want?" I asked. "A full rundown of my evening?"

"Rroww," he rumbled.

"You're worse than Maggie," I said, running my fingers through my hair. "Okay, Marcus made stir-fried chicken with noodles. It was very good."

Owen waited a moment, then pawed at my left leg. Cat for "And then what?"

"We had Eric's chocolate pudding cake for dessert."

He licked his lips, but his gaze didn't move from my face.

I scratched behind his ears and he started to purr. I leaned a little closer. "And you were right. That was a button you dug up this morning." He ducked his head for a moment, giving me a sideways glance with one eye. "Yes, I know, modesty prevents you from saying, 'I told you so.'"

I yawned. "Then Marcus gave me that box of comic books." I gave the cats a brief summary of all the deals that had led to Marcus ending up with the old Batman comics. Neither one seemed very interested.

"And that was pretty much it." I linked my fingers together and stretched my arms out in front of me. "Oh, and he kissed me."

Owen had just turned to take another look at what his brother was doing. He swung around and almost fell off my lap. Hercules jerked his head out of the box so quickly he banged it on the cardboard flap. Clearly they knew what the word "kissed" meant.

"Don't get too excited," I told them. "It was just one kiss."

The cats exchanged a look then, and if I hadn't known better, I would have almost thought they seemed pleased.

9

I was sweeping the porch stairs the next morning while Owen did his morning survey of our yard and Rebecca's and Hercules perched on the top step and watched for the grackle. Harry Taylor—Young Harry—came around the side of the house. I smiled at him. "Hi, Harry," I said.

"Good morning, Kathleen." He smiled back at me. "Do you have a minute?"

"Sure," I said, leaning the broom against the railing. "What is it?"

"I need a favor."

I nodded. "Okay."

"You might want to hear what it is first," he said. His expression was serious, and it struck me that maybe the favor had something to do with his father, Harrison Taylor Senior.

Harry must have seen something in my expression, because he held up a hand. "Don't worry. The old man's fine. When I left, he was making bread with Elizabeth."

Elizabeth was Harry's half sister, the product of a relationship Harrison had had while his wife was dying. They'd met for the first time just a few months ago.

"But the favor does kind of have something to do with him," Harry said. He swiped a hand over his chin.

I put a hand on my chest. "You know how I feel about your dad. Anything I can do for him, I will."

"Okay. See if you can figure out what happened to Mike Glazer—who killed him—because it's pretty clear someone did."

"The police are investigating that, Harry," I said.

He shoved his hands in the pockets of his blue windbreaker and shifted from one foot to the other. "The police were investigating Agatha Shepherd's death, but if it hadn't been for you, the old man never would have gotten those papers that helped us find Elizabeth."

I shook my head. "That was mostly just being in the right place at the right time," I said.

"More like the wrong place, Kathleen. You almost got blown to pieces."

"But I didn't," I said. "Harry, I'm not a cop. And why do you care so much about what happened to Mike Glazer? And why would your father?"

"Elizabeth." He exhaled slowly. "Have you met Wren Magnusson?"

"At the library."

"Boris had a run-in with a porcupine a while back. Elizabeth came with me when I took him down to Roma."

I winced and shot Hercules a warning look not to make any editorial comment. He didn't like Harrison's German shepherd any more than Owen did, even though the big dog was gentle and even-tempered. Herc glared back at me and then became very interested in one of his feet.

"Wren was at the clinic. The two of them hit it off. They're both crazy about animals. Thing is, Wren used to be close to the Glazers."

"I heard."

"She's upset. So's Elizabeth, and that makes the old man upset. There's talk that Glazer's death wasn't an accident. Paper said it's under investigation."

"There's always talk going around town about something," I said.

"Kathleen, people tell you things," Harry said. "You're the one who figured out how Tom Karlsson ended up buried out at Wisteria Hill. You figured out who killed him." He put one foot up on the bottom step. "Look, I'm not asking you to sneak around behind Marcus Gordon's back. I know there's something starting between the two of you. Just ask a few questions and tell him what you find out, whatever the heck that ends up to be. That's all I'm asking. Please."

It was a very bad idea. I wasn't a police officer. I was a librarian with a couple of inquisitive cats that had questionable magical abilities. I'd told Marcus that I'd stay out of his investigation. I wasn't sure he'd understand. And I really wanted to repeat that kiss from last night.

I knew I had to tell Harry no, but when I opened my mouth what came out was "Yes."

The cats let the alarm clock wake me up on Monday morning. When I reached over to shut it off, there was Hercules, sitting by the door.

"I'm awake," I told him, rolling over onto my back. I knew he was likely to stay there until I was actually out of the bed. "Where's your brother?" I asked.

Herc looked over his shoulder toward the hallway. Owen was probably downstairs in the kitchen, not so patiently waiting for breakfast. I threw the blankets back and got up. I wasn't going to find any insights staring at the ceiling.

I was right. Owen was in the kitchen, sitting right beside his dishes.

"I'm not late," I told him as I put out food and water for both cats. "You're up early." He ignored me. Owen wasn't really a morning person.

As I reached for the oatmeal in the refrigerator, it struck me that one of Eric's breakfast sandwiches would taste pretty good. And if I was going to ask some questions about Mike Glazer's death, the diner was a good place to start.

Claire was pouring coffee for a couple at a table by the window when I walked into the restaurant. "You can sit anywhere, Kathleen," she said, smiling at me.

Eric was behind the counter, and I walked over to say hello. He had a cup of coffee poured before I even sat down on one of the shiny silver stools.

"Good morning," he said, setting the heavy china

mug in front of me. He was wearing his normally close-cropped salt-and-pepper hair a little longer and it suited him.

"Good morning and thank you," I said, reaching for the cream and sugar.

Eric waited while I added both to my cup, stirred and took a long drink.

"Mmm, that's good," I said with a sigh of satisfaction.

"What can I get you?" he asked. "An omelet, maybe? I have some nice orange peppers."

I propped my elbows on the counter. "I was thinking about one of your breakfast sandwiches."

"Good choice," Claire said as she passed behind Eric with her half-empty coffeepot.

He smiled and headed back to the kitchen. "It'll just be a couple of minutes."

I was wondering how to bring up the subject of Mike Glazer's death as Claire set a napkin-wrapped bundle of utensils by my right elbow. She gave me a thoughtful look and then said, "Kathleen, is it true that you found Mr. Glazer's body?" Her face flushed. "That was a tacky question, wasn't it?"

"It's okay," I said. "And yes, I did find his body." I didn't bother adding the part about my cat finding it first.

"The guy was obnoxious, but"—she gave a little shudder—"no one deserves to die all alone like that."

I nodded, remembering how the body was slumped in the plastic chair in the dim light of the tent. "It seems like he rubbed some people the wrong way," I said, reaching for my coffee.

"More like everybody." She shot a quick glance past me to make sure the other customers weren't trying to get her attention. "He wasn't in here five minutes and he was telling Eric how he needed to change the menu and update the decor."

I looked around. "What's wrong with the decor?"

Claire gave a snort of laughter. "He thought we should go for a Parisian bistro look."

"In Minnesota?"

She reached for the coffeepot and topped up my cup. "If people want a Parisian café, they'll go to Paris. Tourists who come here are looking for a small-town restaurant with comfort food they recognize."

Eric came out of the kitchen then. "You must be talking about Mike Glazer," he said, as he slid a heavy plate in front of me. I could smell bacon, tomatoes and maybe a little thyme. The thick-cut sourdough bread had been pan-toasted—crisp and golden on the outside and soaked with tomatoes and spices on the inside.

I took a large bite and sighed with happiness. How could Mike have found fault with this?

Claire grinned at me and headed for the table by the window with the pot.

"I take it Claire was telling you about Glazer's suggestions," Eric said.

"Parisian bistro?" I said, raising my eyebrows.

He crossed his arms over his chest. "He also thought we should get rid of all the 'old-fashioned' stuff on the menu, like the chocolate pudding cake."

"Did he have any idea how popular that is?"

Eric shrugged. "Wasn't interested. I made that recipe

three times a day during the music festival last month. It was almost eighty degrees outside and the tourists were still ordering it." He gave me a sideways smile. "By the way, how was last night's batch?"

"Good," I said.

His smile widened, and I knew I'd just been hooked in a fishing expedition. "Susan was positive it was you Marcus Gordon was trying to impress. As my grandmother used to say, are you and the detective keeping company?"

"No comment," I said, bending my head over my plate. "And tell your wife she's going to be dusting every single shelf in the library today."

Eric laughed and gestured to my half-empty plate. "Would you like anything else?"

I shook my head. "No, thank you." I took another bite of the sandwich while Eric started a new pot of coffee.

"Are you still going to do the food tasting?" I asked.

"We are," he said. He turned to look at me over one shoulder. "If Liam and his group can pull this together, it could be good for the town. And I know it sounds awful, but it'll be a lot less of a hassle without Glazer."

I reached for my cup. "Do you think it was just the small-town boy trying to show off his big-city polish?"

"It's possible. Not such a good idea, if you ask me, considering he might have been leaving the big city."

"What do you mean?"

Eric stopped to wash his hands and then came back over to the counter. "Friend of mine has a restaurant in

Chicago. I called him when we knew this pitch to Legacy was a go. He said there was some talk going around that Glazer's partners wanted him out of the company. Nothing specific, mostly just talk."

Before I could ask if he knew why, Claire came back with an order for the three men—town workers—who had just come in.

Eric headed for the kitchen. "Have a good day, Kathleen," he said. "And remember, Susan's bringing lunch. Let me know what you think of the soup."

Claire took my empty plate and I pulled out my wallet to pay for breakfast.

"Kathleen, are you going to be seeing Maggie anytime soon?" she asked.

"Tomorrow night at tai chi class," I said. "Why?"

"Her boyfriend left his travel mug here last week. I thought he'd be back in, but I haven't seen him. Or Maggie."

"You mean Liam?"

She nodded, reached under the counter and brought up a sleek, shiny stainless-steel mug with a comma-shaped handle and rubber grip strips. "He probably forgot where he left it. He was pretty angry after everything. He didn't even finish his meal."

I frowned. "What do you mean, 'after everything'?"

"He was here, at that table." She pointed to the front window. "Next thing I know, he's outside on the sidewalk having some kind of heated conversation with Mike Glazer. He was right in the guy's face. When he came back inside, he just tossed some money on the table, grabbed his jacket and left." She shrugged. "I think he just forgot that he'd asked me to fill his mug, and I couldn't catch him. We're usually not that busy on a Wednesday, but we were that night."

"You're probably right," I said. "I can give it to Maggie."

Claire smiled. "Hang on a sec and I'll get you a bag." She moved over to the cash register, where the take-out bags were stacked on a shelf. "Do you want a take-out cup to go?" she asked, gesturing at the coffee with her elbow.

"Umm . . . yes, thank you."

She put the travel mug in a bag, got me a large cup of coffee to go and brought both over to me. I paid for breakfast, wished Claire a good day and headed out.

I'd left the truck at the library, but I didn't mind the walk. The sun was shining for now, although my wrist still insisted it was going to rain later.

I let myself into the building and relocked the door, leaving the alarm off. After flipping on the downstairs lights, I headed up to my office. It was still early. I put my things on the desk and hung up my jacket. Then I tucked Liam's mug in my briefcase so I'd remember to give it to Maggie.

As I picked up my cup again, I thought about what Claire had said about Liam's argument with Mike Glazer. Mike had clearly pushed Liam's buttons somehow if Liam had left without finishing his meal or getting his coffee. He worked part-time tending bar at Harry's Hat, so he was used to dealing with people who were behaving badly; he didn't lose his cool that easily. *I couldn't catch him,* Claire had said. Then I remembered the rest of the sentence: *We're usually not that busy on a Wednesday, but we were that night.*

I leaned back against the edge of the desk. Wednesday night was the night Mike Glazer had been killed. And he'd had an argument with Liam.

No. That didn't mean Liam had killed him. It wasn't a cause-and-effect thing. Liam wasn't the only person who'd had words with Mike. He wasn't the only person who didn't like the man. Mary had threatened to drop-kick Mike between a couple of lampposts and I didn't think she'd killed him.

Plus Liam was the one who'd come up with the idea of pitching a tour built around Mayville Heights to Legacy Tours in the first place. Why would he kill Mike? It didn't make any sense. For all Liam knew, if Mike was dead, that would be the end of any deal with Legacy.

I looked at my watch. Mary and Abigail would be arriving anytime now and so would our new co-op student and her teacher. I took one last long drink from my cup and headed downstairs.

Harry Taylor—Junior, not Senior—came into the library just after eleven o'clock with Elizabeth.

"I have a couple of books your dad requested," I said, walking over to meet them by the circulation desk. I smiled at Elizabeth. "Hi."

She smiled back and Harry nodded. "Mary called. That's what we came to get." He took a library card out of his shirt pocket and handed it over to Abigail, who was working checkout; then he turned back to me. "There're a couple of things I wanted to ask you."

"Go ahead," I said.

"Do you mind if I start cleaning out those flower beds at the front tomorrow and getting them ready to get the bulbs in?"

"That's fine with me," I said. "Do what works best for you, but don't forget it's story time tomorrow. You might end up with some little helpers."

Harry smiled. "I don't mind." He glanced at Elizabeth. "The other thing is, I was wondering if Elizabeth and one of her friends could come meet your cats sometime. They're thinking about helping out at Wisteria Hill."

I was guessing the "friend" was Wren Magnusson and this was Harry's way of giving me a chance to talk to her.

"Absolutely." I turned to Elizabeth. "Owen and Hercules came from Wisteria Hill. The only thing you have to remember is that they don't like to be touched by pretty much anyone but me. But they do like company."

"Did one of them really go and get Harry when someone broke into your house?" She shot her big brother a skeptical look.

I nodded, my hand automatically going to rub my left wrist. That encounter just over a year ago was when it had been broken. "Hercules," I said. "Harry was mowing the lawn at my backyard neighbor's house. Hercules got in front of the lawn mower and made so much noise, Harry came to see what was going on."

"I figured either something had happened to Kathleen, or Timmy was stuck in the well and the cat fancied himself to be Lassie," Harry said dryly. Abigail handed him the two books and he thanked her.

Elizabeth smiled and made a face at her brother before shifting her gaze back to me. "Is after supper tonight too soon?"

"No, it's not," I said. We settled on a time and I gave her directions. "Tell your dad the other book he wanted should be here next week," I told Harry.

"I will," he said. His eyes darted sideways to Elizabeth for a moment. "Thank you."

I spent most of the morning teaching our new student intern—whose name was Mia—how the computerized card catalogue worked. Like most teenagers, she had good computer skills and she picked it up easily. She was well spoken and well read, conservatively dressed in a black skirt and long-sleeved white blouse. After working with her for a couple of hours, I felt Mia was going to fit in just fine, although her neon blue hair was probably going to get more than a second glance. I sent her to shelve books with Mary and walked over to the circulation desk.

"What time is Susan bringing lunch?" Abigail asked.

I glanced up at the clock. It was almost eleven thirty. "About an hour," I said.

She swept her braided hair over one shoulder. "I don't suppose there are any muffins in the lunchroom, are there? I'm hungry now."

I shook my head. "Sorry. To paraphrase Dr. Seuss, the only crumbs in our lunchroom are crumbs that are even too small for a mouse." Then I remembered that description pretty much described my kitchen and I'd invited Elizabeth and Wren over. I made a face. "Crap on toast!"

"It's okay," Abigail said. "I'm not going to pass out from hunger in the next hour."

"I'm glad," I said. "But I just realized that I invited Harry's sister and her friend over tonight, and there isn't so much as a brownie crumb in my kitchen."

Abigail smiled. "I could call Georgia and see what she has for cupcakes. I don't mind holding the fort here so you could run over there. She's just over on Washington Street."

That sounded a lot better than having to make coffee cake the moment I stepped through the door. "Please," I said.

She reached for the phone. "And if you decided to reward my brilliance with a double-chocolate cupcake, I would be filled with gratitude."

I smiled and shook my head. "You're full of something."

Good fortune was on my side. Georgia had just finished frosting a batch of cupcakes and I could have half a dozen. And Washington Street was close enough that I could walk. "I shouldn't be much more than half an hour," I told Abigail. "Mia is helping Mary."

"Take your time," she said. "I wouldn't want you to smush the icing or anything. You know, for your guests."

I waved at her and headed out the door.

Washington Street was a couple of streets above Main, two blocks east of the library. Georgia was working out of a blue-shingled two-story house that, like most of the other buildings on the street, had a business on the main level and apartments on the second floor. Abigail had told me to go to the back, and as I stepped onto the small verandah, I could see Georgia through the screen door, filling a pastry bag with what looked like chocolate frosting.

She looked up when I knocked on the doorframe and beckoned me inside. The kitchen smelled of a delicious mix of chocolate, vanilla and caramel.

"Mmm, it smells good in here," I said.

Georgia made a swirl of dark chocolate on the top of a dark-chocolate cupcake and set the pastry bag on the counter. "That's probably my cupcakes and Liv's caramels," she said with a smile.

"You share this space with Olivia Ramsey," I said. "I thought the address sounded familiar."

She nodded, icing sugar dusting her dark curls. "Actually, there are three of us: Decadence—that's Olivia—me, and Earl of Sandwich. I've been here only a month."

Olivia Ramsey was a chocolatier who specialized in handmade truffles and caramels. Decadence's reputation was beginning to spread outside the state. Earl of Sandwich ran two lunch wagons that serviced pretty much all the construction sites in the area. And yes, the owner's name really was Earl.

I looked around the kitchen. The walls were painted a pale creamy yellow, like whipped butter. The appliances were all gleaming stainless steel. At the far end of the space, I could see two brick ovens built into the wall.

Georgia followed my gaze. "They still work," she said. "This was a pizza place at one time, I guess." She gestured at two wire racks to her left on the long butcher-block table. "What would you like? The ones with the green frosting are Chocolate Mint Madness and the others are Devilishly Decadent Chocolate."

"Could I have half a dozen of each?" I asked.

"Absolutely," Georgia said. She brushed off her hands and reached for a couple of flattened boxes from a nearby shelf.

"Are you ready for the food tasting?" I asked.

"I think so," she said, glancing up from the box she was folding into shape. "I'm doing six different cupcakes. And Liam rearranged things so now I'm next to Molly's Coffee, which should be good for both of us."

"I hope everything works out," I said.

Georgia set the finished carton aside and started bending the other one into shape. "I think it will . . . now."

"Mike Glazer made things difficult."

She nodded, keeping her head bent over the half-formed box. "Nothing seemed to satisfy him. He was on Liam about every little thing. Then he started in on Mr. Chapman about the style of the tents and if looks could kill—" She realized then what she'd said. "I'm sorry. That was insensitive." There were two blotches of red high on the cheekbones of her otherwise pale face. She wiped her hands on her long white apron.

I gave her a small smile. "It's okay," I said. "I think Mike had alienated pretty much everyone who was involved with the tour project."

Georgia finished the box and reached for the cupcakes. "He stuck his nose into things that were none of his business, and now he's dead." She exhaled slowly and looked at me. "He just shouldn't have done that." I was a bit taken aback by the intensity in her voice.

Georgia finished boxing the cupcakes, and I paid her and put them in the canvas shopping bag I'd brought with me. She walked me to the door.

"Thanks," I said. "I'll look for you at the food tasting. I hope it goes well."

She wiped her hands again on the front of her apron and gave me a small smile. "I think it will, now," she said.

Walking back to the library, I thought again how sad it was that Wren Magnusson was the only person who seemed to feel any grief about Mike Glazer's death. Georgia certainly didn't seem sorry, although to be fair, she'd barely known the man. I thought about the tension in her voice when she'd commented that Mike had been sticking his nose into things that were none of his business and the way that she'd kept wiping her hands nervously on her apron. What had happened had clearly left her feeling unsettled.

Back at the library, I stashed the cupcakes in my office and took over from Abigail at the front desk. Susan came in at twelve thirty, carrying a large crock of soup—the lunch Eric had reminded me about. He was testing a new recipe and we were going to be his guinea pigs. She smiled sweetly as she passed me on her way to the stairs. A small feather duster with Kool-Aid-orange feathers was stuck through her topknot.

Obviously Eric had repeated my threat about dusting all the shelves.

"So not funny," I called after her. She didn't even turn around, but I saw her shoulders shake with laughter.

The soup—chicken with spinach dumplings—was delicious, no surprise. So were Georgia's cupcakes. I spent the afternoon doing paperwork and working on the list of new books I wanted to order.

It was raining when I left the library, fat drops that splattered on the windshield of the truck. As I hurried around the side of the house, I could see Hercules's black-and-white face peering through the porch window. I shook my umbrella before I stepped inside the porch; then I picked him up off the bench under the window. He didn't even object to the dampness of my jacket. Instead he peered at my face and then looked over at the door to the kitchen. Something was up.

"What did your brother do?" I asked. Herc looked back over my arm as though there were something incredibly fascinating all of a sudden on the floor behind us. "It can't be that bad." I stuck the key in the lock. He rested his chin on my shoulder and made a noise that sounded suspiciously like a sigh of resignation.

It was that bad. It looked liked catnip-loving zombies had attacked. There were bits from at least two—or maybe three—of Owen's Fred the Funky Chickens spread all over the kitchen. Yesterday I thought I'd found—and gotten rid of—all the chicken parts he had hidden around the house. Obviously I was wrong.

Tiny bits of Big Bird–yellow fabric littered the floor,

and there were flecks of dried catnip everywhere, as though an overzealous chef had been flinging herbs wildly into the air. A yellow feather was floating in Owen's water dish. The end of his tail was in Herc's bowl. Owen himself was on his back, gnawing on what I was guessing was part of a chicken head, held in his two front paws, while his hind feet circled lazily through the air as though he were aimlessly pedaling a bicycle.

Hercules made a sour face as I set him on the floor. He didn't like mess and he didn't like catnip, either. He headed out of the room, working his way around the mess, stopping twice to lift up a paw and shake it.

I set down my briefcase and the cardboard boxes of cupcakes, crossed my arms over my chest and glared at Owen, who hadn't seemed to register that I was actually home. "Owen, what the heck do you think you're doing?" I said.

He looked over at me, his eyes not really focusing. He shook his head, rolled over and got to his feet, the chicken head hanging out of his mouth. He looked like a drunken sailor after a raucous night of shore leave.

"Bring that over here," I said.

He squinted up at the ceiling as though I hadn't spoken.

I walked over to him, bent down and held out my hand. "Let's have it, Fuzzy Wuzzy."

He made a growly noise and bit down even harder on the bright yellow fabric.

I leaned sideways, looked past him and said, "Whoa, big mouse!"

Owen's furry head whipped around so fast, he had

to take a step so he didn't fall over. The dismembered chicken head dropped out of his teeth, and I scooped it up before it hit the kitchen floor.

He yowled his anger, but it was too late. I took a couple of steps sideways and the late Fred's head was resting in the garbage can. I turned around and crouched down so I was at the cat's level. His eyes were almost slits and his mouth was pinched into a sour pucker. He looked liked a sulky child, and he wouldn't meet my gaze.

"You are in so much trouble," I told him. "Why did you do this?" He kept his focus on the cupboards. "Is this because I threw away the two chicken heads I found under the sofa yesterday?" I didn't say I'd also tossed a whole chicken that was in my winter boots and a body minus a head that had been behind a box in the bedroom closet.

Owen made a huffy noise out through his nose. I sighed and shifted sideways so I was in front of him again. "Okay, I'm sorry I did that without telling you, but those things were covered in cat spit and they'd already been overpowered by the dust bunnies. And they smelled."

One ear twitched, but it was the only sign he was listening. "You could have made your point without spreading catnip and chicken bits all over the kitchen." I reached over to stroke the fur on the top of his head with one finger. "I'm going to get the vacuum and clean this up," I said. "Then we're going to have supper and maybe, maybe you can have a taste of that new kitty kibble I bought."

He rubbed his head against my hand without looking at me; then he headed for the living room, walking slowly and deliberately because he still had a little catnip buzz going.

I sat back on my heels and looked around. Owen had flung catnip chicken bits all over the kitchen, so why was I the one doing the vacuuming and coaxing him back into a good mood? In my next life, I was going to be the cat, I decided as I got to my feet.

Thirty minutes later, the kitchen was more or less cleaned up and I was at the table with a plate of spaghetti. Hercules was next to my chair, watching me eat and probably hoping I'd drop a meatball, while Owen was sprawled under the other chair, making a half-hearted effort to wash his face. I'd already told them what I'd learned at the café. Owen's ears had perked up when I'd shared Claire's story about Liam arguing with Mike Glazer out on the street in front of the diner, but I suspected that was mostly because I'd also mentioned Maggie's name.

I leaned sideways in my chair and looked down at both of them. "We have company coming after supper."

Owen immediately sat up, looked around and started washing his face in earnest. Hercules looked at his brother and then he looked at me. In Owen's kitty mind, the word "company" meant one person: Maggie.

"Yes, I know what he's thinking and he's wrong," I said quietly to Herc. "Should we tell him, or wait until he gets cleaned up?"

He stared at his feet, whiskers twitching, almost as

though he were considering my question. I waited, giving him time to think—just in case he really was; then he meowed softly.

"Okay," I said. I tapped my fingers on the edge of the table to get Owen's attention. He looked over at me, one paw raised in the air. "Not Maggie," I said, shaking my head. He took one more pass at his face, dropped his paw and stretched back out on the floor with a sigh.

Hercules head-butted my leg and meowed, his way of asking, "So who is it?"

I reached down and scratched the top of his head. "Harrison Taylor's daughter, Elizabeth, and her friend will be here in a little while. They want to meet the two of you."

Hercules made a satisfied rumble in his throat, tilting his head so I'd scratch behind his ear. Owen, meanwhile, made a show of stretching, sitting up and starting on his face again as though that had been his intention all along.

I picked up my fork and speared a meatball. Out of the corner of my eye, I saw Herc start to wash his own face.

I'd just finished the dishes when I heard a knock on the porch door. The boys were sitting side by side next to the end of the table. Faces washed and paws spotless, they were the poster children for cat adoption. "Very nice," I said approvingly as I went to answer the door.

Elizabeth smiled when she saw me. "Hi, Kathleen," she said. "This is my friend Wren. I think you met at the library."

"Yes, we did." I smiled. "Hi, Wren. Come in, please. The cats are in the kitchen."

Wren Magnusson gave me a small smile. She looked tired. There were dark smudges under her eyes, and I noticed that she kept running her thumb back and forth along the side of her index finger.

"Thank you for letting us come and see them," Elizabeth said, stepping into the porch. "I hope Harry didn't put you on the spot."

"He didn't," I said. "It's not a big deal. Harry's come through for me more than once. And your father is one of my favorite people."

She shifted uncomfortably from one foot to the other, her expression still serious. "Harrison said that he never would have found me if it hadn't been for you."

I ducked my head, suddenly feeling a little embarrassed. "All I did was find a few papers."

She pressed her lips together before speaking. "He said it was a lot more than that. He said that you helped the police figure out who killed my birth mother." She stumbled a little over the word "mother." "And you were almost caught in an explosion." She swallowed. "I, uh, don't know how to thank you."

I hesitated and then lightly touched her shoulder. "You just did," I said. "And I have all the thanks I'm ever going to need just seeing how happy finding you has made Harrison."

She nodded.

We stepped into the kitchen. Owen and Hercules hadn't moved. They looked curiously at the two young women. Wren immediately looked at me. "Liz said we can't pet them, but is it okay if I get a little closer?"

"Go ahead," I said.

Both cats were watching her intently.

Wren stopped about three feet away from them and dropped down to her knees.

"That's Owen," I said, pointing. He turned his face toward me for a moment and then gave all his attention to Wren again. I gestured at Herc. "And that's Hercules." He bobbed his head in acknowledgment.

Wren smiled at them. "Hi, guys," she said.

Owen craned his neck and sniffed. He seemed to like what his nose told him because he took a step forward.

Wren turned to look at me. "He's so cute," she said.

He knew the word "cute." He dipped his head for a moment, trying to give the appearance of being modest, too.

Hercules raised a paw in a bid to get Wren's attention. "I see you," she said. "You're just as handsome as your brother." He murped his agreement.

"You found both of them at Wisteria Hill?" Elizabeth asked as Wren continued to talk to both cats, leaning forward with her arms propped on her thighs.

"I think it's more like they found me."

I told her the story of how I'd gone exploring out at the old estate a few weeks after I'd arrived in Mayville Heights—had it really been a year and a half ago?—and Owen and Hercules, just tiny kittens then, had persisted in following me until I'd scooped them up and brought them home.

"And there's seven more cats still out there?" Elizabeth asked. Hercules took a couple of steps sideways and looked at her, green eyes wide with curiosity. She crouched next to Wren and extended her hand. He sniffed it and then sat down again.

"That's right," I said, leaning back against the kitchen counter. "I guess you could call Lucy the alpha cat of the group. Where she goes, the rest of the family pretty much follows."

Wren shifted so she could look at me. "What happens in the wintertime? How do they stay warm?"

I explained about the shelters Rebecca and Roma's other volunteers had made and how Harry used straw bales for insulation in one corner of the carriage house.

Wren frowned, two lines forming between her eyebrows. "Why doesn't someone just adopt them? I'd take one. I'd take two."

"They aren't like an average house cat," I said. "They aren't even like these two. They're not going to bond with you. They're not going to curl up at your feet and start purring." I pointed at Owen. "He likes you. Most people don't get that close to him, but I promise if you try to pet him, he will scratch you."

"It just seems . . . cruel," Wren said, "you know, to leave them outside to fend for themselves."

This wasn't the first time I'd heard that reasoning. "They don't have to fend for themselves. Volunteers go out every day with fresh food and water. If the weather is too bad for a four-wheel drive to get up the driveway, Harry uses his snowmobile. The carriage house and the shelters keep them dry and warm. And now

Roma's going to be living out there." I braced my hands against the counter on either side of me. "Wisteria Hill is the cats' home. What would be cruel would be forcing them to live somewhere else, to be what we think they should be instead of who they are."

Elizabeth looked up at me with a wry smile. "That's what Harrison said."

I nodded. "He's pretty smart."

I reached behind me for a bag of sardine cat treats, took out a couple for each cat and handed them to Wren. "Owen's stinky crackers," I said, "but Hercules likes them, too."

Wren handed two of the crackers to Elizabeth, and then she held one of the two she had left out to Owen. His whiskers twitched and he looked from Wren to me; then he pawed the ground with one foot.

"He wants me to set it down, doesn't he?" she said.

"Yes," I said. "Don't worry. It won't hurt anything."

She set the cracker down on the floor. Owen hesitated, but not for long. He picked up the cracker, took three steps backward and set it down again. Then he dropped his head and carefully sniffed it. I wondered sometimes what he thought his keen nose was going to discover.

By this time Hercules's patience was almost worn out. One paw moved through the air as though he were reaching for the crackers Elizabeth had in her hand. She held one out to him, her fingers just touching the corner edge, and to my surprise, after hesitating for a minute, he took it from her.

"He almost never does that," I said. "I think you've made a friend."

She offered the other treat, and this one he took without any hesitation at all. Elizabeth smiled, clearly pleased.

"How about a mint-chocolate-chip cupcake?" I asked. "And I have tea or hot chocolate."

Wren looked at Elizabeth. "Do we have time?"

She nodded.

"Hot chocolate, please," Wren said to me. "If it's not too much trouble."

"It's not," I said.

"Me too," Elizabeth said, brushing her hands on her jeans and getting to her feet. "Could I help?"

I pointed to the bubble-glass plate sitting on the counter. "You could put the cupcakes on the table."

Wren sat on the floor, talking to Owen and Hercules until the hot chocolate was ready; then she stood up and joined us at the table. I showed them a couple of pictures I'd taken of Lucy walking in the long grass behind the carriage house. Both Wren and Elizabeth had a lot more questions about the cats, and I tried to answer them all as honestly as I could.

Hercules came to lean against my leg, and I reached down to stroke his fur. I noticed he was watching Wren. Owen sat halfway between my chair and Wren's, watching her too, but not with the same goofy adoration that he gave to Maggie. If he'd been a person instead of a cat, I would have said that he seemed concerned. Wren had an air of sadness about her, and given that both cats seemed to be able to sense someone's mood, maybe he *was* concerned.

After a few minutes, Wren grew silent. She was rubbing her thumb against her finger again. A couple of times she caught the edge of her lower lip between her teeth.

"Wren, is there something you wanted to ask me?" I said. Twice it had looked like she was going to speak but then she hadn't.

She traced the rim of her cup with a finger. "Yeah," she said, "but it's not about the cats."

"That's okay," I said, folding my hands around my own cup. "What is it?"

She took a deep breath as though she were trying to work up her nerve. She seemed very fragile. "Is it true that you found Mike Glazer's . . . that you found him?"

I nodded slowly. "Yes. It is."

Elizabeth reached over and gave her friend's arm a brief squeeze.

"Did he . . . did it look like he . . . suffered? I hate thinking he just lay there alone for hours." Wren lifted her head to look at me, and I could see the grief in her pale blue eyes.

I took a moment before I answered. I wanted to say something that might make her feel a little better, but I didn't want to make up a story, either. "From what I saw, I don't think so," I finally said. "I didn't see anything that made me think he'd had a fight with someone. There were no signs of a struggle. No overturned furniture. He was just there. There wasn't any blood."

She swallowed a couple of times, gave Owen—who was still watching her—a small smile and then looked at me again. "Just so you know, I, uh, I'm not trying to be some kind of a ghoul. When I was little, I was really close to Mike and his family."

"I know about Mike's brother," I said.

"I hadn't seen Mike in a long time . . . years," she said. She picked up the cupcake on her plate, broke it in half and set it back down again without taking a bite. "I was so happy when I found out he was involved in this tour thing. I thought about going to see the whole family a bunch of times, but I didn't exactly know how to find them and I didn't want to make anybody feel bad."

She shrugged. "It probably sounds dumb, but us both being here at the same time just kind of seemed like a sign."

"It's not dumb," Elizabeth said. She might not have been raised by the Taylors, but like her father and her half siblings, Elizabeth seemed to be fiercely loyal to the people she cared about.

"No, it's not," I agreed.

Wren took a sip from her hot chocolate. "I know that people are saying he was a jerk, but he really wasn't." She twisted a lock of hair around her finger. "I was going to see him that night, you know. I'd already missed seeing him once. But I had car trouble . . ."

She swallowed again and stared at the ceiling for a moment. "I was going to see if we could have lunch and catch up."

"I'm sorry that didn't happen," I said. Both cats were sitting next to Wren's chair now. It was impossible not to be touched by the pain she was feeling.

"Things didn't exactly turn out the way I thought they would," she said.

Elizabeth cleared her throat. "We should get going," she said, touching her friend's shoulder.

Wren nodded. She leaned over and smiled at Owen and Hercules. "It was nice to meet you," she said. Owen meowed and Herc lifted one paw.

"They feel the same way," I said. "You're welcome to come and visit anytime."

Wren smiled, the first real smile I'd seen that hadn't been directed at a cat. "Thank you," she said, getting to her feet. "I might do that."

"Thanks, Kathleen," Elizabeth said. She looked down at the boys and waggled her fingers good-bye at them.

"You're welcome," I said. "If you'd like to go out with me sometime to feed the cats, just let me know."

"I will," she said.

The cats and I walked them to the back door and said good night. Owen climbed up on the bench to look out the window. I carried Hercules back into the kitchen and dropped into my chair. Wren was so wounded, she reminded me of the tiny birds that shared her name.

Herc studied my face. "We have to figure out what happened, don't we?" I said. He meowed his agreement and laid his head on my chest. I stroked his soft black fur. "Yeah." I sighed. "I was afraid you were going to say that."

10

Hercules went back and forth from the bedroom to the hallway while I got dressed in the morning, which I didn't seem to be doing fast enough for him. Now that he'd met Wren, he was clearly motivated to help her and he wanted to get going. The third time he went into the hall, he didn't come back. I figured he'd given up and gone to wait for me downstairs.

I found him sitting next to my briefcase underneath the coat hooks. Since he knew my laptop was inside, I wondered if he was suggesting I get started on some research.

Owen seemed to have other priorities. He'd nosed his food dish into the middle of the floor and was waiting beside it.

Hercules meowed the moment he caught sight of me. Owen leaned over so I couldn't miss seeing him and meowed as well, just a little louder. But Hercules was a cat on a mission. He stalked across the floor and sat in front of Owen's bowl, looking up at me with serious green eyes.

They weren't brothers for nothing. Owen immediately began pushing the dish around his brother. I could see the fur was going to be flying—literally—in just a minute if I didn't step in. I held up one hand. "Stop, stop, stop," I said sharply.

They didn't even look at me. Owen was staring at Hercules through slitted golden eyes. Hercules glared back, unmoving except for his tail. I clapped my hands together, which made them both jump.

"Cut it out!" I said.

I pointed at Hercules. There was something a little self-righteous in the way he sat there perfectly straight, head up, neck a smooth expanse of white fur. "I know you want to help Wren," I said. "So do I. But these are not the Middle Ages and we are not the Knights Templar. We have time for breakfast."

He dropped his eyes and meowed softly.

"Your heart's in the right place," I told him.

Owen lifted his head, his eyes darting sideways to his brother. I crossed my arms over my chest. "Hang on a minute, Fur Ball," I said.

He turned his attention to me, at the same time setting a paw on the edge of his bowl. "You are not starving to death. I know breakfast is the most important meal of the day, but you can wait five minutes while I figure out what I'm going to do first."

I pressed my lips together and shook my head. Had I actually just told a cat that breakfast was the most important meal of the day?

Owen took a step forward then—or at least tried to—except he ended up putting his weight down on the side of the bowl where his left paw had been resting. I don't know if it was all the stinky crackers he'd been eating, or the extra racing around the backyard, but he seemed to have more strength than he realized. The plastic dish somersaulted into the air end over end like it had been launched from a catapult. I lunged for it, but I was too slow. It landed, upside down, on Owen's head and slipped a bit sideways so it looked like a jaunty, oversize beret. He gave a yowl of outrage and shook his head furiously, which just made the bowl dip down over his eyes. I grabbed it before he got any madder.

And he was mad. His gray fur was standing on end, one ear was turned inside out and a bit of something— a crumb of cracker maybe—was stuck to a whisker.

"Are you all right?" I asked, swallowing down the bubble of laughter that was threatening to get loose. Hercules had wisely become engrossed in sniffing the end of his tail and wasn't even looking at us.

Owen bobbed his head and sneezed away whatever had been stuck to his whiskers. I reached over and fixed his ear, smoothing down his fur while he made huffy noises of indignation. His dignity was wounded, but otherwise he seemed to be okay.

I got breakfast for both cats, setting Owen's dishes in the usual place, but moving Hercules's a bit farther away. "You are the soul of discretion," I whispered to Herc, giving him a little scratch under his chin as I put the food in front of him.

I washed my hands and stuck my oatmeal in the microwave. I turned around in time to see Hercules pick up a couple of pieces of cat kibble, carry them over and drop them by Owen's bowl, then go back to his own food. After a moment, Owen sniffed the peace offering, moved each triangle a couple of inches and ate them.

All was well in my small corner of the universe.

I had more than an hour before I had to leave for the library, so after we'd all had breakfast and washed hands (me), and face and paws (Hercules and Owen), I got the laptop so I could do some research into Legacy Tours. It took some digging, but I finally found what I was looking for in a six-month-old article in the archives of an online business magazine.

"Listen to this," I said to Hercules, who had been sitting patiently at my feet.

Legacy Tours had been started by Alex and Christopher Scott while the twins were still in university. The company had found its niche putting together all-inclusive getaways for corporate clients. Almost three years ago, Mike Glazer, an old friend from law school, had joined Legacy as a full partner. According to the article's author, the new collaboration hadn't worked from the start. About a year ago—six months before the piece had been written—the rumblings about Mike Glazer had turned from hints that the Scott brothers were planning to buy out their old buddy to whispers that Mike had been taking kickbacks from businesses the tours patronized and was about to be ousted. The author even cited a couple of his "questionable" deals. But in the six months since, nothing had changed. The rumors persisted, but Mike had remained at Legacy.

Hercules moved closer to my chair. I patted my thighs and he jumped onto my lap and immediately leaned forward, as if he wanted to read the article for himself. Feeling a little foolish, I scrolled down the screen.

"You think it's possible his partners had something to do with Mike's death?" I asked. Hercules didn't seem to have an opinion.

"I don't see it," I said, stretching my arms over my head. "Why kill him? The business was doing well. If they wanted Mike out, they could have just bought him out. And if he was taking kickbacks, they could have had him arrested. Heck, they should have had him arrested."

Hercules touched the screen with one paw.

I leaned in to see what had caught his attention. It was a photograph of Mike Glazer at some kind of travel conference, smiling at the camera. He was flanked by his partners, who, it turns out, were identical twins. But that wasn't what made me stare at the computer and then click on the picture to enlarge it so it filled the screen.

I had no idea which one, but one of the Scott brothers had been in Mayville Heights. I'd spoken to him. He was the man I'd talked to at the library, the same one I'd seen at Eric's getting directions from Claire the night Marcus and I had gone for dinner.

The night Mike Glazer had died.

"Holy molars, Batman," I said to Hercules, who looked at me blankly.

My brother, Ethan, had reintroduced me to the campy sixties TV show when I was back in Boston. Unlike his brother, Herc didn't see the fun in watching old episodes of *Batman* online, although I suspected what Owen really liked was sprawling across my stomach and getting scratched behind his ears.

Owen wandered in from the living room, pretending he needed a drink. I knew what he really wanted was to see what Hercules and I were doing. Seeing him reminded me about the button he'd found. Like I'd told Marcus, it didn't look like something plastic or mass-produced.

I closed my eyes and tried to picture the jacket whichever Scott brother I'd seen had been wearing— red and black wool and denim collar and cuffs. It had struck me as being something Ethan would wear. I was pretty sure it hadn't been mass-produced either.

Finding photos of Alex and Christopher Scott online was surprisingly easy. Scrolling through to see if I could find one of them wearing that jacket wasn't. Hercules's furry black-and-white head kept getting in the way.

"I appreciate your help, but you need to get down," I told him. Muttering, he jumped to the floor.

I found what I was looking for on the fourth page: Alex Scott wearing the red and black jacket at a fundraiser for the children's hospital. I enlarged the picture and studied the buttons. I'd gotten only a quick look at the one Owen had found, but these seemed to be the right size and color.

As I sat there staring at the screen, Owen leaped into my lap. He looked expectantly from the computer to me. He was the one who'd discovered the button and gotten the best look at it. Feeling more than a little silly, I pointed to the photograph. "Does that look like the button you found?"

He squinted at the image, his face just inches from the screen, and then he pulled his head back and looked at me kind of cross-eyed. It could have been a yes.

I looked at my watch. It was almost time to leave. "Thank you," I said. I set him on the floor and he headed for the living room. "And thank you, too," I told Hercules. "You were a big help."

He rubbed against my leg and then went through the kitchen door into the porch. I wondered what it said about me that seeing him literally go through a door had just become a regular part of my day. I shut down my computer, put it back in my briefcase and got my sweater from the living room closet.

"I'm leaving," I called. After a moment, there was a muffled meow from Owen. He was either in the living room closet or looking under the couch for more catnip chicken parts.

Hercules was on the bench by the window in the porch. I stopped to pet the top of his head. "Have a good day," I said. He jumped down and walked me out, waiting for me to open the porch door instead of just walking through it. With the sun shining and the grass dry, I knew he'd probably walk over and take a nap in Rebecca's gazebo.

Abigail and Mia were waiting for me by the steps

when I pulled into the library lot. Tuesday meant story time, so the first thing we did was get the puppet theater out of the storage room and set it up in the children's section.

"Could I borrow Mia?" Abigail asked. "I could use an extra set of hands with the little ones."

"Absolutely," I said. I figured Mia, with her electric-blue hair, would be a big hit with the preschoolers.

With story time, a group of seniors checking out our meeting room to see if it would work for their Spanish class and what seemed like more traffic than usual for a Tuesday, it was noon before I realized it. I'd worked for Susan a couple of weeks earlier and she was repaying the favor, which meant I could go out to Wisteria Hill for a late lunch with Roma. She was standing by her SUV as I bumped my way up the rutted driveway, and she walked over to meet me as I got out of the truck.

"Hi," I said.

"Hi." She had a grin that matched the sunny day. She held up both hands and looked around. "I still can't believe this place is mine. I have the urge to jump up and down and squeal. Is that silly?"

I shook my head. "No. I think it's wonderful that this place isn't going to be lonely and empty anymore." I'd worried that Roma might regret her decision to buy the property. After all, her biological father's remains had been found in the field out behind the carriage house. But putting him to rest—literally and figuratively—had been good for her.

In a misguided attempt to keep Rebecca from learning about her mother's part in the death of Roma's father, Everett Henderson had left the old estate unoccupied for a very long time after his mother died and the caretakers of the old house retired. But when Tom Karlsson's remains were unearthed back in the spring, the truth about Ellen Montgomery had been exposed as well. There were no more secrets to hide. Everett and Rebecca had decided to make their life together in town, and now Wisteria Hill would be Roma's home.

"Do you want the tour first, or do you want to eat first?" Roma asked as we walked across to the old house.

"Tour, of course," I said. I'd been inside more than once while I was helping Rebecca clean everything out, but I wanted to walk around with Roma and hear what her plans were.

The house was more than a hundred years old, and like a lot of homes of that vintage, pieces had been added to it over the years. Roma pointed to a small porch on the far side of the building. "That's coming down," she said. "Oren said it's not even on a proper foundation, and the floor is half-rotten anyway."

We stepped onto the verandah that ran across the front of the house and down one side. Roma reached over and put a hand on the railing. "This needs to be replaced as well, but Oren says he can duplicate the original design."

Oren Kenyon was an extremely talented carpenter. He'd created a beautiful sunburst to hang above the main door just inside the library entrance. He was also Roma's cousin in the convoluted way that everyone seemed to be related to everyone else in Mayville Heights.

Roma unlocked the side door and we stepped into what I guessed had originally been the pantry. "I may make this into a mudroom," she said. "Or I might just knock the wall down and make it part of the kitchen."

The country kitchen was a big, bright space with windows that looked out over the backyard, or would once the overgrown garden was cut back. There was also a dining room, a living room and a small parlor on the main floor. Upstairs, I knew there were four bedrooms and a big bathroom with a huge claw-foot tub.

Structurally, the house was sound. The old stone foundation didn't leak, and there was no rot in the floor joists. The ceilings were high, and the wide wooden floors just needed to be refinished. The rooms were filled with light, and if there were any ghosts, well, they must have been friendly ones, because there was nothing foreboding about the place.

I stood in the middle of the living room floor and turned in a slow circle. "I love this house," I said to Roma, smiling because her grin seemed to be contagious. "If you don't jump up and down and squeal, I might."

"How about we eat first?" she said. She led the way back into the kitchen, where she'd left a small cooler on the round wooden table in front of the window overlooking the backyard.

"Let me guess," I said. "Rebecca gave you the table and chairs."

Roma nodded, opening the lid of the cooler. "She said Old Harry made them for Everett's mother—he turned the legs on a hand lathe—and the table belonged here. Eddie said he'll refinish it for me."

"Is there anything he can't do?" I teased.

Her cheeks turned pink. "No," she said with a smile, setting salad and a corn bread muffin in front of me. "He's just about perfect. Well, except for the spiders." She handed me a napkin roll of utensils and took a thermos and a couple of cups out of the cooler.

"Spiders?" I said. "What does he do? Raise them as a hobby?" I took a bite of my salad. It was good: turkey, apple and dried cranberries mixed with lettuce and carrots and tossed with a citrus dressing.

Roma gave a snort of laughter. "No. I'm pretty sure he has a bit of a phobia about them."

"Why?" I asked, breaking my muffin in half.

Roma hooked her chair with a foot and pulled it closer so she could sit down. "Because I caught him stomping on something in one of the upstairs bedrooms. He said he was trying to push a nail back into one of the floorboards."

"Maybe he was," I offered. "Or maybe he's auditioning for the road company of *Riverdance* and didn't want to spoil the surprise."

She shot me a skeptical look and picked up her fork. "Of course. That sounds so much like Eddie."

The thought of Eddie Sweeney—all six foot four inches of muscled hockey player—being afraid of a little spider made me smile. He was so perfect in every other way; he cooked, apparently he could refin-

ish furniture, he was a star hockey player for the
Minnesota Wild and a romantic boyfriend, plus he
looked like he should be on the cover of *GQ*, not *Sports
Illustrated*.

"Have you talked to Marcus?" Roma asked.

"We're taking it really slowly," I said. "We've had
dinner a couple of times, but that's all." Except for a
kiss that had made me forget, momentarily, the thirteen
times table, my own name and how to breathe. But I
didn't say that out loud.

"Good to know," she said. "But I meant, have you
talked to him about Mike Glazer?"

"I think he's waiting for something official on the
cause of death," I said.

She frowned, chewing on her bottom lip.

"What is it?" I asked.

"Nothing," she said. "Probably." She reached for the
thermos and poured iced tea for both of us.

"Tell me."

"I feel like an old busybody."

"You're not an old busybody," I said. Roma knew
more about what was going on around town than most
people did. Half the town was in and out of her clinic
with their pets and she still made house calls, but she
kept what she heard and saw to herself. "C'mon. What
is it?"

She exhaled slowly. "Okay. Last Wednesday night, I
was late getting out of the clinic, and Eddie's at training
camp, so I decided to have supper at Eric's. I parked
the truck and I walked down to the corner first to mail
a letter. When I turned around, Mike Glazer was out-

side the restaurant and he was arguing with Liam, Maggie's boyfriend or whatever he is."

"I know," I said.

Her eyes narrowed. "What do you mean 'you know'?"

"Claire was working that night. Liam was so distracted by whatever happened out on the sidewalk that he left his coffee mug behind. She gave it to me to give to Maggie."

"Did Claire hear what they were saying?" Roma asked.

I shook my head. "I don't think so."

"Well, I did. They were pretty loud, and I felt awkward about just walking up to them, so I stepped into the alley." She ran a finger up and down the side of her glass. "I wish I hadn't, because even from there I heard Liam tell Mike to leave town—except he didn't put it quite that nicely. He told Mike to forget about the food tasting and the art show—everything—it was all over."

"You think he was serious?" I asked.

"Very." Roma traced a scratch on the tabletop with two fingers. "He said if he saw Mike on the street, he might just forget what the brakes on his truck were for."

"And the next morning . . ."

"Mike Glazer was dead."

"Roma, you need to tell this to Marcus," I said.

She brushed a strand of dark hair off her cheek and sighed. "I know. I was trying to convince myself that what Liam said didn't mean anything. People say things like that all the time when they're angry."

"I know that," I said. "And I'm not saying that I think Liam had anything to do with Mike Glazer's death. It's Marcus's job to figure that out."

"You're right," Roma said, picking up her fork again. "I'll call him after lunch." She leaned an elbow on the table and propped her chin on her hand. "Let's talk about something else. So, you've had two dinners with Marcus." Her eyebrows went up on "two." "Just exactly how slowly are you two taking it?"

"Very, very slowly," I said, making a face at her. "I don't know what's going to happen."

"What would you like to happen?" This time she wiggled her eyebrows at me.

"I would like to eat my lunch," I said, feeling my face get red.

She laughed, and I knew that when she and Maggie found out Marcus had kissed me, they were going to giggle like a couple of sixth graders.

We finished lunch—there was rice pudding with peaches for dessert—and then Roma walked me around the yard and told me about her plans for the outside of the old house. As we came around the side of the carriage house, she stopped suddenly and put a hand on my arm. "See that?" she asked, pointing to the old lilac hedge. The long grass moved, and I saw what looked like a flash of ginger fur.

"Is that another cat?" I asked.

She nodded. "I don't know if it's feral or someone abandoned it, but this is the third time I've seen it." She started walking again. "It's a little marmalade tabby, about half-grown. I've been calling it Micah."

"For the biblical prophet?" I asked.

"More for the mineral. It was the way the cat's fur seemed to glisten in the sun." She gave a half shrug and looked a little embarrassed. "Eddie likes to collect rocks."

We walked back to the driveway. "I'm so glad you're going to be living out here," I said as the two of us stood by my truck. "I'm glad the cats will be safe. And if I can do anything, anything to help, please ask."

"Can you paint?" she asked.

"Roller, brush and sprayer." I held up one, two and then three fingers.

"You're hired," she said with a laugh.

"Anytime," I said. I hugged her. "Thanks for lunch. I'll see you at class tonight."

Roma waved as I started down the rutted driveway—the first outdoor project on her list. In the rearview mirror, I saw her pull out her cell phone and I hoped that was because she was calling Marcus. I had meant what I'd said to her. Just because Liam had told Mike if he saw him again he might forget what the brakes on his truck were for didn't mean that Liam had had anything to do with Mike's death.

I spent the afternoon cleaning out the flower beds in the backyard, getting them ready for the bag of compost Harry had promised to drop off to me. Owen and Hercules helped.

Owen's idea of helping was to pounce on every dead and dried-up plant I pulled out of the ground. Hercules took a more paws-off approach, sitting on one of the wooden Adirondack chairs and meowing comments from time to time.

I was putting my tai chi shoes in my bag and complaining about Cloud Hands to Hercules, who wasn't even pretending to listen, when the phone rang after supper. It was Rebecca.

"Hello, Kathleen," she said. "Are you going to class tonight?"

"I am," I said. "Would you like a ride?"

"I would, please." I could hear her smile through the phone. "I was going to walk, but I'm feeling a little lazy and I don't want to take my car because I'm meeting Everett later."

Rebecca was many things, but lazy wasn't one of them. I knew if I questioned her, I'd find out she'd done more all day than I'd done in the past three days. "I'm leaving in about ten minutes," I said. "I can come around and pick you up."

"You don't need to do that," she said. "I'll come through the back. It'll give me a chance to see the boys."

"All right," I said. "I'll see you in a minute."

I went back into the kitchen and wasn't at all surprised to see "the boys" waiting by the back door, Owen giving his face a quick wash so he'd look presentable for Rebecca. They followed me into the porch.

Rebecca was making her way across the backyard. Even with arthritis, she moved like a much younger woman, a combination, she said, of good genes and regular tai chi practice. She was wearing gray yoga pants and a gray sweater over a rose-colored T-shirt and carrying a wildly colored, crazy-quilted tote bag.

"Thank you for giving me a ride," she said as reached the back steps.

"Anytime," I said.

"Everett and I are trying to decide on a wedding date," she said. "After class, we're going to sit down with our calendars." She rolled her eyes just a little when she said "calendars."

"Are you thinking next spring?" I asked.

She smiled at Owen and Hercules, who both gave her adoring looks, then looked at me. "To tell the truth, Kathleen, all I'm thinking is, Let's get on with it."

I laughed.

"Do I sound like—what's the word—a 'bridezilla'?"

I shook my head. "No. I think you're the opposite of a bridezilla."

"Everett is determined that we're going to have a 'wedding.' I'd be happy with just Ami and the boys and a few close friends like you." She shook her head. "Sometimes that man can be unbelievably stubborn."

"He loves you," I said.

She smiled again and it lit up her entire face. "I know," she said, a tinge of pink coming to her cheeks. "Isn't it wonderful?"

I couldn't help grinning back at her. "Yes, it is." I gestured toward the kitchen. "I just have to get my keys and my bag."

"Take your time, my dear," Rebecca said, setting her tote on the window bench. "I'll just catch up with Owen and Hercules."

I went back into the kitchen, stuffed a towel and my water bottle in with my shoes and wallet and got my keys from my purse. Liam's coffee mug was in the bottom of the bag. I made sure both cats had a drink and then I went back out into the porch. Rebecca was sitting on the bench, hands folded in her lap, talking to Herc and Owen, who seemed to be listening intently. Both cats were purring like twin diesel engines.

I held the kitchen door open. "Time to say good night," I told them.

Rebecca got to her feet. "Come over for tea some morning," she said.

Owen meowed with his usual exuberance. He knew tea with Rebecca usually meant a catnip chicken. He was so busy looking back at her over his shoulder that he almost walked into the doorframe. He pulled up short and shook himself. Hercules looked from Owen to me, and I thought I saw an almost imperceptible head shake.

I locked both doors, and Rebecca and I walked around to the truck. "I like your bag," I said as we backed out of the driveway.

"It is beautiful, isn't it?" she said, smoothing the fabric with one hand. "I kind of got it under false pretenses."

"You?" I shot her a quick glance. "I don't believe that."

"It's a piece from the art show," Rebecca said. "I was helping Ruby unpack everything last week, and I fell in love with it the moment I saw it. Ella King made it."

"She does beautiful work," I said.

"Yes, she does. When it looked as though the show and the food tasting were going to be canceled, Ruby let me buy the bag, but I wonder if I should let her have it again now that everything is back on."

"It's probably not the only bag Ella made, but why don't you ask Ruby."

"That's a good idea," she said. "That's what I'll do." She rubbed her right wrist.

"Is your arm bothering you?" I asked. My own wrist felt fine now. I stopped at the bottom of the hill and waited for a couple of cars to go by.

"Just a little," Rebecca said. "I was helping Mary this afternoon. We were ironing all the backdrops for the booths in the two tents. Mary had ironed every single one of them last week and hung them on a couple of racks in the tent, but of course the police had to look through them and they got wrinkled again. I think I'm a bit out of practice. I don't iron many things these days." She laced her fingers in her lap. "That was so sad about Michael."

I turned right, glancing over at her as I did. "You knew him?"

"Heavens, yes," she said. "I gave Michael his first haircut and every one after that until the family left Mayville Heights. He was so full of life." Out of the corner of my eyes, I saw her hold up one hand. "And yes, Kathleen, I've heard what people have been saying around town about Michael—that he was rude and insulting and no one really wanted to work with him." She sighed softly. "All I can say is, that's not the young man I knew."

"What was he like when you knew him, when he was younger?" I asked, looking ahead for a parking spot.

"Full of life," Rebecca said. "He could hardly sit still

in the chair for me to cut his hair—not because he had a problem paying attention. It was just that he was so full of energy and there were so many things he wanted to do. He was on the ski patrol. He helped his old coach at every track-and-field event the little ones at the elementary school had."

I spied an empty parking space, big enough for the truck, a couple of doors down from the tai chi studio and backed into it.

"You've probably heard what happened to Michael's brother," Rebecca said.

I nodded.

"He was different after that. But then, how could he not be?" She looked at me, her blue eyes warm and kind, as always. "But I think that young man who was so full of life was still somewhere inside. Maybe if Michael had had a little more time here, he would have come out."

I reached over and patted her arm. "That's a nice thought," I said.

When we got out of the truck, Ruby was coming up the sidewalk, and we waited by the door for her. Her hair was in three ponytails sticking out from her head at odd angles. "Hi," she said. She gestured to her hair. "Thank you for the conditioner," she said to Rebecca. "I can't believe how soft my hair is."

"Oh, you're welcome," Rebecca said. She held up her bag. "Now that the show is on again do you want this back?"

Ruby shook her head, making her little ponytails bounce. "No. I have more of Ella's bags. What I want is for you to make sure you have that bag with you at the show and that you tell people you like it." She frowned at Rebecca. "You do like it, right?"

"Heavens, yes," Rebecca said. They started up the stairs, discussing the merits of Ella King's tote bags. I followed them.

Rebecca saw the best in everyone and everything. That was one of the many things I liked about her. But she was also a very good judge of people, and if she said that Mike Glazer was a good person at heart, I had to believe she'd seen some goodness in him.

Maggie had decided we were going to spend the class working on our weak areas. I knew for me that would be Cloud Hands. After the warm-up, we spread out and she moved from one person to the next, watching, encouraging, making small adjustments. By the time we finished the form at the end of the class, my T-shirt was blotched with patches of sweat.

"Your Cloud Hands look better," Maggie said, holding her arms out and shaking them as she walked over to me.

"Seriously?" I said.

"I wouldn't say they did if they didn't." She pulled both hands back through her blond hair. "Could you give me a ride?" she asked. "I have three bags of cotton stuffing in my office, and I don't really want to carry them."

"Sure," I said. "That reminds me. I have Liam's coffee mug in my bag."

"Why?" The bridge of her nose wrinkled as she frowned at me.

"Because he left it at Eric's and hasn't been back. Claire gave it to me to give to you."

"He's had a lot on his mind," Maggie said with an offhand shrug. "Thanks for bringing it."

I didn't see any point in bringing up the argument Liam had had with Mike. Maggie had a lot on her mind, too. "What are you going to do with three bags of stuffing?" I asked instead. "Are you working on another piece like Eddie?"

Maggie's life-size Eddie Sweeney had been part of last winter's Winterfest display at the community center. And he'd indirectly been the reason Roma and the real Eddie had started going out. The last time I'd been at Maggie's apartment, Eddie had been sitting in her living room with his skates propped on a footstool.

Maggie grinned and gave her head a little shake. "Don't tell Roma, but I'm actually working on Eddie. He needs a little bodywork"—she patted her hips with both hands—"if you know what I mean. Eddie—the real one—wants stuffed Eddie as a housewarming gift for Roma."

"Aww, that's so romantic," I said, using the sleeve of my shirt to wipe sweat off the side of my neck.

"It is, isn't it?" Maggie said as we started for her office. She bumped me with her hip. "Kind of like offering to put the pieces of an old rocking chair together for someone."

I shot her a daggers look. She held up both hands as though she were surrendering. "I'm just saying," she said.

We carried the three bags of cotton stuffing out to

the truck. Mags put two of them in the middle of the bench seat and fastened the lap belt around them. The third bag she jammed down by her feet.

Maggie's apartment was on the top floor of an old brick building that had been a corset factory at one time. The stairs came out onto a landing with a huge window that flooded the space with light. To the left was a small bathroom and an equally small bedroom.

Straight ahead, down two steps, was the living space, dark hardwood stretching all the way to the other end of the long room. Maggie's dark chocolate dining room table and chairs were in the area next to the stairs where the wall jutted inward to make room for a small roof terrace outside.

An old Oriental rug, which Mags had confided she'd scavenged from the dump and half carried, half dragged home, marked the living room space. There were two deep blue sofas and a square-shaped leather chair in front of the built-in bookshelves with their beveled glass doors. Faux Eddie was in the chair, skates up on the dark blue footstool. Maggie had somehow fastened a copy of the *Wall Street Journal* to his hockey gloves. From the front it actually looked like a real person sitting there reading the financial news in skates and full hockey gear.

At the end of the long room there was a small galley kitchen with a dropped hammered-tin ceiling.

"How about some hot chocolate?" Maggie asked, setting the two bags of stuffing she'd been carrying on one of the sofas and heading for the little kitchen. She set Liam's coffee mug on the counter.

"Sounds good," I said. I put the bag of stuffing I'd been holding next to the other two, sat on the empty sofa and studied Eddie. He really did look like the real thing.

I watched Maggie move around the tiny kitchen, shifting her weight instead of stretching and overreaching. It made me wonder if eventually all the tai chi practice would have me moving like that. "That's really nice of you to let Eddie have Eddie," I said. "I had lunch with Roma out at Wisteria Hill today."

Maggie turned from the refrigerator, a container of milk in her hand. "I know," she said. "Roma called me—before she called Marcus."

"She told you about seeing Liam arguing with Mike Glazer." So she knew after all. I kicked off my shoes and curled my feet up under me.

"She did. I know he was angry about the way things were working out. Mike was driving everyone crazy." She shot me a sidelong glance. "That's why he left his mug at Eric's, isn't it?"

I nodded. "Claire said he just tossed some money on the table and left before she could catch him."

She sighed. "Kath, Liam's not the kind of person who would hurt someone, let alone kill anyone. People say a lot of things they don't mean when they're angry." She got the marshmallows out of the cupboard over her head. "I got mad at Jimmy Harrison in third grade and told him I was going to stuff him in the toilet and flush him to China."

"You didn't, did you?"

"Of course not," she said. "You can't flush someone

to China. And anyway, eight-year-old boys don't fit in elementary school toilets."

"I'm not going to ask how you know that," I said.

Maggie just laughed.

I looked over at Eddie. Straight on, it looked like he was reading the news, but from this angle it seemed as though he were watching me out of the corner of his eye, over the top of the newspaper. "Mags, is Eddie watching me or am I just imagining things?" I asked.

"Very good," she said with a smile. "You're the first person to notice that, or maybe I should say you're the first person to say you noticed it. Everyone else has just moved to the other end of the sofa."

"So you did it on purpose?"

She picked up one of the heavy pottery mugs and brought it over to me. "It was an experiment. Remember me telling you about the art show I went to in Detroit?"

"There was a painting—a landscape. You said it made you uncomfortable, but you couldn't figure out why at first."

She nodded. "It turned out there was a person in the image, almost lost in the shadows of the picture. Wherever you stood in the gallery, it felt as though that figure were watching you." She picked up her own mug. "Close your eyes."

I closed them. The feeling I was being stared at seemed stronger now that I couldn't see Eddie.

"Don't look," Maggie said.

I folded my fingers tightly around my cup, and after

a minute I felt Maggie sit down. "Okay, open your eyes," she said.

The first thing I did was turn my head toward Eddie. I had no idea what she'd done, but he wasn't watching me anymore. That unsettling sensation, like someone's breath on the back of my neck, slipped away.

"What did you do?" I asked.

Maggie was curled into the opposite corner of the sofa. "I just moved his head, maybe an inch or so down and about the same amount to the side."

I leaned forward. "It's almost like he's smiling at me now."

"I know," she said. She grinned and took a sip of her hot chocolate.

"Mags, do you know much about Legacy Tours?" I asked.

"A little," she said. "Why?"

I hesitated. "This stays between us?"

Her expression turned serious. She put one hand over her heart. "Of course."

"Harry Taylor—Junior—asked me to poke around a little and see if I could maybe figure out what happened to Mike."

"Why?"

I leaned back against the arm of the couch. "Because his sister, Elizabeth, is friends with Wren Magnusson, and Wren's pretty much the only person who really feels bad about Mike Glazer's death."

"And if Elizabeth is upset, then so is Harry Senior."

"He's a good person. I couldn't say no."

Maggie shook her head and gave me a half smile.

I shrugged. "Okay, I could have said no, but I care about Harry. He feels like family to me."

"You care about Harry. Harry cares about Elizabeth. Elizabeth cares about Wren. It's getting complicated, Kath."

"If I find out anything, anything, the information goes to Marcus." I took another sip from my cup.

Maggie wrinkled her nose at me. "So I'd be wasting my time telling you what a bad idea this is."

"Pretty much," I said.

She pulled her feet up so she was sitting cross-legged. "Okay. Most of what I know about Legacy Tours comes from Liam. You know that they specialize in putting together travel packages for corporate clients."

I nodded. "I did a little research. I know that Alex and Christopher Scott started the company and they brought Mike in about three years ago."

Maggie propped her cup on one knee. "Did you know that the company was having financial problems at the time?"

I sat up a little straighter. "No."

"Legacy wasn't the only company Liam considered for this tour pitch. He checked every one of them very carefully. He knows someone who works for one of the big banks in Chicago. Liam found out that before Mike became a partner, Legacy had a high expense-to-revenue ratio, but in the last eighteen months things had turned around."

She peered into her cup, frowned and got up for another marshmallow. Then she settled back on the sofa again. "I know the major reason Liam thought Legacy was the best choice for this whole tour idea was because Mike Glazer had grown up here, but I also know it was important to him that Mike was a good businessman."

My foot was going to sleep. I stretched out my leg and rolled my ankle in slow circles. "I found an article online that hinted that Mike was taking kickbacks from some of the businesses he was dealing with."

Maggie nodded and took another drink. "It's probably the same article Liam found. I know he spoke to the writer. He said all the guy had were rumors and loose talk."

"Did you know that either Alex or Christopher Scott was here the day Mike died?" I asked.

"Are you sure?"

I shifted against the arm of the sofa. "Positive. I spoke to whichever one of them it was at the library."

Maggie started nodding her head. "I remember Liam saying that Alex was getting an award from some service organization. There was a big dinner in Minneapolis. It's only an hour's drive. He probably came to see Mike about something."

I made a face and stared up at the ceiling for a moment. If Alex Scott had been at a dinner in Minneapolis, he couldn't have been here when Mike Glazer died. But maybe his twin could have been.

"Kathleen, you don't really think it was one of Mike's partners who killed him, do you?" Maggie asked.

"I don't know," I said. "It sure would be a nice, simple solution though, wouldn't it?"

She nodded, lacing her fingers around her cup. "It would," she said. "But it seems to me that when someone dies around here, there's nothing nice or simple about it."

11

Marcus came into the library about nine thirty the next morning. Mary was working at the circulation desk. She gave me a sly smile as I walked over to meet him.

"Hi," he said. "Do you have a few minutes?"

I noticed he was carrying a small paper bag from Eric's, and I could smell cinnamon.

"I do," I said. "How about a cup of coffee?"

He smiled. "That would be good."

I turned to Mary. "Susan is reshelving books and Mia's helping her. Do you need anything?"

"No, I'm fine," she said. Then she turned to look at Marcus, gesturing to the bag he was holding. "Did you bring enough to share with the class, Detective? Or just sweets for the sweet?"

His eyes shifted from me to Mary. "Excuse me?" he said.

"Never mind," I said to Mary. "I smell cinnamon

and just a hint of vanilla, which most likely means there are cinnamon rolls in that bag. Cinnamon rolls that Eric made from the 'secret' recipe that you gave him and that neither one of you will share with anyone else." I made a face at her, and she looked back at me all wide-eyed, nurturing grandma. "And now that I'm thinking of it, you smelled like cinnamon and vanilla when you got here this morning." I crossed my arms over my chest, so I probably looked like every carica-ture of the stern librarian. "Do you have anything up-stairs in your bag that you'd like to share with the rest of us?"

Mary cocked her head to one side and gave Marcus a sweet albeit slightly fake smile, eyes sparking with mischief. "Enjoy your coffee, Detective," she said.

I inclined my head toward the stairs. "C'mon up to my office," I said to Marcus.

"What was that about?" he asked, as we started up the stairs to the second floor.

"A little meddling," I said, feeling my face get warm. While we were emptying the book drop before the li-brary opened, Mary had asked if Marcus and I were a couple now. "We're taking it slowly," I'd told her.

"Well, if you decide you want to speed things up a lit-tle, I could teach you a few things," she'd said. She'd pan-tomimed pulling off a glove with her teeth while I stood there, dumbstruck. Then she'd winked and wheeled the cart over to the checkout desk.

"Because we had dinner together at Eric's," he said.

I nodded as I unlocked my office door. "Have a seat and I'll get the coffee," I said.

He held up the brown paper bag. "You were right, by the way: Eric's cinnamon rolls. They're still warm." He rolled his eyes. "I suppose this will have people talking, too."

"Probably," I said.

A slow smile stretched across his face as he shrugged out of his jacket. "It's a good thing no one saw us in the driveway then," he said, his eyes locked on mine.

For a moment I just stood there, looking at him and indulging in a Walter Mitty–esque fantasy in which I backed Marcus up against my desk and kissed him until his knees wobbled.

I shook my head to get rid of the picture. Okay, not something I should even be thinking about doing in the library in the middle of a workday. Or in the middle of any day, for that matter.

I gestured over my shoulder and cleared my throat. "I'll, uh . . . I'll be right back."

When I came back with our coffee, I found Marcus standing beside my desk holding the picture frame that had been sitting next to my phone. He looked up at me. "This is your family."

I smiled. "It is." I set the cups down on the desktop and leaned over to look at the photograph. My friend Lise had taken it when I was back in Boston during the summer. We'd been down on the Common, throwing around a foam football and generally acting like goofy kids. In the photo, Sara and I were tackling Ethan, trying to get the ball while Mom and Dad cheered us on. We were laughing, the sun was sparkling, and looking at the picture, I felt a small ache of homesickness.

"Sara and Ethan are twins, right?" Marcus asked.

I nodded. "I think I told you that my parents were married, divorced and then they got married again. After the divorce, they started seeing each other—no one knew—and then all of a sudden Ethan and Sara were on the way. I was a teenager. I was mortified." He handed me the frame, and I set the picture back on the desk again. "Mom said she decided it didn't matter how crazy my father made her; she was just happier with him than without him."

Marcus picked up his coffee, and I gestured to one of the two chairs in front of my desk.

"I just realized that I don't know if you have any brothers or sisters," I said.

"I have one sister," he said. "She's younger."

I waited for him to say something else, but he didn't. I reached for my own cup and sat down. He took the two buns out of the paper bag and set them on the plate I'd brought in.

"So what's up?" I asked.

"What makes you think something's up?" he asked. "Maybe I just wanted to bring you a cinnamon roll. You've brought me coffee lots of times."

I leaned over and broke off a piece of one of the buns. It was so good. Better than any cinnamon roll I made. I'd never been able to duplicate Mary and Eric's secret recipe, and when I asked Mary why that recipe was always so much better, she'd just grin and say, "Because we make them with love." I always made mine with a couple of cats eyeballing my every move.

"I have gotten you coffee lots of time," I said. "I just

brought you that cup." I gestured to the mug in his big hands. "And the cinnamon roll is delicious. Thank you. Now, what's up?"

He smiled and shook his head. "You were right. The button Owen found came from a jacket that belongs to one of Mike's partners—Alex Scott."

"He was here in Mayville Heights the day Mike died. I saw him at the library, and he spoke to me on his way out at Eric's. Do you remember?"

Marcus nodded. "But he wasn't actually in town when Glazer died."

"Are you sure?"

"I'm positive. He was in Minneapolis at a benefit dinner. There are photos and video online."

That's what Maggie had said. Marcus was good. "Alex and Christopher Scott are identical twins," I said. "One of them could have been at that benefit and the other could have been here."

"They were both there."

"Maybe one brother was pretending to be both brothers while the other was here." It sounded silly even to me.

Marcus pointed at my laptop. "Could I borrow your computer for a second?"

"Go ahead," I said.

He went around the desk and leaned over the keyboard. After a minute, he beckoned to me. I went to stand beside him. An image of Alex and Christopher Scott, grinning and soaked with sweat, arms around each other's shoulders, filled the screen.

The two men were the spitting image of each other,

down to their close-cropped hair and stubbled chins—except one of them had an elaborate dragon tattoo curling around his right arm.

Marcus held up a finger. "Hang on." He brought up another photo. This one, I guessed, had been taken at the benefit in Minneapolis. One of the two Scott brothers was standing with three other people, a drink in his hand. He wasn't wearing a suit jacket, and the cuffs of his white shirt had been rolled back. There was no tattoo.

"That's Alex," Marcus said. "And this"—he clicked the mouse pad—"is Christopher Scott."

It could have been the same person. Christopher Scott was wearing the same dark pants and white shirt. His sleeves weren't rolled back, but I could see a bit of the dragon tattoo beyond the edge of his shirt cuff.

"So much for wrapping up the case in a nice, neat package." I moved back around the desk.

"It doesn't usually work that way," Marcus said, leaning against the side of my desk.

"There's something else you should know," I said, breaking off another bite of the cinnamon roll before I sat down again. I knew Roma had spoken to him, but I didn't want to keep secrets.

"What is it?"

"Liam Stone had an argument with Mike on the sidewalk in front of Eric's Place. I'm not saying I think he had anything to do with what happened to Mike; I'm just trying—"

"—not to interfere in my case?" he finished. He gave me a smile that made his blue eyes crinkle. "I know about the argument. Roma called me, and more than one person heard them." He looked expectantly at me.

"What?" I said.

"Aren't you going to tell me that really you think Liam had nothing to do with Glazer's death?"

I shook my head and took another sip from my mug. "No."

"No?"

"I don't know who killed Mike," I said, setting my cup back on the desk. "I like Liam, but I don't know him that well." I smiled sweetly at Marcus. "So I'm not going to waste a perfectly good argument." I held out the plastic top to the mug he was holding. "Here."

"What is it?" he said, taking it from me.

"The lid. It's a travel mug. You can take the rest of your coffee with you."

"Are you trying to get rid of me?" He couldn't quite stop the beginnings of a smile from pulling at his mouth.

"No," I said. "But in the last couple of minutes you've scratched your arm twice so you could check your watch."

He stared at me for a minute. He rarely blushed, but there was a flush of pink on the tops of his cheekbones. "I only scratched it once," he said finally. "The second time I was pushing my sleeve back." The smile got loose completely then. "I do have to go, though."

He leaned across the desk and broke the second cinnamon roll in half. Then he snapped the lid on the coffee mug, setting the bun half on top. Straightening up, he took a couple of steps closer to me. He was so close, I could feel the warmth coming off his body. "Thank you for the coffee, Kathleen," he said.

My mouth was dry and I had to swallow before I answered. "You're welcome," I said. "Thank you for the cinnamon roll."

We stood there for a long moment, looking at each other, just a little bit closer than we probably should have been standing, and maybe in another minute or so I really would have backed him against the desk and given him a good romance-novel kissing, but I didn't get the chance because Mary cleared her throat in the doorway. Marcus immediately took a step backward and we both turned to look at her.

"I'm sorry to interrupt," she said.

She didn't look sorry. She looked like a smug little elf. All she needed was a pair of curly-toed shoes.

"Is something wrong?" I asked.

"There's a bit of a problem with a book delivery."

"I didn't order any books," I said.

Mary nodded. "I know. That's the problem. Delivery guy says he has six boxes of books for us."

"I have to get back to work," Marcus said.

I smiled at him. "Thank you."

He raised his cup and eased by Mary, smiling at her as he passed. I grabbed my keys and locked my office door while Mary waited, the same smug elvish grin on her face.

"I really am sorry I interrupted you two," she said as we started down the stairs. "I hope it wasn't an important conversation." She put a little stress on the word "important."

"I'm ignoring you," I said darkly, keeping my eyes forward.

She gave a snort of laughter. "That never works, Kathleen." She scampered down the last four steps ahead of me. At the bottom, she looked back at me over her shoulder and gave me a saucy wink.

The day of the annual library book sale, at the beginning of the summer, Susan had shown up wearing her favorite *Younger, Stronger, Faster* T-shirt. Mary had taken off her sweater to show off her own shirt. It said, *Old, Sneaky and Stubborn*. At least three people had tried to buy it from her.

It took me a while to straighten out the mix-up with the book delivery. The last two boxes were going out the door as Elizabeth came in. She raised a hand when she caught sight of me and walked over to the circulation desk.

"Hi, Kathleen," she said. "Is it possible to request a book for Harrison? I don't have his library card."

"What would he like?" I said.

"He's already halfway through the book we picked up for him. I thought maybe I'd request the next one in the series for him."

"I already did," I said.

"Thank you," she said, giving me a small smile. "I guess you know him pretty well."

"He's one of my best readers."

She tucked her hands into the front kangaroo pocket

of her red sweatshirt. "Thank you for letting us meet your cats the other night. Wren loved them."

"You're welcome," I said. "Come back and visit anytime. They love people who make a fuss over them."

Elizabeth's expression grew serious. "And thank you for answering Wren's questions about"—she stopped and stared at her feet for a moment—"about finding Mike Glazer."

I hesitated; then I reached out and laid my hand on her arm. "I hope it helped."

She nodded. "It did. It's been really hard for her. Everyone says he was a jerk." She shrugged. "Maybe he was. I don't know. All I know is that Wren was really happy to be going to see him, and when she found out he was dead, she almost passed out from the shock."

"I'm so sorry," I said. "I know the police are working on the case. Maybe they'll come up with some answers that will at least put her mind at rest."

She made a face. "It said in the paper that his death is still under investigation. Isn't that just a polite way of saying they think someone killed him but they don't want to actually admit that for some reason?"

I chose my words carefully. "I think they need to look at all the evidence before they say anything."

"This not knowing is eating a hole in Wren," Elizabeth said. "First her mother dies and now this. It's not fair. I just wish somebody would figure out something."

She looked so much like her father and had the same deep loyalty to the people she cared about as he had.

And like Agatha, she seemed to inspire that in other people, too.

"Somebody will figure out something," I told her.

What I didn't say was maybe that somebody would turn out to be me.

12

There were no dismembered chicken parts strewn around the kitchen when I got home, although I did find what looked to me to be gray fur on the seat of the big chair in the living room. "Were you sleeping on my chair?" I asked Owen.

His whiskers twitched, as though he were thinking about my question. Then he gave a sharp, short meow.

I reached for the little clump of cat hair. "Okay, so you might not have been sleeping," I said. "But I know you were up here." I turned around and discovered I was talking to myself.

Hercules kept me company while I made supper, and Owen prowled the backyard, poking around the flower beds and chasing the odd bird. While I ate, I told them what I'd learned from Marcus about the Scott brothers. "How are we going to figure out who killed Mike Glazer?" I asked them.

Hercules meowed softly. I leaned sideways to see

what he was looking at. I'd brought home two books and a DVD from the library. They were sitting on one of the kitchen chairs, which Hercules seemed to be staring at.

"You think a book on Scottish history would help?" I asked.

The look he shot me was clearly disdainful.

I reached for the DVD. It was *Young Sherlock Holmes*. "You think we should play Sherlock Holmes?"

"Merow," he said.

I leaned back in the chair. "So what do you think we should do? Round up the usual suspects?"

Herc looked up at the ceiling. Could cats roll their eyes?

"Oh, right," I said. "That's *Casablanca*, not *Sherlock Holmes*."

The cat brought his gaze back to me, not at all impressed with my sense of humor or my knowledge of old movies.

I reached down to stroke the top of his head. "Okay, no more teasing," I said. "So who are our suspects?"

Owen chimed in then with a loud meow.

I looked over at him trying to work something sticky off the side of a back paw. "Liam?" I asked.

He meowed again and went back to his cleanup routine.

I straightened up in the chair. "Okay, Liam," I said to Hercules. "Maybe Abigail's friend Georgia, and maybe even Burtis. Who else?" He looked at the books again. "Not Mary," I said. "I know she threatened to launch Mike Glazer between two streetlights like she was kicking for three points in the Super Bowl, but I refuse to believe she'd kill anyone."

I laced my fingers together and rested my hands on the top of my head. "I know Marcus said the Scott brothers couldn't have had anything to do with Mike Glazer's death, but I'd still like to know more about them."

Hercules lifted one paw and looked at me. Feeling kind of silly, I leaned down and held out my hand. He put his paw on my palm. It looked like we had a plan.

The phone rang just as I was starting the dishes. "Hello, Katydid," my mother's voice said, warm somehow against my ear.

I dropped down onto the footstool. "Hi, Mom," I said. "How's LA?" My mother was in Los Angeles, reprising the role she'd created on a soap opera early in the year.

"Warm and sunny," she said. "At least I'm assuming it is. I'm at the studio."

"How's everything going?"

She laughed. I loved the sound. My mother had a great laugh—big and deep and warm. "Wonderful. I could very easily turn into a diva. I have a gorgeous suite. They send a car for me every morning. And my dressing room is bigger than our first apartment." She paused. "Or our second apartment, or our third."

I laughed too. "I get the picture, Mom."

"I read in your paper that there was a dead body found in the downtown," she said. "You wouldn't know anything about that, sweetie, would you?"

My mother read the *Mayville Heights Chronicle* online

so she could keep up with what was happening in town.

"How do you do that?" I asked.

She laughed again. "Mother's intuition. Did you find the body, or is the dead man connected to someone you know?"

I stretched my feet out across the hardwood floor. "Actually, Hercules found the body."

"Your cat?"

"Uh-huh."

"Most people just buy their cats a couple of rubber mice and a ball of yarn to entertain them, Katydid," she said dryly.

"It's kind of complicated, Mom."

"The best stories always are."

I explained about Ruby's paintings, Hercules bolting across the street, and Mike Glazer's body being in the tent. I even filled her in on the proposal for Legacy Tours.

"So what happens to the tour idea now?"

"It's still on," I said, rolling my head from one side to the other. "One of the other partners is coming to town."

"My fingers and toes are crossed for all of you," she said.

"Thanks, Mom," I said. "Now, how about a couple of hints about your story line? Maggie's going to ask me."

Mags had become a loyal *Wild and Wonderful* fan after she'd started watching to see my mother in action.

"I could never give away story line secrets," Mom said, and I pictured her with her hand over her heart. I waited. "But if I were to do it . . ." She went on to tell me a couple of surprises planned for her character that I knew would have Maggie glued to her DVR.

"I have to go," Mom said. "They're going to be calling me to the set soon. I love you, and I sent you something in the mail."

"You sent me something? What?"

"Now, if I told you, it wouldn't be a surprise, would it?" she said. "Call your father and your brother and sister. I'll talk to you soon." With that, she was gone.

I hung up the receiver, wondering what she was sending me. Knowing my mother, it could be anything. I looked at the phone. Now that I'd talked to my mom, I wanted to talk to the rest of the family.

Ethan answered the phone. "Hey, Kath," he said.

"How did you know it was me?" I asked. "Do you have Mom's ESP?" Our mother had this spooky ability to somehow know when it was one of her kids on the phone.

"No," he said. "We have this little invention called caller ID here in the big city. I know you probably don't have that kind of thing out there in the sticks."

"Yeah, we just make do with tin cans and string."

"I figured," he said. "And for the record, when I talked to Mom earlier, she did say you'd call around now."

"Doesn't surprise me," I said. "So what are you up to, baby brother?"

"Still working on the video. And now Sara's got this

idea of making a video about making the video. Oh, yeah, and I cut my hair."

"You cut your hair?" I said.

"Well, technically it was cut by a redhead with—"

I cleared my throat.

"—a very nice smile," he finished. I could hear the laugher in his voice.

He spent a few minutes telling me more about the video. Then he said, "Sara wants to talk to you. She keeps poking me in the back of the head with her bony old-woman fingers."

There were sounds of a scuffle and then Sara came on the line. "Hi, Kathleen," she said. "Ignore Ethan. He's a wuss."

"Hi," I said. "How's the video going?"

"Good. Ethan doesn't pay attention to what I tell him to do, but everyone else is pretty easy to work with." I heard something in the background. "Just a sec," Sara said.

"Sorry," she said more clearly a moment later. "We shot some of the scenes at the warehouse today. I'm e-mailing you photos."

The band's song was called "In a Hundred Other Worlds." Sara's idea for the video had different versions of the band singing the song—the bands in the hundred other worlds. They were doing most of the filming in an old warehouse that Ethan had been able to rent for almost nothing.

"I can't wait to see them," I said.

"Yeah, well, if you'd been here, you would have

seen way more of the guys than you ever wanted to, because I certainly did."

"Do I want to know what you mean?" I asked. Hercules came in from the kitchen and leaned his black-and-white head against my leg. I reached down and lifted him onto my lap.

"I mean Milo, Devon, Jake and our baby brother without their shirts on." Sara was older than Ethan by close to four minutes and never let him forget it.

"Why?" I said.

She laughed. She sounded so much like Mom. "Because I had to airbrush them from the waist up. Well, not Ethan. I got a friend of mine to come do him."

"Airbrush?" I said.

"Makeup." Sara worked as a makeup artist to support her filmmaking. "I needed the tattoos and the piercings gone for one of the scenes in the video. They're supposed to look like seventeenth-century pirates in frilly shirts open to the waist. The piercings were easy; they just had to take out all their hardware. Best way to cover up all their ink was to airbrush. It did a great job, but none of those guys were on my list of men I wanted to see without their shirts."

I couldn't help it. I laughed. I got a mental picture of Sara airbrushing makeup onto Ethan's band mates while they stood around bare-chested, cringing. It's not that they weren't all exhibitionists to some degree, but I knew each one of the guys had a bit of a crush on her, and as for Ethan, the only thing that would have been more embarrassing was if it had been Sara spraying him with makeup instead of her friend. It still made him squirrelly when I reminded him that I'd changed his diapers.

"I don't know whether to be glad I wasn't there, or sorry I missed it," I said.

"Don't worry. I'm sending you pictures of them in their frilly shirts," she said.

In the background, Ethan yelled, "No, you're not."

I talked to Sara for a few more minutes. She promised she'd tell Dad I'd called, and I promised to turn the most embarrassing shot of Ethan in his ruffled shirt into my screensaver.

I put the phone back on the table. I missed them. And I couldn't stall much longer on giving Everett my decision on whether or not I was going to stay in Mayville Heights. The whole thing had gotten a lot more complicated since I'd gone back to Boston to see everyone during the summer.

"They were different," I said to Hercules. "I didn't feel like I had to take care of everybody and everything." He walked his front paws up my chest and licked my chin. "Okay, maybe it was me that was different."

I picked him up and went out to the kitchen. I'd miss my little house and my friends if I went back to Boston, and I had no idea how Owen and Hercules would adjust to being in the city. And if I stayed, then I was always going to be a little homesick to see Sara and Ethan and Mom and Dad. There wasn't any easy answer.

I scratched Hercules's chin and he made a contented sigh. "When I was in Boston, no one ever asked me to figure out why someone got killed," I said.

Herc turned his head to look at the volunteer schedule for feeding the cats at Wisteria Hill. Marcus and I were up on Friday morning. I laid my cheek against the top of the cat's soft, furry head. There was no playing Sherlock Holmes in Boston, but there was no Marcus, either.

13

Maggie called first thing in the morning while I was standing bleary-eyed in front of my closet, trying to decide what I was going to wear. "Did I wake you?" she asked.

"No," I said. "Owen did that. He seemed to think that if he was awake then everyone should be awake. He sat by the bed and he was either meowing the 'Toreador Song' from *Carmen* or 'Old MacDonald Had a Farm.' I'm not sure which."

"Aww, I bet he was adorable." Maggie thought everything Owen did was sweet or adorable. Mr. Adorable himself was coming across the floor to me with that uncanny radar he had that always told him when it was Maggie on the phone.

"If by adorable you mean annoying, then yes," I said.

She laughed. "I need your truck, Kath, if that's okay."

"Sure," I said. "I could pick you up on my way to the

library and then you could bring the truck over whenever you're finished with it." Owen's back end was twitching, but before I could lean over and scoop him up, he jumped onto my lap.

"Don't you want to know why I want your truck?" she asked.

"I'm guessing you need to move something."

I heard her breathe out and guessed that she was stretching while she talked to me. "I need to get a couple of collage panels over to the community center, and Ruby's gone to Minneapolis for the day, so I can't use her truck."

Owen was trying to worm his way to the telephone receiver. He almost succeeded in bumping it out of my hand. "Sorry," I said to Maggie. "Owen's here."

"Hold the phone up to his ear."

"You're not serious."

"Don't pretend you don't talk to Owen and Hercules like they can understand you," she said. "Kath, put the phone by his ear."

"All right." I looked at Owen. "Maggie wants to talk to you," I said, realizing as the words came out of my mouth that I had just proved Maggie's point.

I held the receiver next to the cat's furry, gray ear. A moment passed. He meowed and then he started to purr. Clearly he recognized Maggie's voice.

I waited. Owen turned to look at me, and then he jumped down to the floor and headed out of the room. I put the phone back to my own ear.

"Owen's gone," I said.

"I know. I told him to go finish his breakfast," Maggie said. "And I told him I'd see him on Friday." I'd invited Mags and Roma for supper on Friday night.

"He was purring."

"The little fur ball is a charmer," she said, and I could hear the smile in her voice.

"I'll come pick you up," I said. "I just have to have some breakfast and get my things together. I should be there in about half an hour."

"Thanks, Kath," she said. "I appreciate it."

I went back to the kitchen to make myself a bowl of oatmeal. Owen was happily moving food from his dish to the floor. Hercules had already finished eating and gone somewhere to do cat stuff.

Maggie was waiting out front when I got to her place. "Hi," she said as she slid onto the front seat. "Did Fuzz Face finish his breakfast?"

I nodded. "He did. He's probably rolling around on the footstool or the chair right now, trying to get as much cat hair on it as possible."

She laughed. "That's one of the things I like about Owen; he has that rebel cat streak."

I shook a finger at her as I pulled away from the curb. "That's because you don't have to vacuum the cat hair off the footstool."

That just made her laugh harder.

"I talked to my mother last night," I said.

Maggie immediately sat up straighter. "And?" she prompted.

"And she's having a good time in Los Angeles. She said her dressing room is huge and the network sends a car for her each morning."

"Did she at least tell you who she's sleeping with?"

I shot her a quick look.

Mags waved a hand in the air. "I don't mean your mother. I mean her character."

"Sorry." I shrugged. "She didn't."

She slumped back against the seat. "I was kind of hoping she'd go for Billy. They had great chemistry the last time on the show."

I stopped at the corner and looked both ways before heading through the intersection. "She did tell me who Jack's going to sleep with," I said, keeping my eyes on the road. That got her attention.

"Who?" she asked.

I told her what my mother had said.

"On Victor's desk?" I nodded, and she chortled with laughter and all but squirmed in her seat.

She badgered me with questions the rest of the way to the River Arts building. "Next time I talk to Mom, I'll put you on the phone," I said as I backed the truck into Maggie's parking spot behind the building.

"Seriously?" she said.

I nodded.

"Could we call her tomorrow night?"

The look on her face reminded me of Owen when he was trying to wheedle a stinky cracker out of me. "Maybe," I said, and she gave me a goofy grin of happiness. Maggie's newly discovered love for the *Wild and Wonderful* was a lot like her undying affection for Matt Lauer—one of those things that I was never quite going to understand.

I took the truck keys off my key ring. "Here," I said.

"Bring the truck back when you're finished. I'm at the library all day."

She hugged me. "Thanks. I should have it back to you by lunchtime."

I grabbed my briefcase and got out of the truck. "I'll see you later," I said with a wave.

I walked down to Main Street and stopped at the corner to look out over the water. It was a gorgeous fall day. The white tents on the green grass against the backdrop of the deep blue water looked like a painting. If I didn't stay in Mayville Heights, this was one of the many, many things I was going to miss. I wondered if Mike Glazer had missed Mayville. Was that one of the reasons he'd agreed to come and hear Liam's tour proposal?

I was about to head down the street to the library when the end flap of the closest tent lifted and Oren Kenyon stepped out. I raised a hand in greeting, and he started toward me. There were no cars coming, so I crossed the street and met him on the sidewalk.

"Good morning," I said.

He gave me a small smile. "Hello, Kathleen," he said. Oren was tall and rangy with sun-bleached blond hair. His large hands had long, slender fingers, and he was an accomplished pianist as well as a talented carpenter. He turned and looked back over his shoulder at the tent.

"Is something wrong?" I asked.

"I'm not sure," he said. "Do you have your cell phone with you? I don't have one."

"It's right here." I pulled the phone out of my pocket.

Oren wiped his hands on his brown work pants and then looked at them. They were streaked with dirt. "Kathleen, would you mind calling the police?" he asked. "I was moving some of the booths—getting them leveled and secured a little better. I found something that might be important. I don't know."

"What was it?"

Oren glanced at the tent again. "I thought I saw a glint of something shiny by one of the end tent pegs when I was tying back the sides to let some sun in, so I went to take a look." He made an apologetic shrug. "Maybe it doesn't mean anything, but it looks like there's a knife stuck in the ground."

"A knife?"

"A butter knife, I think. I'm not sure. It's small with a thin blade." His shifted his weight from one side to the other. "Thing is, I tied that line myself and there sure as heck wasn't any knife in the ground when I did."

I nodded slowly. "I'll call Marcus," I said.

I punched in the number with a strong feeling of déjà vu, thinking maybe I should put Marcus on speed dial. The phone rang half a dozen times before he answered it. I explained where I was and what Oren had found.

He exhaled loudly and mumbled something I didn't catch. "Okay, I'm on my way."

"Do you need me to stay here?" I asked. I could hear voices in the background.

"Can you?" he asked.

I looked at my watch. "Yes," I said. "But I do have to open the library and I'm walking."

"I won't be long. I promise," he said, and then he ended the call.

"Marcus is on his way," I told Oren, putting my phone back in my pocket.

"Thank you," he said. He tried to brush more of the dirt off his hands. "I know the police are still investigating Mike Glazer's death. I don't know if that knife means anything or not."

I looked past him at the tent. "Oren, could you show me where it is?" I asked. I held up both hands. "I won't touch anything."

"All right," he said.

I followed him across the grass. He lifted the canvas flap and pointed. "Right there. I'm not sure if you can see it."

"I see it," I said. With the other flaps tied open, the tent was flooded with early-morning sun. The light was glinting off the rounded end of what looked like a knife handle, the blade jammed down into the earth, less than a foot away from where Owen had dug up that brass button from Alex Scott's jacket. How had it gotten there? I'd checked the area very carefully after Owen had discovered the button and there hadn't been a knife, or anything else, stuck in the grass.

Oren looked at me. "You think it's a butter knife?"

"Looks like one," I said. We took a couple of steps away from the tent, and I set my bag on the grass at my feet.

"Doesn't make a lot of sense. If someone was trying to hide it, they didn't do a very good job."

"Maybe it's a coincidence," I said, stuffing my hands

in the pockets of my hooded sweater. "Maybe that knife has nothing to do with Mike Glazer's death."

He gave me an appraising look, eyes narrowed. "Do you really think so?" he asked.

I was spared having to answer because Marcus's SUV pulled up at the curb then. He got out of the car and walked over to us. "Hi," he said softly to me before turning his focus on Oren. "Kathleen said you found something in the tent."

Oren nodded. "I was opening things up so I could get some light inside and see what I was doing. Looks like someone stuck some kind of a knife down in the ground." He made the motion with one hand.

"Show me, please," Marcus said.

Oren led him over to the open end of the tent and pointed inside. "See it? Follow that line."

Marcus leaned forward, ducking his head. "Got it," he said after a moment. He straightened and turned back to me. "Why were you here?" he asked.

"I wasn't," I said.

"She was just headed up the street," Oren said. "I waved her over because I don't have a cell phone."

"All right," Marcus said, pulling his own phone out of his jacket pocket. "You can go, Kathleen." He looked at Oren. "I'd appreciate it if you could hang around for a few minutes, though."

"I can do that," Oren said. He smiled at me. "Thank you, Kathleen."

"You're welcome," I said, picking up my briefcase.

"I'll be over to talk to you about the planters. Maybe after lunch."

"I'll be there all day." I nodded at Marcus and cut across the grass to the sidewalk.

Once I was far enough down the street that Marcus couldn't see me, I jaywalked across Main Street, heading for the library as the crow flies instead of how the streets were laid. Abigail and Mia were waiting on the steps and Susan was hurrying along the sidewalk.

"I'm sorry I'm late," I said as I unlocked the doors and deactivated the alarm. "I had to take Maggie my truck." I didn't say anything about the latest find at the tent. There was enough speculation around town as it was about what had happened to Mike Glazer. I didn't want to add to it.

"You're not late," Abigail said. "It's only five to."

Susan pushed through the door behind us; her top-knot, secured precariously with two bendy straws, waved at us like the top of a bobblehead doll. "I thought I was late," she wheezed, half out of breath.

"You're fine," I said, flipping on the lights. Mia headed for the book drop without even being asked. She was turning out to be the most conscientious student intern I'd ever worked with. Abigail crossed her arms and squinted at the bag Susan was carrying.

"What's in the bag?" she asked, wiggling her eyebrows and grinning.

Susan swung it from side to side with a grin of her own. "Eric's experimenting again. Cheese and bacon muffins."

Abigail's smile got wider. "You do know that I love your husband, don't you?" She put one hand over her heart. "I seriously love him."

Susan started for the stairs, shifting the bag up onto her shoulder. "He snores," she said dryly.

Abigail followed her. "Music to my ears," she said.

"He leaves his dirty socks all over the house."

"I would be honored to pick them up and wash them," Abigail countered.

"He has belly button lint. Lots of it." They were headed up the steps then and I didn't hear Abigail's response, but I pretty much knew what it was going to be. They'd done this routine before.

It was a busy morning. I did a presentation to a group of seniors about the library's e-lending program and got my notes ready for an upcoming meeting with the library board, fortified by one of Eric's muffins that, incredibly, tasted even better than it smelled.

Unlike a lot of small-town libraries, we were doing well, but that was only because Everett Henderson had funded the building's renovation as a gift to the town. Now that the building looked so good, I was determined to keep it running well.

Maggie brought the truck back right after lunch. "Thank you," she said, giving me a quick hug. "I have a meeting, but I'll see you tonight at class."

Oren showed up about midafternoon, and Abigail and I walked around the library grounds with him, looking for the best place to put a raised planter box. Abigail had had the idea to start a small garden with the story time kids in the spring. Oren was going to build the box now so planting could start as soon as the snow was gone and the ground had thawed.

Abigail explained her idea and Oren listened and

nodded, asking a few questions and making a couple of suggestions. Once we settled on the best place for the planter, Abigail went back inside. I held the end of Oren's metal tape while he measured and made notations on the tiny sketch he'd drawn in the small black-covered notebook he kept in his shirt pocket.

"I should have a drawing for you in a couple of days," he said. "And some idea of what it's going to cost."

"Thanks," I said.

"I'm sorry about this morning." He pulled off his cap and raked his fingers back through his sun-bleached hair.

"Don't worry about it," I said. "I was here in time. Did Marcus keep you very long?"

Oren shook his head. "No. I got the feeling he doesn't think that knife really means anything."

I brushed some dried grass off of my pants. "Why do you say that?"

He shrugged and fingered the brim of his cap. "He asked me twice how sure I was it wasn't there when we were setting up the tent."

"It wasn't," I said.

His gaze narrowed. "You found . . . the body, didn't you?"

I nodded. "I did. And something else that turned out not to be important. There wasn't any knife stuck in the ground there. I'm certain of it."

"It was probably just kids or someone goofing around in there."

"Probably," I agreed.

Oren left with a promise that he'd get back to me in the next few days, and I went inside again.

Hercules was sitting on one of the Adirondack chairs in the backyard when I came around the side of the house after work. "What are you doing out here?" I said. He squinted up at the big maple and meowed. I leaned over and scooped him into my arms. "Is Professor Moriarty back?" I asked.

The grackle seemed to think Herc should sit somewhere other than the small wooden bench under the maple tree and dive-bombed the cat to make its point. Herc had pretty fast paws, and more than once he'd almost grabbed the bird. That hadn't dissuaded it at all.

I'd thought that maybe the grackle had a nest in the tree, and once the babies were gone it would give up on trying to chase the cat, but so far that hadn't happened. Hercules made a point of sitting on the bench at least once a day, and the bird, for its part, made at least one low-flying pass over the cat's head whenever they were both in the yard, with appropriate sound effects from both sides. Both the grackle and the cat seemed to know how to hold a grudge.

One of these days one of them was going to win. I still wasn't sure which one to put my money on.

"How was the rest of your day?" I asked as I carried Hercules into the house. He muttered and murped the whole way, so I guessed it had been busy. I set him on the kitchen floor, hung up my sweater and put my briefcase on one of the chairs.

The basement door opened and Owen appeared. He had the end of my favorite purple scarf in his mouth.

I'd been looking for the thing for more than a week. He dragged the scarf across the floor and dropped it at my feet, looking up at me with a self-satisfied expression on his gray face.

I picked up the length of woven fabric. "Thank you," I said. I reached down and patted the top of his head. "I searched everywhere for this. It didn't enter my mind to check in the basement." Owen ducked his head. "You don't have any idea how this scarf ended up down there, do you?"

His furry head dropped even lower over his paws, as though they were suddenly the most fascinating appendages he'd ever seen.

"That's what I thought," I said.

I filled the boys in on Oren finding the knife inside the tent. Mostly I just wanted to say everything out loud to see if it made any more sense than when I just rolled what had happened around in my head.

"The knife wasn't there when you found the button," I told Owen. He was trying to snag part of a Funky Chicken that was poking out from under the stove and lifted his head only long enough to murp his agreement.

"Oren thinks it was probably just kids goofing around." I picked up my fork and then set it back down again. "You know, I can see the attraction of sneaking into the tent for a look around, but what was the point of sticking that knife or whatever it is in the ground? What kid carries something like that around?"

Hercules had been carefully washing his face. He gave one last pass behind his right ear; then he walked over to the coat hooks, jumped in the air and with one swipe of his paw pulled down the scarf that his brother had brought up from the basement. He grabbed one end with his teeth and dragged it across the floor to me. He gave me what I would have called a pointed look if he'd been a person and not a cat, and then he went into the living room.

"Is this supposed to mean something?" I called after him. Since he was a cat and not a person, I didn't get an answer. "Does this mean something?" I said to Owen. He was too busy eating to do more than just glance at me. In other words, "You figure it out."

I picked the scarf up from the floor. I knew Owen had swiped it for cat knows what reason. I suspected he'd pretended to discover the scarf in the basement to divert suspicion from himself. Cat or not, he was more than capable of doing that.

I stared at the woven tangle of purple fabric shot with silver in my hand. If Owen, a cat, was capable of a little subterfuge and diversion, why not the person who had killed Mike Glazer? It felt a little like something from an old Nancy Drew mystery, but maybe that silver-handled knife was a plant designed to reroute the police's interest on to someone else. It was a little outlandish—okay, it was a lot outlandish—but it didn't mean I wasn't on the right track.

"I get it," I called. After a moment there was an answering meow from the next room.

Maggie insisted that she talked to Owen and Hercules like they were people only because I did. I wondered what she'd say if she knew that not only did I talk to them as though they were people, but sometimes I was pretty sure they were answering. I headed upstairs to get ready for tai chi, taking the scarf with me.

I had enough time, so I walked down to class. Taylor King was coming along the sidewalk as I turned the corner. "Hi, Taylor," I said.

"Hi, Ms. Paulson." Her purse slipped down off her shoulder as she reached for the door.

"You can call me Kathleen," I said.

She smiled. "Okay."

I gestured at her bag. "I like your purse. It's vintage, isn't it?" The little copper satin handbag had a gold clasp and fabric strap.

"It's from the nineteen fifties," Taylor said, running her fingers over the smooth fabric. "I collect old purses. I like to think about the women who used to own them—what they were like, what their lives were like."

"The bags have a story," I said.

She nodded. "Yeah, they do."

"I like old things, too," I said, smiling back at her. We started up the stairs. "How do you like tai chi so far?" I asked.

"I like it." She shrugged. "But I don't see how I'll ever learn all one hundred and eight movements."

"I know what you mean," I said. "I thought I was never going to get beyond Cloud Hands." I fluttered my hands in front of myself and she laughed. I laughed too. "But I did and so will you. You're a lot better than I was. And I'm not just saying that to be a polite adult."

"Are there any books about tai chi at the library?" Taylor asked as we got to the top of the steps.

"Four or five," I said, peeling off my hoodie and sitting down to change my shoes. "Would you like me to leave a couple for you at the front desk?"

She nodded, pulling her hair back into a high ponytail. "Yes, please. Sometimes when I get home I can't remember one of the parts of a movement. It would help if I could at least see a picture."

"I'm going over to the library after class. I'll see what we have."

Taylor gave me a little-girl grin, lacing her fingers together. "Thank you. I work for my dad on the weekend, but I'll try to leave early on Saturday and come get them."

"I could take the books home with me and you could stop by my house and pick them up, if that would help," I said, hanging my hooded sweatshirt on one of the hooks and setting my shoes on the floor underneath.

"Seriously?" she asked.

"Seriously," I said, smiling as I straightened up.

"Well." She hesitated. "If it's not too much trouble. I'm trying to show my dad that I'm responsible because I'm going to start driving soon, so I don't really want to ask to leave work early. I promise I'll come get them on Sunday."

"It's no trouble."

"Okay, then, thanks." She hung her little bag on an empty hook and we went into the studio. Ruby waved Taylor over, and Maggie walked over to me, carrying her before-class mug of tea. "I heard that Oren found something in one of the tents this morning," she said.

I tried to keep my face neutral. "I heard the same thing."

"Ruby says Marcus and his cohorts were there all morning."

I couldn't stop myself from smiling at her. "You're fishing," I said.

"Okay, I'm fishing," she said. "I saw you cross the street to speak to Oren this morning. What was going on?"

"He found something. He wasn't sure if it was important or not, so I used my phone to call Marcus because Oren doesn't have one."

Maggie sipped her tea and watched me over the top of her cup. "Was it important?"

I pulled a hand over my neck. "I saw Oren this afternoon and he didn't think that Marcus thought so."

"Do you think so?"

I shrugged. "I don't know."

Maggie sighed. "I'll be glad when this is all over—not just the investigation, but everything: the food tasting, the art show, the whole pitch to Legacy. This entire project has a bad energy to it." She looked up at the clock. "Time to get started." She moved to the middle of the room, clapped her hands and called, "Circle, please."

I slipped in place between Rebecca and Roma. They both smiled at me. Before I could do anything more than smile back, Maggie was calling out instructions.

I worked hard the entire class. It was a good distraction from thinking about Mike Glazer and what had happened to him.

"Good work, everyone," Maggie said when we finished the form at the end of the class. "Work on bending your knees and shifting your weight."

Beside me, Roma stretched out one arm and then the other. "Your push hands are getting better," she said. "We should practice sometime."

I nodded. "Please. I could use some extra practice."

She frowned. "Maybe this weekend. I'll look at my schedule and let you know tomorrow night." We started for the door. "Could I bring anything?"

"Just yourself," I said.

"I have some samples of a new all-natural cat food," Roma said, running a hand back through her dark brown hair. "I thought I'd bring them along for Hercules and Owen to try."

"I'm sure they'd love to be your taste testers."

"I'm not trying to bribe them into liking me." She raised her eyebrows. "Well, maybe a little."

Since Roma wasn't one of the cats' favorite people, a visit to her vet clinic always involved treats, subterfuge on my part, a fair amount of yowling and a Kevlar glove. But when Roma had been dealing with the death of her birth father, it almost seemed as though Owen and Hercules had tried to be nice to her.

"Don't underestimate the power of a good bribe," I said with a laugh. "Owen's affections can be swayed—at least temporarily—although with Maggie in the room, he might just eat and ignore you."

"In other words, it'll be just like my dating life before Eddie," she said, with a glint in her brown eyes.

"How is Eddie?" I asked as I stepped out of my tai chi shoes.

The sound of his name made her face light up. "Wonderful," she said. "I'm going to see him next weekend." She searched my face. "How's Marcus?"

I put my shoes in my tote bag. "Annoying. Cute . . . Did I say annoying?"

Roma laughed.

"He made me dinner. He gave me a box of Batman comic books. Then he turns into Robocop."

Roma bent down to tie her red canvas sneakers. "Have you kissed him?" she asked.

I hesitated just a second too long. She snapped upright like the top half of her body was attached to a spring. "You did!" she said, a grin spreading across her face.

I felt my own cheeks burning. "No comment," I said.

She glanced at her watch. "You're off the hook for now because I have somewhere I have to be, but I will be expecting details tomorrow night." She grabbed her bag and headed down the stairs. "Lots of details," she said over her shoulder.

Halfway down, she stopped and turned to look at me. "That means you have twenty-four hours to do any additional research you might need. There will be questions about technique and style."

I leaned over the railing. "You're enjoying this, aren't you?" I hissed.

"Let me see . . ." She scrunched up her face in a mock frown. "Yes, I think I am." She was down the last few steps and out the door before I could say anything else.

I pulled the elastic off my ponytail and combed my

fingers through my hair while I made a mental change to the menu for supper Friday night. Brownies. I was definitely going to need brownies.

The only person who was going to get more delight than Roma out of Marcus and me sharing a kiss was Maggie. She would be bouncing with happiness over this "proof" that Marcus and I were oh so right for each other, and I was going to require more than one brownie to get through all the insistence on details.

14

Marcus was waiting at Wisteria Hill when I pulled up in the morning, leaning against his SUV. Roma's comment about doing more research into his kissing technique flashed through my mind.

Stop that, I told myself sternly.

The water jugs were on the hood of his car. He grabbed them and walked over to meet me. "Good morning."

I smiled. "Good morning."

We started for the carriage house. Marcus looked around. "Roma isn't going to need all of us once she moves out here, you know," he said. "We'll have to stop meeting like this." He smiled at me.

"There's a lot of work that needs to be done before she can move in," I said, inclining my head in the direction of the old farmhouse. "I think it's going to be a while." I didn't add that I'd miss feeding the cats with Marcus. Our friendship had developed in the old carriage house, watching Lucy and the others.

We put out the cats' food and water and then re-treated, as usual, back by the side door to wait for them to come out to eat. I stood close to the wall. Marcus leaned his arm against the weathered gray boards over my head. He was so close, I could smell his aftershave and what I guessed was cinnamon-flavored gum.

"I'm sorry I didn't get over to the library yesterday afternoon," he whispered.

"I told you everything there was to tell," I said. "Oren waved me over. I looked in the tent, but I didn't go in. I called you."

Lucy was coming from the cats' sleeping area, and I studied her carefully, watching for any sign that she was injured or sick, but she looked fine. She glanced over at us, meowed—her way of saying "Good morn-ing," I guessed—and continued to the feeding station.

"You didn't see anyone besides Oren?"

I shook my head. "No." The other cats were coming out, and just like I had with Lucy, I studied each one in turn. They all seemed well.

"Do you think the knife's important?" I asked.

He shifted behind me. "The problem is, there's no way to know how long it was there."

I twisted around to look at him. "Yes, there is. It wasn't there when Owen found that button from Alex Scott's jacket."

"You don't know that for sure."

I narrowed my eyes. "I do know that for sure," I said. "That knife was stuck in the ground less than a foot away from where that button was. I was right there. I would have seen it."

He pressed his lips together, took a deep breath and exhaled slowly. "There wasn't that much light in the tent, Kathleen," he said.

I glanced over at the cats and then came back to Marcus. "There was enough. I was right at that spot. My hand was on the ground. If the knife had been there I would have seen it. It. Wasn't. There."

He rubbed his chin. "I don't want to argue with you," he said quietly.

I looked up at him. "Then don't." I crossed one arm over my chest. "Marcus, I would have seen a knife jammed into the dirt if it had been there—I probably would have put my hand on it—and Owen would have been trying to dig it up, just the way he did with the button. Not to mention, wouldn't one of your investigators have found it? Can't you at least try to keep an open mind?"

He pushed off the wall and leaned sideways to check out the feeding station; then he turned his attention back to me. "I don't have a problem keeping an open mind, but not so open that my brains run out my ears." He shook his head. "You can't swear with one hundred percent certainty that knife was not stuck in the ground when Owen was in the tent, not considering how dim the light was. Yes, we searched the tent and the grounds and I don't think we missed anything, but we didn't take that tent down—which we should have done—so I can't be positive. And I'm sorry, but a cat is not exactly a credible corroborating witness. No lawyer is going to accept that."

There was a sudden bitter taste in my mouth. I chose

my words carefully before I answered him. "I'm not asking some lawyer to accept that I know what I saw. I'm asking you to accept it," I said.

He shoved his hands in his pockets and looked up at the ceiling in frustration or something else, I wasn't sure.

I turned around to see that the cats were finished eating and were already headed back to their shelters, Lucy trailing all the others. She stopped and looked at me, tipping her head to one side. Had she caught the tone of our conversation, if not the actual words? I knew the little calico cat had exceptional hearing. After a moment, she followed the rest of the cats, and I immediately headed for the feeding station. I scooped up a couple of bits of dropped cat food and collected the dishes. Marcus refilled the water bowls, silent beside me.

Once we were outside the carriage house, he touched my shoulder. "Kathleen, look, I do believe that you think there was no knife stuck in the ground when Owen found that button, but I wouldn't be doing my job if I based an investigation on something I know a good lawyer could tear apart. And it's not like that knife is what killed Mike Glazer; you know that."

"Yes, I do know that," I said. "I think Mike suffocated in some way." I held up my free hand. "And before you say you can't tell me whether or not I'm right, I wasn't asking." I was holding on so tightly to the bag with the dishes and cat food, I could feel the strap cutting into my palm. "Marcus, I think someone jammed that knife down in the dirt on purpose, so it would be found, so it would direct attention away from the person who killed Mike and on to someone else."

He didn't say anything, and his mouth was pulled into a thin, tight line.

"I know," I said. "It's not any of my business." It always came back to that. And maybe there wasn't any way to come to a compromise. I turned and started down the path.

Marcus caught up with me as I was setting the canvas carryall on the seat of the truck. Roma was just coming up the driveway. She waved and I raised a hand in hello.

"I don't want to argue with you over this," he said. His hands were jammed in his pockets. "It's stupid."

"Yes, it is," I agreed, shifting my keys from one hand to the other. "So I'm not going to. I'm just going to go. I don't want to say something that'll just make this worse."

I climbed in, fastened my seat belt and started the truck. Marcus took a couple of steps backward. I bumped my way down the rutted driveway. I didn't look back over my shoulder. I didn't check the rearview mirror.

Even though it was my morning off, I ended up going into the library early. Owen had disappeared into Rebecca's backyard and Hercules was sitting on the bench under the maple tree, eyeing the butter-yellow leaves over his head, watching for the grackle. I wasn't sure how to resolve things with Marcus other than to distance myself from his case, and I couldn't do that. I'd given Harry my promise that I'd see what I could find out and I wasn't going to go back on it.

I pulled into my parking spot at the library and stretched across the bench seat to retrieve my purse, which had dropped down onto the passenger-floor mat. When I straightened up, I caught sight of Lita, Everett Henderson's assistant, standing by her car, two rows over in the small lot. She was talking to Burtis Chapman. He said something and Lita smiled. Then she reached over and touched his cheek.

I froze and then, because I was so shocked at seeing such an intimate gesture between those two, I did the next stupidest thing I could think off: I dove down onto the seat, out of sight. I lay there for a minute, face against the woolen blanket that covered the old vinyl upholstery, thinking this was a lot like the time Maggie had dragged me along to hijack Roma and her SUV because she had the idea the three of us could be Charlie's Angels. It turned out we hadn't been nearly as skilled at subterfuge as we'd thought.

Slowly, I sat up again, hoping neither Lita nor Burtis had seen my swan dive onto the bench seat of the truck. There was no sign of Lita or her little car. I didn't see Burtis either.

I grabbed my purse and briefcase and locked the truck. Were Burtis and Lita a couple? I wondered. Maybe I'd misinterpreted that small gesture between them. The two of them, as my father liked to say, were as different as chalk and cheese.

Inside, Mia was working the circulation desk, with Mary supervising. "Good morning," Mary said. "You're early."

I patted my briefcase. "I brought brownies."

"Did I ever tell you I like you best?" she said.

I laughed. "I think you did the last time I brought brownies."

Mary smiled. "There's coffee upstairs." She reached under the counter. "And this parcel came for you." She handed me a small padded envelope.

I recognized my mother's handwriting. "Thanks," I said. I started for the stairs just as Burtis came around the end of a shelving unit.

"Hello, Kathleen," he said. "You're just the person I need."

"How can I help?" I asked.

He smiled, which made him seem a lot less intimidating. "I was looking for a DVD," he said. "Computer says it's here, but I can't find it."

"People pull the cases out and then put them back in the wrong place," I said. "Let me see if I can find it." I started for the shelves where we kept the DVD collection. "What movie was it?" I asked.

"*Pale Rider*," Burtis said. "Clint Eastwood. You seen it?"

I cleared my throat. "Twice. It's a good movie."

I'd probably seen every movie Clint Eastwood had ever been in or directed at least once, thanks to Maggie. She was a big fan of the actor-slash-director, and we'd spent a lot of Friday nights the previous winter watching the DVDs with Owen and Hercules. I think Maggie had turned Hercules into a fan as well. He'd watch the TV screen intently, meowing and pawing the air at the most suspenseful moments, much to Maggie's delight.

The thing was, I happened to know that Maggie and Herc weren't the only huge Eastwood fans in town.

Lita was maybe the biggest fan. Maybe I hadn't mistaken what I'd seen after all.

The missing DVD case was at the end of a row, three shelves above where the titles beginning with the letter P were shelved. I pulled it out and handed it to Burtis. "Thank you," he said. "You'd think people would put things back where they found 'em."

"Most people do," I said.

"My mother—rest her soul—always said, 'There's a place for everything and everything in its place.'" He smiled again. "She had a way of looking at you that didn't make you want to argue."

It occurred to me that some people would say the same thing about Burtis.

We started for the front of the library. "You decided if you're going to stay with us yet, Kathleen?" he asked.

"I'm still thinking about it," I said.

He looked around. "All this wouldn't have happened without you. I know it was Everett Henderson's money, but you're the one who made sure the work was done. You turned the library back into an important part of this town. I hope we don't lose you."

For a moment I was speechless. "Thank you, Burtis," I finally managed to get out. "That means a lot."

"I'm just telling the truth," he said, "but you're welcome. And don't forget that invitation to breakfast still stands. Lot better way to start your day than finding a dead man."

"You heard?" I said.

"I did. I get around. I hear a lot of things, like maybe that Glazer boy's death wasn't an accident. I hate to think him dying is going to mess up the idea of bringing some tour business into town." Nothing in his expression gave away what he was thinking.

I gave him a long, steady look. "Burtis, you of all people ought to know that when you're trying to get your hook into something, you need to use the right bait."

He laughed, a deep rumble that seemed to start way down in his steel-toed work boots and roll around his barrel chest. "I'll remember that." His face grew serious. "It's still the truth, though. The longer the police have Glazer's death 'under investigation,' the less likely it is that anyone is going to want to start bringing tourists here. And the town really could use that money coming in."

I pushed a strand of hair off my face. "I don't know how Mike died," I said. Not officially I didn't.

Burtis studied my face. "But I'm betting you have your suspicions." He raised a hand before I could respond. "I'm not askin' you to tell me. All I'm saying is you seem to have a knack for getting yourself mixed up in this kind of thing and maybe this time it would be better if you took a step back. Glazer pretty much pissed off everyone he had anything to do with from the moment he came back to town. He didn't know when to shut up. So maybe somebody showed him. And I'm not saying that was right, but it happens."

He squeezed the brim of his Golden Gophers cap in his massive hand. "Right now Mayville Heights is your home—I hope it'll keep on being that—and the sooner this Glazer business goes away, the better it'll be for everybody."

I wasn't sure if he was giving me a warning or just making conversation. I did know it wasn't a good idea to be on Burtis Chapman's bad side.

He held up the movie. "Thanks for finding this. You have a nice day, Kathleen." Then he turned and headed for the checkout desk.

I watched him hand the DVD case over to Mia, and I thought about his hand wrapped around the brim of his cap. I couldn't help wondering: It hadn't squeezed the life out of Mike Glazer, had it?

15

I went upstairs to my office, put my things away and then sat in my desk chair, swinging around to look out the window over the water. I didn't really think that Burtis had had anything to do with what had happened to Mike. He was an intimidating man, yes. But kill someone? I just didn't see Burtis doing that. I could picture his sinewy hand tightening into a fist and making contact with Mike's face, but I couldn't see it slowly and deliberately blocking his nose and mouth so he couldn't breathe.

On the other hand, I didn't really think Burtis had just been making friendly conversation with me, either. He was deeply loyal to the town and its people and I'd just been told to back off. That made it twice in one morning. In my mind I could see Marcus standing by his SUV, hands in his pockets, shoulders hunched. I hated how his cases always seemed to come between us.

I wondered what Burtis would do if I didn't stop asking questions about Mike Glazer's death. I rocked back in the chair. I was going to find out because I wasn't going to back off. Burtis wasn't the only one with a loyal streak. I'd given Harry Taylor my word that I'd see what I could find out about how Mike Glazer had died, and I hadn't exhausted all the possibilities yet.

I twirled around in the chair and reached for the phone.

Lise Tremayne answered on the fifth ring. "Hi, Kath," she said. "How are things in the Hundred Acre Wood?"

"Beautiful," I said. "The sky is blue. The sun is shining. And I think Pooh and Piglet just walked by my window."

Lise laughed. "No fair. It's rainy and windy here."

"You could always come for a visit."

"I should do that," she said. "Before you come home."

Lise was my closest friend in Boston. She assumed I'd be heading back to the city when my contract expired. So did Ethan and Sara. I knew my dad wanted me closer, but he wouldn't say it. And my mother, who had an opinion on everything, was for once keeping her opinion to herself.

"Lise, I need a favor," I said.

"Favors are my specialty," she said. I pictured her in her office at the university, her feet in some ridiculously high heels propped on the edge of her desk.

"I'm looking for some information. Do you have any contacts in Chicago?"

"Absolutely. What do you need?" Lise had contacts everywhere. She came from a big family—eight brothers and sisters. Her husband was a very talented jazz guitarist who had played all over the place. And she was warm and down-to-earth. She could talk to anyone about anything.

"Anything you can find out about Alex and Christopher Scott. They own a tour company in Chicago."

"Wait a second. Are they both lawyers?"

"Yes," I said, stretching one arm up over my head. "But as far as I know, they're not practicing. Why? What do you know?" Not only did Lise know people everywhere; she also had a mind like the proverbial steel trap. I heard a squeak, which told me she was leaning back in her desk chair.

"Do you remember about five or six years ago there was a story that went viral online? This guy talked himself into a job with one of the top law firms in Chicago by paying off the caddy of one of the managing partners and then somehow improving the man's golfing score so he won a bet with some other lawyer. The partner was impressed with the would-be lawyer's initiative."

"The story sounds familiar," I said. "Then didn't it turn out that the guy failed the bar exam?"

Lise gave a very unladylike snort of laughter. "Five times. Someone from his class outed him online."

"It was one of the Scott brothers."

"Uh-huh. I'm pretty sure it was Alex. And even more embarrassing, his brother passed the first time."

"Ouch."

"It gets better," Lise said, "or worse, depending on your perspective. Their father was a lawyer and his father and his father. And no Scott had ever not passed the bar exam on the first try."

I switched the phone from one hand to the other so I could stretch my other arm. "That's a lot of pressure."

"It is. So what do you want to know?"

"Anything you can find out about their business, Legacy Tours. Rumors, gossip, anything that's not common knowledge."

"I'll see what I can do," Lise said. "You notice I didn't ask if this has anything to do with a dead body."

"I appreciate that," I said, wishing I could somehow reach through the phone and hug her.

"I'll talk to you soon," she said.

The parcel from Mom was sitting on my desk. I reached for it, wondering what she'd sent me as I pulled the tape off the end flap.

It was a small picture of a tiny cottage, with two cats sitting on the front steps and the caption *Home Is Anywhere You Are.* I felt the pinch of tears and had to swallow and blink a couple of times. I knew this was my mother's way of saying she'd support whatever decision I made. It made me miss her even more.

I took a deep breath. Then I got up and set the picture in my briefcase. I took the foil-wrapped package of brownies down to the staff room, where I put one on a plate and left the rest in the middle of the table. I poured a cup of coffee and took it and my brownie back to my office, where I ate lunch backward—brownie first, salad last—and went over paperwork.

At twelve thirty I took over the circulation desk so Mary and Mia could have their lunch. Later Abigail and I did a presentation on podcasts for one of the seniors' book clubs. When I headed for the parking lot at quarter after five, I was glad I'd left dinner in my slow cooker. I'd hoped that Marcus might stop by, but I reminded myself that we'd disagreed about my getting involved in his cases before, and we'd always worked it out.

Owen was sitting on the top step by the back door when I got home. As soon as I unlocked the door, he followed his nose and went over to the counter to stare up at the slow cooker. The kitchen smelled like tomatoes, onions and spices. Owen tipped his head back and closed his eyes. If it smelled delicious to me, how good did it smell to him?

"That's not for you," I said. "That's for Maggie." Immediately he leaned back to look around me. "She won't be here for another hour," I said. "And Roma's coming as well."

The cat narrowed his eyes, whiskers twitching.

"Hey, I like Roma," I said, kicking off my shoes. "And don't forget Maggie likes her."

Owen made a huffy noise that rumbled in his chest.

"Suit yourself," I said, going over to peek through the glass lid of the cooker. "Roma was hoping you or your brother would try some cat food samples she was sent, to see if you liked them, but you don't have to."

There was a meow from the direction of the living room. Hercules was sitting in the doorway. He came about halfway across the room and meowed again.

"Would you like to be Roma's taste tester?" I asked.

He sat down, curled his tail around his back legs and licked his lips.

I smiled at him as I went to the sink to wash my hands. "Thank you. Roma will appreciate that. I think there's some kind of salmon-flavored bits and maybe chicken. I'm not sure."

Out of the corner of my eye, I saw Owen's head whip around at the word "salmon." His third favorite word after "sardines" and "funky chickens." Fourth favorite if you counted "Maggie."

He galloped across the floor, legs high in the air, and then sat down next to his brother, wiggling his back-side and bumping Hercules with his hip, which got him a withering look.

"Oh, so you are interested in helping Roma?" I said.

He licked his lips just the way Hercules had done.

"Your brother volunteered first," I told him as I dried my hands. "But if Roma needs a second opinion, you'll be it."

Owen glared at Hercules. Herc flicked the tip of his tail in return and came over to rub against my leg.

I told the cats about seeing Burtis with Lita in the library parking lot as I peeled the potatoes. "Do you think those two could actually be a couple?" I asked.

Hercules closed his eyes as though he were trying to imagine the two of them together. Owen, who was still sulking under the table, didn't even look in my direction.

Then I told them about my conversation inside the library with Burtis. "He is right that the library is an important part of Mayville," I told Hercules as I got the makings for a salad out of the fridge. "The usage numbers have gone up and they've stayed up."

"Merow," he said with enthusiasm.

"It wouldn't have happened if Everett hadn't paid for the renovations as a gift to the town and if people like Oren hadn't worked so hard to see the work get finished. Everybody here cares about Mayville Heights. And so do I."

I took down four tomatoes that had been ripening on the kitchen windowsill. "I'm thinking that maybe, maybe if I can figure out what happened to Mike Glazer, it could do more than put Old Harry's mind at ease. Maybe it could somehow help save the tour proposal."

Hercules put a paw over his face. Was that his very polite cat way of saying "Are you out of your mind?"

"It might help," I said a little defensively. All I could see around the paw was one green eye looking at me.

I put the tomatoes on the cutting board and scooped the cat into my arms. He nuzzled my chin. "I could do it," I said. "I could figure out how Mike died, and Maggie and Liam can convince his partners that basing a tour around Mayville Heights is a great idea." I scratched the spot above his nose where his black fur gave way to white. "All I need is Wonder Woman's Lasso of Truth and her bulletproof bracelets."

He scrunched up his furry black-and-white face and tilted his head to stare at the ceiling.

"And the invisible plane would be good, too," I said with a laugh. I put him back on the floor.

Maggie arrived about quarter after six. Owen was waiting for her by the back door.

"Hey, Fuzz Face," she said, bending down to smile at him. As usual, he got all twitchy and started to purr. "Mmmm, something smells good," she continued, stepping into the kitchen with the cat three steps behind her. "Is it that beef dish you made before with onions and mushrooms and tomato sauce?"

I nodded. "It is."

She looked down at Owen. "This is going to be good." Then she looked at me. "What can I do?"

Just then Roma knocked on the back door.

"You could put the knives and forks on the table," I said as I went out into the porch to let her in.

Roma was carrying a string grocery bag and a bottle of wine. "This is Ruby's latest vintage," she said. "I'm driving and I see Maggie is, but I thought you could save this to enjoy with . . . someone else."

I took the bottle and mock-glared at her. I knew she meant Marcus. Then again, maybe I could share the bottle with him as a peace offering.

I hung up Roma's coat while she said hello to Maggie. I knew it was only a matter of time before she outed me on kissing Marcus. For a moment I considered turning around, flinging out my arms and announcing it, but that seemed a tad melodramatic.

When I did turn around, Hercules was sitting in front of Roma. She opened the top of the string bag. "Hello, Hercules," she said. "I need your opinion on these cat food samples."

"I think the word you're looking for is 'bribe,' not

'samples,'" Maggie said. She looked down at Owen and raised her eyebrows conspiratorially. She'd pulled out a chair and was sitting, one leg tucked underneath her, not unlike the way Owen was sitting on the floor beside her, his tail curled around his feet. He was sneaking little looks in Roma's direction, I noticed.

Roma pulled a cardboard box stamped with paw prints out of the string bag and opened the top flap. "This isn't a bribe," she said to Maggie. "I need an honest opinion. Another vet I know is developing a line of all-natural, organic cat food. It's not as though I can try it and decide if it's any good."

Maggie leaned forward, snatched a piece of star-shaped kibble out of the box and popped it in her mouth before Roma could react.

She chewed and then wrinkled her nose. "Needs salt," she said.

Hercules's head swiveled from Roma to Maggie and back again. Roma shook her head with a wry smile. "Maggie Adams, I can't believe you just ate cat food," she said.

Mags pointed at the box. "It's not like the stuff is made of bug parts," she said. "Which wouldn't be so bad because I have eaten a bug once."

Owen gave her a look of pure, unadulterated adoration. I had no idea how much of the sentence he understood, but he definitely knew the word "bug."

Hercules, who also knew the word, dropped his eyes. I think he would have blushed if he could have. Hercules had eaten a bug once too—a very hairy caterpillar. It hadn't exactly lain well on his stomach.

The light on the slow cooker went from red to amber as the heat went from "cook" to "warm." I grabbed a spoon and lifted the lid for a taste. It was Lise's recipe, and as usual, it tasted as good as it smelled. The sauce was perfect. I didn't even need to adjust the seasonings.

"Roma, it's in her hand," I said, turning on the oven light so I could peek in to see if the roasted potatoes looked done. They did.

"What's in her hand?" Roma asked, frowning. Hercules was frowning too and sniffing in Maggie's direction. Unlike Roma, he knew what I meant.

"The cat kibble thing."

Maggie laughed and looked at me. "How did you know?"

I gave my best impersonation of Mr. Spock from *Star Trek*, complete with one raised eyebrow. "No crunching," I said. "You did a very good fake chew, but I didn't actually hear you eating."

She looked down at Owen and nodded. "We have to remember that for next time," she said. She turned her gaze to Roma again. "And why is it okay for you to bring them treats, but you give me a hard time when I do it?"

Roma folded her arms over her chest. "Eric's sausage-filled panzerotti are not a suitable treat for cats."

With exquisite timing, Owen yowled his objections. Even Roma laughed. Then she shook a few of the star-shaped bits of cat kibble onto the floor near the cats' food dishes and took a couple of steps back. Hercules gave her a long, thoughtful look. Then he went over to the pile and sniffed. "Salmon," Roma said helpfully.

Owen's gray ears twitched. I could see the tension in his small furry body.

Hercules looked back over his shoulder at Roma. Then he took a cautious bite. The second bite wasn't nearly as restrained. The third bite was actually more like shoving his face in the small pile. He sighed with happiness.

Roma smiled. "Hercules doesn't seem to think they need salt," she said to Maggie. She looked at Owen and held out the box. "Would you like to try them?"

His expression was pained. On the one hand, there was a box of fish-flavored cat food. On the other hand, the hand holding the box belonged to Roma, the woman who poked him with needles and tried to cut off his access to sausage panzerotti and frozen yogurt.

"Here," Maggie said. "Try this one."

She held out the little star she'd palmed in her hand and then let it drop to the floor in front of Owen. He looked uncertainly at it, sniffed it and then gave it a careful lick. It disappeared from the floor faster than if I'd sucked it up with the vacuum.

Roma dumped a few more bits onto the floor in front of him.

"I think your friend just got two paws-up," I said to her, setting the salad bowl on the table.

Roma pulled out a chair and sat down as I filled the plates, handing one to her and another to Maggie, before setting my own on the table.

Mags took a bite, gave me a blissful smile and waved her fork approvingly at me.

"This is good," Roma said after her first taste. "Could I have the recipe?"

"Absolutely," I said. Owen had come to sit next to Maggie's chair, the way he always did when she had dinner with us. Hercules was next to the refrigerator, washing his paws. Maybe I'd gotten lucky and the little cat food drama had made Roma forget about me kissing Marcus.

She turned to Maggie, fork poised over her plate. "So how was your week?" she asked. "I know Kathleen was kissing Marcus. What have you been doing?"

Or maybe it hadn't.

For a moment Maggie was as still as a stone statue. Then she squealed, flinging both hands in the air like she was about to do a victory dance in the end zone. "Finally," she exclaimed. "I was beginning to think I was going to have to ask Rebecca if there were any kissing potions in those old notebooks of her mother's." She peered at me across the table. "When did you kiss him? And why didn't you tell me?" Her gaze flicked over to Roma. "And how did you find out?"

Roma shrugged. "I asked. She turned the cutest shade of red." She gestured to me with her fork. "Just the way she's doing now. It was a dead giveaway."

Maggie nodded. "I know. She used to do that all the time whenever I'd say Marcus was just perfect for her. That's how I knew she liked him, no matter what she said."

"I can hear the two of you, you know," I said.

Mags nodded. "We know." She speared a couple of

potatoes, popped them in her mouth and then leaned her elbows on the table, propping her chin on her interlaced fingers. "So?" she said after she'd chewed and swallowed.

"Marcus kissed me. I kissed him back. That's it," I said. "He didn't throw me over his shoulder and swing back to his tree house like Tarzan." It didn't seem like a good time to mention that we'd argued this morning. Again. Maybe I would invite him over to try Roma's wine and this time I'd kiss him.

"I've never thought that sounded very comfortable," Roma said, wrinkling her nose, not unlike the way Owen did when he was inspecting his food. "Hanging upside down over someone's back and whipping through the trees—I think I just might get motion sickness." She made a backward motion with her hands. "I like a nice dip."

"Mmm, yeah." Maggie nodded slowly. "But it's very easy to overextend one's back, and there is more than half a foot difference in height between Kathleen and Marcus."

The two of them stared at me. "You're wasting your time," I said. "I don't kiss and tell." They exchanged shrugs and picked up their forks again. "But if I did," I continued, "I'd say, 'Wow!'"

They both howled with laughter.

"Now why don't we talk about your love life?" I said to Maggie.

"Sure," she said, "except I don't have one."

"What do you call Liam?" I asked.

"Cute as a bug's ear?" Roma said. Maggie and I both

looked at her. "Just because I have Eddie doesn't mean I can't appreciate cute."

Maggie nodded. "Liam is a sweet man, but all we are is friends." She squared her shoulders and held her head high. "I want what you and Marcus have."

I frowned across the table. "What do we have?"

"Passion," she said. "It's the difference between a plain brownie and one with nuts and chocolate frosting. I want the nuts and the chocolate frosting."

"You are nuts," I said. "Marcus and I don't have passion."

Laughing, Roma shook her head. "Wisteria Hill? This morning? Something was going on between the two of you, although it didn't look like something that was going to end with Marcus flipping you over his shoulder and swinging through the trees."

"That wasn't passion. That's this case—Mike Glazer's death. I just kind of stumbled into it." Hercules lifted his head and meowed softly. "And it really wasn't me. It was Hercules."

The cat went back to washing his paws now that he'd been acknowledged. Owen, on the other hand, immediately moved into Roma's line of sight, lifting a paw almost as though he were saying "I did something too."

"And Owen, too," I added.

Roma's head was bent over her plate. She didn't even look up. "I know I'm going to be sorry I asked this," she said, "but what do you mean 'and Owen too'?"

Before I could answer, the cat did. He stalked over to

Roma's chair, looked up and meowed at her. Then he sat down and looked expectantly across the table at me. Clearly it was my job to fill in the details.

I gestured at the little gray tabby. "Owen found something that could have been a clue, but it turned out not to be."

"I'm not even going to ask how that happened," Roma said.

Mags smiled at Owen and gave him a thumbs-up. Then she straightened up in her chair. "I don't suppose these two could figure out what happened." She shook her head and sighed. "I'm sorry. That isn't very nice of me. Mike's dead and I'm thinking about the tour pitch."

"Is it really that big a deal?" Roma asked.

"It could be," Maggie said. "At least that's what Liam believes. You know how quiet it is around here in the fall. Anything that could bring in tourists has to be good. He and Mary and Ruby, a couple of people from the hotel, Thorsten—they've put so much time and energy into this pitch."

"I think you do like Liam," I said teasingly.

She rolled her eyes. "Not in the way you mean. It's just for fun between us. Liam likes to rescue damsels in distress and I'm not really the damsel type." I saw her hand move and knew she'd just managed to slip Owen something from her plate. "For instance, last Thursday I'm meeting him for lunch at Fern's, and as I'm coming from the parking lot, I see him with Wren Magnusson of all people, heads together, talking about something." She gave her own head a little shake. "Turns out she'd had a flat the night before and Liam had stopped to help. Then, of course, Liam being Liam, when he saw her the next day, he had to make sure she'd gotten a new tire. He's always doing things like that."

"He sounds like a nice guy," I said.

Maggie wiped a dab of sauce off the side of her mouth with her napkin. "He's got a big heart," she said. "I wouldn't want him to be any different." She gestured at Roma with the napkin. "It's just that when Roma walks into a room, she's the only person Eddie sees."

Roma grinned and her cheeks got pink.

"And you and Marcus, I swear, the two of you could be standing in the middle of a hurricane and all you'd notice is each other." She shot me a warning look. "Don't say it's not true, because the entire town thinks you two should just get on with it and admit you're nuts about each other."

"Well, Mary did offer to teach me a few things," I said.

"What kind of things?" Roma asked, her voice edged with suspicion.

I did a little shimmy in my seat and copied Mary's tugging-off-the-glove motion.

Roma covered her eyes. "Way more information than I need," she said.

"Did you say yes?" Maggie asked, a teasing gleam in her eyes.

My cheeks were burning. "No, I didn't," I said. "Time to change the subject."

"Kathleen, have you decided what you're going to

tell Everett?" Roma asked, pushing back her empty plate.

I dipped a potato wedge in the last bit of sauce on my plate. "There's a lot to think about," I hedged. "I like Mayville Heights, and I can't imagine not sitting here with the two of you, or going to tai chi, or being at Eric's for lunch."

"So stay," Maggie said quietly.

"I miss my family," I said. "I didn't realize how much until I went back to Boston to see them. They drive me crazy, but I do love them. And my life was in Boston for a long time. I have connections and people I care about there, too."

Roma tipped her head to one side and smiled. "Do what feels right, what makes you happy. We'll be friends no matter what you choose."

Maggie stuck out her fork into the middle of the table.

"If you're still hungry, there's more in the pot," I said.

She made a face. "No. We're the Three Musketeers. You know, all for one, one for all."

"I thought we were Charlie's Angels," I said.

"This isn't going to end with you two hijacking my car, is it?" Roma asked.

"You're both so awful at the symbolic moment," Maggie said. She wiggled her fork. "C'mon. All for one."

I looked at Roma. "She isn't going to give in until we do this." I picked up my fork and stretched across the table so it rested on Maggie's fork.

Roma looked at the two of us and shook her head; then she picked up her own fork and leaned forward until the tines were resting on the other two. It would have been far more dramatic with fencing foils.

"All for one," Maggie said with a grin.

"And one for all," Roma and I joined in, laughing.

In that moment, whether or not I should stay seemed so simple.

16

Both Harry Taylors—Senior and Junior—came into the library Saturday morning just after we opened.

I put my arm around the older man's shoulders and gave him a hug. "It's so good to see you," I said.

"It's good to be seen," he said. "I was getting so tired of being cooped up in the house. I figured I was going to have to use a soup spoon to tunnel my way out when my keepers were asleep."

"You can see he's feeling much better," his son said dryly, heading over to the desk to give Mary three hardcover books and a couple of DVDs.

Harrison had just gotten over a second serious middle ear infection that had left him unsteady on his feet and caused at least one blackout that I knew of. He was using his cane, but he wasn't relying on it quite as much as the last time I'd seen him.

"I'm not planning on being a customer of Dan Gunnerson anytime soon," he said tartly.

"I'm very glad to hear it," I said, smiling at him. Dan Gunnerson ran Gunnerson's Funeral Home.

"I have a few more bulbs I want to put in," Harry said. "Dad figured he'd come along and freeload a cup of coffee he shouldn't really be drinking off of you."

"First of all, if a cup of coffee once in a while was going to kill me, Gunnerson would have planted me— probably in some ridiculously overpriced box—years ago," the old man said. "And second, Kathleen enjoys my company." He winked at me. "I'm very charming."

The younger Harry shook his head and headed for the door. "He's all yours, Kathleen," he said over his shoulder. "I won't be long."

I offered Harrison my arm. "Are you actually allowed to have a cup of coffee?" I asked.

"Depends on how you define 'allowed,'" he said, as we made our way to the seating area overlooking the water, at the end of the double row of computer desks.

I narrowed my gaze. "Am I going to get in trouble if I get you one?"

He gave me a sly grin. "Not with me you won't." With his snowy beard and mischievous blue eyes, he looked like Santa Claus without the red suit. And he really was charming.

I got Harry settled in front of the high windows and then went upstairs and got him half a cup of coffee, partly because I knew he probably shouldn't be drinking it and partly because having it downstairs, even away from all the books and the computers, was against library rules.

He took a long sip from the cup and sighed with

pleasure. "Now, that's a cup of coffee; a lot better than that decaf stuff the boys and Elizabeth are trying to get me to drink." He balanced the stoneware mug on his knee and turned to look at me. There was a question in his deep blue eyes. I waited for him to ask it.

"So, what have you found out about the Glazer boy's death?" he said.

I knew there was no point in trying to bluff him. He might have been old, but he was as sharp mentally as a man half his age.

"How did you know?" I asked, shifting sideways in my chair and crossing my legs.

He took another sip from his cup. "There's nothing wrong with my hearing, and just because it looks like I'm asleep doesn't necessarily mean that I am. So what do you know?"

"Not very much," I said.

"It wasn't an accident." He wasn't asking a question.

"What makes you say that?" I asked. Had he heard some bit of gossip I'd missed?

"Because if it was, Marcus Gordon would have said so by now."

I nodded. "No, I don't think it was an accident."

Harrison stroked his close-cropped beard. "You think it was someone in town or someone from away? I hear the boy was pretty much making an ass of himself. More than a couple of people had words with him."

I slid my palms over the armrests of my chair. "His two partners were at a fund-raiser in Minneapolis in front of a couple hundred witnesses. As for the people who had words with Mike Glazer, Liam Stone was helping someone who'd had a flat tire. That leaves me with Mary"—I dipped my head toward the circulation desk—"Burtis Chapman and the woman who's the new baker over at Fern's, who doesn't look like she's big enough to kill a grasshopper."

He gave a snort of laughter. "Mary wouldn't kill anybody. She might have left him singin' soprano, but that's about it." He frowned in thought. "Baker over at Fern's? Didn't she do those fancy cupcake things for the reception after the music festival?"

I nodded. "That's her. Her name's Georgia."

Harrison took a long pull from his coffee. He folded his hand around the mug. The skin on his hand was heavily lined, like a close-up of a street map. "She's about the size of a piece of dandelion fluff. I can't see her killing Glazer. Why would she want to? Because he didn't like those little chocolate sprinkles?"

I put both feet on the floor and leaned forward. "Tell me about the Glazers. I know about the accident that killed Mike's brother."

He sighed and fingered his beard again. "That was a terrible thing. If anyone had predicted that one of the Glazer boys was going to end up dead the way he did, well, no one would have figured it to be Gavin. It tore that family apart. And now both boys are dead." He shifted in his chair. "You know, Kathleen, when you have kids, you love them for different reasons. Hell, they're different people. When I met Elizabeth for the first time—" He patted the left side of his chest. "It was as though a little part of myself that had been missing had been given back to me. But that didn't mean I loved my other children one bit less."

"It wasn't that way in Mike's family," I said.

Harrison shook his head. "I'm sorry to say it wasn't. I can't say I know what it's like to lose a child, because I don't and I hope I never find out. But I know what it's like to be without a child, and you just don't hold that against your other ones."

"Gavin Glazer was the golden boy."

"And I guess you could say Michael was young and reckless." He drained the last of his coffee. "I had a bit of a reckless streak myself when I was young," he said, the twinkle coming back to his blue eyes. "I grew up, and who's to say young Michael wouldn't have done the same thing, except Gavin died, and once he was dead, well, I don't mean to criticize, but some people turn the dead into saints."

"Do you think it was just a coincidence that Mike died here in Mayville Heights?" I asked.

Out of the corner of my eye, I saw Harry Junior come in the front door; at the same time, the old man reached for his cane and pushed himself to his feet. I wasn't sure if he'd seen his son or somehow just known he was coming. I offered my hand and he took it, giving it a squeeze.

"I don't put a lot of stock in coincidences, Kathleen," he said. He handed me his cup. "Thank you for the coffee."

"Ready to go, Dad?" Harry said.

"Would it matter if I said no?" the old man asked.

"Not in the slightest," Harry said. He smiled at me. "Thanks, Kathleen."

"Anytime," I said.

Harrison stopped at the desk where Mary was working. I saw him smile at her and thought—not for the first time—what a handsome man he must have been in his prime. Even stiffened with arthritis, he was striking.

"Mary, you make a fine cup of coffee," I heard him say. "If you weren't a married woman, I'd be camped on your doorstep."

Mary gave him a flirtatious smile. "If I weren't a married woman, you wouldn't be camped out there very long." She winked. He laughed, and Harry Junior looked back at me and shook his head.

I took the empty cup and headed upstairs, thinking about what Harrison had said about coincidences. Was the fact that Mike Glazer had died here, not somewhere else, not anywhere else, important? Was that the key to figuring out why he'd died and who had been involved?

17

When we closed the library at one o'clock, I decided to walk over to Eric's for lunch. As I came down the steps of the building, I saw Abigail and Georgia on the sidewalk. Georgia looked troubled, dark hair wind-blown, shoulders hunched, her arms crossed tightly over her chest.

Abigail saw me and motioned me over to them. "Kathleen, please tell Georgia that Marcus Gordon is one of the good guys," she said.

I gave Georgia a small smile. "He is." There were tight lines around her mouth and eyes. She didn't look convinced. "Is something wrong?" I asked.

Georgia's gaze flicked to Abigail, who gave an almost imperceptible nod. Georgia looked at me again. "The police found something of mine . . . in the tent where they found Mike Glazer's body. It was a little spatula I use for spreading frosting."

The knife that Oren had found. It wasn't a butter knife—it was a spatula.

She pulled a hand over her neck. "I wasn't in that tent. I was over at the community center, where the art show is going to be, but I wasn't in the tent and I have no idea how that spatula ended up there."

"How did the police figure out it belonged to you?" I asked.

Georgia looked down at her feet. "My fingerprints," she said.

That meant her fingerprints were in the system. She might have been no bigger than a piece of dandelion fluff, as Harrison Taylor had described her, but it wasn't her first encounter with the police.

"Georgia was arrested for assault, when she lived in Chicago," Abigail said quietly. "The charges were dropped."

Georgia lifted her head and met my gaze. "They were dropped because I didn't assault anyone. The thing is . . ." She hesitated. Then she took a deep breath and uncrossed her arms, lacing her fingers together in front of herself. "I changed my name. I'm not really Georgia Tepper. My real name is Paige Wyler."

I shook my head. "It's not really any of my business."

"Everyone's going to find out," she said. "I may as well start by telling you." Her eyes darted for a moment to Abigail. "Abigail says I can trust you."

"Go ahead then," I said. "I'm listening."

"I was married," she said. "My in-laws didn't like

me—they'd wanted their son to marry someone else—but it didn't matter as long as he was alive."

"He died?"

"Our daughter was only six months old. His parents tried to get custody. When that didn't work, they tried to kidnap her. That's where the assault charge comes from."

She was twisting a narrow gold and platinum ring around her right ring finger. I wondered if it was her wedding ring, moved from her left hand.

"I left Chicago in the middle of the night with Emmy—that's my daughter. We moved around for a while. Eventually we ended up here. The police think I knew Mike because I used to live in Chicago."

I shifted my briefcase from one hand to the other. "Did you?" I asked.

Georgia shook her head. "But the company my former father-in-law works for has used Legacy Tours; at least that's what that detective told me." She held out both hands. "I know it seems like a lot of coincidences, but that's what they are. I'd never met Mike Glazer before, and I didn't know about any connection between his company and the one my former father-in-law works for. I haven't had any contact with my husband's parents other than through my lawyer."

She didn't shift her feet or look away from me. There was no hesitation in her words. I believed her, which is what I said.

"The police are going to check out everything you told them. All they want is to get to the truth. No one is going to try to railroad you."

She exhaled slowly. "I hope you're right," she said. "I really like it here, but . . . I've been thinking maybe it would be better if Emmy and I just moved on again."

I gave Georgia a small smile. "I hope you don't," I said. "There are a lot of good people in Mayville Heights." I glanced at Abigail. "Including Detective Gordon. I'm not going to tell you to relax, because I know you can't, but I think it'll be okay."

Abigail reached over and gave my shoulder a squeeze. "Thanks," she said.

"What I don't understand is how a spatula belonging to me ended up in that tent," Georgia said, rubbing the back of her head with one hand. "I wasn't anywhere near it."

"Maybe someone else borrowed it and then dropped it and didn't notice," Abigail offered.

I realized they didn't know the spatula had been stuck into the ground, not just left in a booth or on the grass. "What's the last place you were that you were using a spatula?" I asked.

Georgia shrugged. "Well, over at Fern's, because I did a couple of caramel fudge cakes." A couple of frown lines appeared between her eyes. "I did decorate a batch of cupcakes in the kitchen at the community center—one of the other partners from Legacy came for a quick meeting with us all, and Liam asked me to put together a little food for after. But that was a couple of days after Mike was already dead."

"Were you missing the spatula then?"

"Honestly, I didn't miss it at all. I think I have at least half a dozen exactly alike."

An idea was starting to form in my head, like a snowball rolling downhill, gaining size and form as it went.

"Detective Gordon—Marcus—will get to the bottom of this," I said. "He's not just a good police officer; he's my friend. You can trust him."

"Okay," Georgia said. She pressed her lips together and then gave me a small smile. "Thank you for . . . for listening and for believing me."

"If I can help at all, please ask," I said. I pointed over my shoulder at the library building. "I'm here most of the time when we're open and Abigail knows how to get in touch with me when I'm not."

I turned to Abigail. "I'll see you Monday," I said. I smiled at Georgia one last time and headed for Eric's.

It was past one thirty, so the lunch rush was over when I stepped into the café. There were five people at one of the tables by the window, including a couple of artists who had studio space at River Arts. Marcus was sitting alone at a table by the end wall. He looked up when I walked in and smiled. Then he pushed back his chair and got to his feet. My feet had already started walking over to him.

"Hi," he said.

I couldn't help smiling back at him. "Hi."

"Kathleen, I'm sorry," he said.

I hadn't been expecting that. "What for?" I asked.

"Could you sit down for a minute?" he asked, gesturing at the table.

I nodded and pulled out the other chair.

Marcus leaned one elbow on the table. "Look," he

said. "I keep saying, 'Stay out of my case,' but I do know that you're not getting mixed up in my investigations on purpose."

I could see the sincerity in his blue eyes. I owed him the same thing in return. "Sometimes I am," I said.

His expression changed to surprise. He straightened in the chair and put a hand on each armrest. "Okay. Would you like to explain?"

This time I leaned forward. "Marcus, Harrison Taylor is very important to me," I said.

He nodded. "I know. You risked your life to get those papers about his daughter."

For a minute I was back in the old cabin in the woods, smoke slowly seeping into the small, dark basement where I'd been trapped. I swallowed and gave my head a little shake.

Marcus must have seen something in my face. "You all right?" he asked.

I nodded. "I'm okay. I was just thinking how happy I was to see you coming through the snow that day."

"I was happy to see that you were alive," he said quietly.

"You know I'd do anything that I could for Harrison, for any of the Taylors." I cleared my throat. "Harry—Harry Junior—asked me to see what I could find out about Mike Glazer's death."

Marcus rubbed a hand across his chin. "You said yes."

I nodded. "Have you met Wren Magnusson?"

"I've spoken to her."

"She's friends with Harrison's daughter, Elizabeth."

"And Mike's brother, Gavin, was almost her stepfather."

"Yes."

Behind the counter, over Marcus's shoulder, Claire held up a turkey sandwich and gave me an inquiring look. I nodded and focused on Marcus again. "People tell me things. Maybe it's because I'm from away and they think their secrets are safe with me. Or maybe it's because I'm a good listener." I shrugged. "And I'm pretty decent at spotting a liar. I've been watching people pretend to be someone they're not all my life." I wished I had a cup or a glass so I'd have something to do with my hands. "Harry didn't ask me to keep anything I learned from you, and I haven't."

Marcus continued to silently watch me. I could tell from the line of his jaw that he was clenching his teeth together.

Claire came over to us with the coffeepot. She poured a cup for me and topped up Marcus's. "Your sandwich will be ready in a couple of minutes," she said.

"Why didn't you tell me this before?" Marcus asked once Claire was back at the counter.

A good question, although I wasn't sure he was going to like my answer. I folded my hands around my cup, lacing my fingers together. "Because I knew that no matter what you said to me, I was going to see what I could find out. I didn't want to argue with you and I also didn't want to ruin this"—I made a back-and-forth motion in the air—"whatever this is between us."

I studied his face. "Can you accept the fact that I

can't just stand around making stinky cat crackers when people I care about need help?"

"I don't want you to end up being the one who needs help," he said. "So can you accept the fact that I'm never going to like you getting involved in a police investigation?"

I played with my knife, sending it spinning on the table like the pointer in a game of chance. "I'm trying," I said.

He blew out a breath. "So am I."

Claire appeared then with my sandwich. She topped up my cup, smiled and said, "Enjoy."

"No secrets, Kathleen," Marcus said, his voice and expression serious. "No investigating cabins in the woods with only a cat for backup. I'm not going to tell you not to do this, because I know you're going to ignore me. Just don't go off playing amateur detective by yourself. You find out something—anything—I want to know."

I nodded. "Okay." I picked up half my sandwich. It tasted even better than it smelled and it smelled wonderful. "You don't seriously think Georgia Tepper killed Mike, do you?" I asked after a couple of big bites.

"You talked to her," Marcus said. He didn't seem surprised.

"She was at the library with Abigail."

He shifted sideways so he could stretch out his long legs. "So you know Georgia Tepper—"

"—is really Paige Wyler. I do." I pulled a bit of mushroom out of my sandwich and ate it. "I also know she lived in Chicago and the company her father-in-law works for is one of Legacy Tours' clients."

Marcus tented the fingers of his right hand over his coffee cup. "It is true, you know; people do tell you things," he said.

"I also know Georgia was arrested and charged with assault and then the charges were dropped."

"She threatened her former mother-in-law with a chef's knife."

"That I didn't know," I said. "But according to Georgia, the former mother-in-law was trying to kidnap Georgia's little girl. You can't fault her for protecting her child."

Marcus shook his head. "That's why the charges were dropped." He picked up his cup and drained it. "But you have to admit there's a similarity: a chef's knife, a spatula."

"There's a big difference between a chef's knife and a little spatula used for spreading frosting on cupcakes." I frowned at him. "And Mike Glazer was asphyxiated." I waved the hand that wasn't holding the other half of my sandwich at him. "I know you didn't say that, but I saw the body."

He folded his arms. "No comment." That was usually as good as a yes.

"If Georgia was responsible for Mike's death, then why would she take that spatula and stick it in the ground? It makes no sense. It's a red herring."

"This isn't an Agatha Christie novel, Kathleen," he said.

"No," I said. "But it's the kind of thing that would

turn up in one of her books." I leaned my elbows on the table. "The knife wasn't there the day Owen found the button from Alex Scott's jacket. I know you think I can't be sure of that, but I am. Which means that someone stuck it in the ground later. Why? There's no reason for Georgia to do that."

Marcus brushed crumbs off his tie. "There's no reason for anyone to do that."

I wiped my fingers on my napkin. "Yes, there is. It's a diversion. A distraction. It puts the focus on Georgia instead of the real killer."

"Alleged killer."

"All right, alleged killer," I said.

He looked at his watch. "I'm sorry, Kathleen. I have to go." He got to his feet and grabbed his jacket from the back of his seat. "By the way, your chair's almost finished," he said.

"You mean you've actually been able to put those pieces back into something I'm going to be able to sit on?"

He nodded.

"I can't wait to see it," I said, smiling up at him. "I don't know how to thank you."

He shrugged and his deep blue eyes never left my face. "Maybe you'll think of something."

I immediately thought of his mouth kissing mine and wondered if he was thinking the same thing. "I, uh, I'll try," I managed to get out.

"I'll talk to you soon," he said and headed over to pay Claire.

I watched him go because . . . well, it was fun watching his long legs move. Then I ate the last bites of my sandwich and finished my coffee. I wiped my fingers again and headed up to the counter.

Claire gave me a knowing Cheshire cat grin. "Detective Gordon already got it," she said. She held out a small take-out bag. "This too."

It was a still-warm chocolate-chip cookie. I felt my cheeks redden as I waited for her to say something else, but she just kept smiling at me. I took a step backward and almost fell over a chair.

"I'm just going to go then," I said, gesturing in the general direction of the door. And I did, before I started acting any more like a goofy teenager.

18

Sunday was warm and sunny, and even Hercules was happy to spend most of the day outside while I worked in the yard. I sat on one of the big Adirondack chairs to eat lunch. Hercules took the other, eyeing the big maple for any signs of Professor Moriarty, while Owen roamed between our yard and Rebecca's. By midafternoon I'd cleaned out the last of the flower beds and made a pile of brush and weeds for Harry to take away for composting.

Owen was sprawled over the railing of Rebecca's gazebo, on his stomach, legs hanging down on either side, dozing in the sunshine. Hercules was poking at the compost pile with one paw. My back was stiff from bending over and I needed a break.

I stretched out in the swing, knees bent, one arm tucked under my head. "Hey, leave that alone," I called to Hercules.

He made his way across the grass and came to stand

in front of the swing, green eyes narrowed questioningly. I patted my midsection. "C'mon up," I said.

He jumped onto my stomach, setting the swing swaying gently. I reached out to steady him with my free hand. He leaned his head back and looked all around.

"The bird's not here," I said. "He's hanging out somewhere with his little bird friends. I think you can relax."

He made a sound a lot like a sigh and lay down, stretching across my chest with his chin on my breastbone.

"And please stay out of that pile of branches and dead plants. Harry's coming to get all that tomorrow to put in his compost pile."

I stroked the cat's black fur, warm from the afternoon sun. "I don't have anything to tell him," I said. "Mike Glazer didn't die from anything natural—like a heart attack—but other than that, I don't know what happened to him, or why it happened."

I scratched the top of the cat's head with one finger. "Got any ideas?" I asked.

He squinted at me. Either he was pondering my questions or the sun was in his eyes.

"Mike's partners are out. They both have alibis. They were at that awards dinner in Minneapolis." I sighed. "I keep thinking that it has to matter that he was killed here, in Mayville Heights." I moved my arm a little under my head. "Okay," I said. "There's Liam."

Hercules made a face.

"Yes, I know Maggie likes him, but Liam and Mike

did have that argument outside Eric's Place. Maybe whatever happened was an accident and Liam panicked."

Hercules didn't look convinced.

"Who else?" I said.

He seemed to think for a moment and then he licked his whiskers.

"Georgia?" I said. I shook my head. "I don't think so." She'd been awfully convincing in her explanation about losing the little spatula. Then again, whoever killed Mike had likely convinced *him* they weren't a threat.

He flicked the tip of his tail and gave a snippy meow.

"Fine. Liam and Georgia are both on the list."

Herc put his head back down again.

"What about Burtis?" I asked.

Hercules gave his head a vigorous shake. I wasn't sure if that was a yes or a no.

"What reason could he have had for killing Mike?" The cat didn't have an answer. "Does Burtis strike you as the kind of person who would panic and run if something had happened by accident?" I blew a strand of hair off my cheek. "Liam, Georgia and Burtis," I said. "That's what we have. Or some mysterious person from out of town who followed Mike here to kill him because . . . because . . ." I made a face. "I don't have a 'because.'"

I put my arm around Hercules and sat up. I set him on the swing beside me. He shook himself and looked inquiringly at me. "I guess we might as well start with Liam. What do we know about him?" I held up one finger. "He's a bartender at Barry's Hat." I stuck a second finger in the air. "He's working on a degree in psychology." I held up a third finger. "He's been the driving force behind this whole tour proposal idea."

Herc cocked his head to one side.

I nodded. "Yeah. That might be important."

I knew almost nothing about Liam Stone, I realized, other than he was good-looking and liked to help women in trouble. He hadn't borrowed books or anything else from the library. People's borrowing habits were a good way to get some insight into what secret dreams they had and who they really were.

"Maggie said Liam likes to rescue damsels in distress," I said to Hercules. Then I remembered what she'd also said about Liam rescuing Wren Magnusson the night Mike Glazer had been killed.

I folded one arm over my face and groaned into my shoulder. "Liam has an alibi," I said, letting my hand slide down over the back of my head. I nodded slowly. "I bet Marcus knew that. That's why he didn't seem too concerned about that fight between Liam and Mike."

Hercules put both paws on my leg.

"That leaves us with Georgia, Burtis and some nameless, faceless person from Chicago . . . or, or anywhere for that matter." I rubbed the back of my neck. "Do you know what the problem is?"

He looked around. Searching for an answer to my question or doing a quick spot check to make sure his friend the grackle wasn't back?

"We don't know anything about Mike other than what Rebecca and Harrison told us. And the fact that everyone who'd dealt with him here in town thought he was a jerk."

Rebecca had described Mike as being "full of life." Harry Senior had said he was "young and reckless." And they'd both talked about how the death of his brother had changed Mike.

I closed my eyes for a moment, trying to recall Harrison's exact words: *If anyone had predicted that one of the Glazer boys was going to end up dead the way he did, well, no one would have figured it to be Gavin.*

I opened my eyes and looked down into Hercules's green ones. "Everyone says that Mike changed when his brother died. And Harrison told me no one would have expected Gavin to die 'the way he did.' Maybe that's where the answer to this whole thing is. Maybe what we need to do next is to find out just exactly how Gavin Glazer did die."

19

The problem was I couldn't find any details about Gavin Glazer's death online. His car had missed a turn on Wild Rose Bluff and gone down over an embankment. The weather was good, the road bare and dry. I scrolled through two weeks' worth of newspapers online for the period of time after the accident, looking for follow-up articles and reading the Letters to the Editor. There was some speculation that a deer might have darted in front of the car, and when Gavin had swerved to avoid it, he'd lost control of the vehicle, but that's all it was—speculation.

After supper I'd taken the computer outside to sit in one of the big chairs by the back steps. Hercules was on the wide, flat arm of the other so he could look at the computer screen. "There's something off here," I said to him. "The night of Gavin Glazer's accident it wasn't snowing or raining. He was on a stretch of road he'd been driving since he was sixteen." I touched the screen with one finger. "See that?" I said, pointing to the photo on the front page of the archived issue of the *Mayville Heights Chronicle.* "The embankment is on the left-hand side of the road and it's an open field on the right. If a deer ran out in front of him, where did it come from and why didn't he see it?"

I leaned against the back of the wooden chair. Hercules seemed to be reading the article on the screen, so I left the page open. I knew I was reaching, but something felt off about Gavin Glazer's death. Maybe it had nothing whatsoever to do with his little brother's death last week, but I didn't have anything better to go on.

"I think I'll call Mary," I said.

Hercules stopped reading—assuming he had been reading and not just admiring his reflection in the screen. He jumped down and started for the house. There was an e-mail in my in-box from Lise, I noticed. It was probably the information I'd asked her for about Legacy Tours.

Hercules paused, looked back over his shoulder at me and meowed insistently. I could read the e-mail later, I decided. I shut down the computer and followed him.

I wasn't sure how to explain to Mary why I wanted to know what I wanted to know.

"You don't think Mike's death was an accident, do you, Kathleen?" she asked.

"I don't know for sure," I said. "Maybe I'm just grasping at straws."

"I just can't see how it all goes together."

"How what goes together?" I asked. Hercules was

on my lap, green eyes focused on my face as though he were following the conversation.

Mary sighed on the other end of the phone. "Kathleen, at the end of the day, this is all just gossip, but my mother always used to say, where there's smoke, there's fire."

She was silent for a moment and I waited, knowing she'd tell me in her own way. "Gavin was crazy about Wren's mother, Celia. She was older than he was and she had two kids, but he didn't care. The boy was smitten. Instead of going out with his friends on a Saturday night, he was calling bingo at the senior's center with Celia—lovin' it and her." She sighed again very softly. "Not everyone thought it was a good match."

The hairs came up on the back of my neck. "Mike."

"They were Irish twins," Mary said. "Less than a year between them. And as close as real twins before Gavin met Celia, even though they were so different. Night of the accident, Gavin had driven Mike home. He had a part-time job at the St. James. Parents weren't there. The boys ate supper and then Gavin headed back into town to pick up Celia."

"Mike was the last person to see Gavin alive."

"Yes." There was silence for a moment. "Kathleen, Gavin had been drinking."

"That wasn't in the newspaper," I said. I leaned my elbow on the arm of the chair.

"He wasn't over the legal limit," she said. "I don't know how his family kept it out of the paper, but they did. The only reason I knew was because back then I worked at the courthouse. I heard a lot of things that way. In fact, it's how I really got to know Celia. She worked there, too." She lowered her voice. "Celia didn't drink, mostly because her father had drunk enough for two people. So Gavin didn't drink anymore. The night of the accident, the boys had stopped for a pizza to take home for supper. A couple of people had heard Mike telling Gavin he was whipped, that a beer or two wasn't going to turn him into a drunk."

"Mary, do you think that Mike kept at Gavin until he had a drink just to shut Mike up?"

"They were both barely adults—they were babies really. Full of testosterone." She sighed. "I can see how that could happen."

I thought about my brother, Ethan, and some of the stupid choices I'd seen him make because his friends were bugging him. Luckily, his dumbest was coloring in the patchy mustache he was trying to grow with a permanent Sharpie and discovering he was allergic to the marker ink.

An idea was turning over in my head. "Mary, is it possible that Wren and her family suspected?"

"I've often thought Celia did." Mary took a deep breath and slowly let it out. "She didn't sit with the Glazers at the funeral, and she didn't speak to them. I know they sent presents for the kids that Christmas. I was there when the mailman brought the box. She handed it to me and asked me to drop it off at the fire station's toy drive. I asked her why, and all she said was, there was nothing inside she wanted. It was like trying to get answers out of a stone wall."

"Would Celia have told Wren?" I asked.

"No," she said. There was silence for a minute. "No," she repeated, and there was more certainty in her voice.

"Did Celia keep a diary or anything like that?"

"She did," Mary said after a long moment. "She called it her journal. She had them going back to when she was a teenager. They were all in an old leather steamer trunk."

"Wren's been cleaning out the house," I said. "Maybe she found them, read them."

"Uh-uh," Mary said at once. "The trunk isn't there. I know that because I walked through the house with her when she came back last month. Celia must have destroyed the journals and gotten rid of the trunk when she got sick." I heard her shift the phone from one hand to the other. "Even if you're right and someone did kill Mike, it wasn't Wren, Kathleen. She's maybe half his size, for one thing. And she's the only person who seems upset about his death. You heard how she talked about him. She was thrilled at the idea she'd get a chance to reconnect with him. I don't see how Gavin's death could have anything to do with Mike dying."

"Thanks," I said. "Like I said, I'm just grasping at straws."

"I wish you could figure out for certain what happened to Mike," Mary said. "I think it might give Wren a little peace. She's a sweet child. You know, she brought me some of her mother's jewelry this afternoon. She said she was never going to wear it and she wanted me to have it."

"I like Wren," I said. "She's already had way too much grief in her life."

"She told me she met Hercules and Owen." I could hear the smile in her voice. "Thanks for that."

"Anytime," I said. "I'll see you tomorrow." I hung up and set the phone on the footstool. Hercules was still staring intently at me. I glanced up at the ceiling for a moment. "I don't know," I said.

I looked at the cat again. "What do you think? It wasn't the Scott brothers. It couldn't have been Liam. It wasn't Wren. So who killed Mike?"

After a moment, he hung his furry black-and-white head.

I reached over to stroke his fur. "I know," I said softly. "I don't know either."

20

Just then there was a knock at the back door. Hercules leaned sideways and looked in the direction of the kitchen.

"That's probably Taylor," I said. She'd called to say she'd be over after supper.

It was Taylor. Her long red hair was in a loose braid over one shoulder, and she was wearing jeans and a lime green sweatshirt.

"C'mon in," I said. "The books are in my briefcase in the kitchen."

She smiled. "Thank you so much for bringing them home with you. Now I can practice before the next class."

"It was no problem," I said. My bag was on the floor under the coat hooks. I reached down to get the books. Hercules was sitting in the doorway to the living room, watching us.

"That's Hercules, right?" she asked.

"Yes, it is," I said. The cat came about halfway into the room, sat down and studied Taylor.

She put the strap of her purse over her shoulder and leaned forward, hands on her thighs, to smile at him. "Hi, Hercules," she said.

"Merow," he answered, whiskers twitching.

She looked back at me. "Hercules was the son of Zeus, wasn't he?"

"Yes, he was," I said. The fact that I'd been thinking mostly about actor Kevin Sorbo when I'd named Herc really wasn't relevant.

"Yeah, we did Greek myths last year in English," she said. She straightened up, turned and took the books from me.

"I like your purse," I said. It was a brown leather bucket bag with a braided leather strap and four rows of what looked to be wooden buttons around the top edge.

Taylor slid a hand over the caramel-colored leather. "It's from the nineteen eighties, as far as I can tell," she said. "I just got it today and I didn't have time to do any research, but for ten dollars I figured it was okay."

"It's in great shape," I said. "Where did you find it?"

"My dad has a building up on the highway where he rents storage space."

I nodded.

"Someone's been clearing out one of the units for the past couple of weeks, and she has some great stuff from back in the seventies and eighties." She shrugged and the strap of her bag slipped down her shoulder a little. "The first time I asked her about maybe buying a couple of the bags she said no, because they were her mother's, but then today she said if I still wanted the bags I could have them." She frowned. "I kind of felt like maybe I was cheating her, you know, because all she wanted was ten dollars for this one and a little black evening clutch purse, but Wren said no, she didn't want any of the stuff anymore."

"Wren Magnusson?" I said.

Taylor was smiling again at Hercules, who had moved a little closer to us. "Uh-huh," she said. "The stuff all belonged to her mother. You wouldn't believe some of the things that she'd kept—platform shoes, hot pants, elastic belts. There was a big old trunk and even a pair of roller skates. Wren just packed most of the stuff in big garbage bags and took it to Goodwill." She turned to look at me again. "I should get going," she said. "Thank you again for getting the books for me. I'll see you at class on Tuesday."

I walked her out, and when I turned around, Hercules was behind me. I dropped onto the bench and pushed my bangs off my forehead. He jumped up and sat beside me. Uncertainty was gnawing at a point just under my breastbone.

I looked at Herc. "You heard what Taylor said. Wren might as well have just given her those two purses. All she asked for was ten dollars. And she did give Mary some of her mother's jewelry. Not to mention she took the rest of her mom's stuff to Goodwill."

He didn't say anything. He just nudged my hand with his head. I started absently stroking his fur. Maybe the fact that Wren was giving away things that had been important to her meant nothing. Maybe it meant that she wanted a clean slate so she could move on with her life. Or maybe . . . maybe it meant she didn't want to move on . . . didn't want to go on.

I closed my eyes and went back over the conversation I'd had with Wren when she and Elizabeth were here. Her sadness over Mike Glazer's death had been genuine. I was certain of that. I remembered her asking if I thought he'd suffered. And then I remembered what else she'd said: *I hate thinking he just lay there alone for hours.*

I opened my eyes. Hercules was watching me. "Mike's body was in a chair," I said. "So why did Wren say she hated to think he'd lain there alone for hours?"

I remembered feeling for a pulse against Mike's skin, cold and waxy under my fingers. I remembered seeing the injury to the back of his head. "As though he'd fallen backward and hit his head," I said aloud to Hercules. My stomach tightened, and I could feel a lump pressing in the middle of my chest. I swallowed a couple of times, but it didn't move.

"Wren was there," I said slowly. The problem was, Wren had an alibi. "Except she was supposed to be out on the highway with a flat. Remember what Maggie said? Liam rescued Wren."

Hercules watched me, his green eyes fixed unmoving on my face. I thought about Wren's expression, her body language and her words each time I'd seen her. I thought about her genuine grief over Mike's death and how she'd been giving away her mother's things. Each little piece fit with the next. The only explanation I could come up with was that Liam was covering for her. But why?

I thought about it, pulling the question apart in my head. "I need to check on something," I told Hercules. He followed me into the kitchen. All it took was a visit to a couple of social-networking sites and I had my answers.

"She was there. She thinks she killed Mike." I could feel the last cup of coffee I'd had, burning at the back of my throat. "Somehow, she found out that Mike had something to do with his brother's death. Someone said something, or—" Taylor's words echoed in my head: *There was a big old trunk and even a pair of roller skates.*

"She found her mother's journals," I said to the cat. "She knew. She went to see Mike. Something happened and she thinks she killed him and . . . and she can't live with that."

My cell phone was on the counter. I punched in Mary's number. She'd know how to find Wren.

The line was busy.

I raked my fingers through my hair. Elizabeth would probably know where Wren was. I took a deep breath and called Harry Taylor. All I got was his voice mail.

"Why isn't anyone answering their phone?" I asked Hercules, sinking onto one of the kitchen chairs.

The cat had been sitting patiently at my feet. Now he stood up on his back legs and put a paw on my cell.

"What?" I said.

He made a noise that sounded a lot like a sigh of frustration. Then I got it. I had Harry's cell phone number.

I found my address book in one of the inside pockets of my briefcase. I sat on the floor and tried Harry's number. Hercules climbed onto my lap, gazing intently at the phone.

"Harry, it's Kathleen," I said when he answered.

"Hi, Kathleen," he said, and there was an edge of caution in his voice. I'd never called his cell before. "Everything all right?"

For a moment I thought about saying yes. I wasn't certain Wren had seen Mike the night he died. I wasn't sure she thought she was responsible for his death. The way the pieces all fit together, that's how it looked to me, but maybe there was another way to look at them. The problem was I couldn't find it.

"I . . . I don't know. Is Elizabeth with you?"

"Sorry, no," he said. "I'm not at the house. And, anyway, she's not either. She went to pick up Wren Magnusson. They're having supper at Eric's. Wren has to go back to Minneapolis tomorrow. Her brother needs her there for something."

My stomach twisted itself into a knot. Wren's brother wasn't in Minneapolis. Mary had told me he was working in Alaska until the end of the month.

"Can you meet me at Eric's?" I asked.

"I can," he said. "I'm up on the bluff, so I'll be a while. What's going on?"

I told him my suspicions about Wren. "I might be wrong."

"You don't think you are."

"No, Harry, I don't," I said, shaking my head even though he couldn't see me.

"I don't think you are, either," he said. "Go. I'll get there as fast as I can."

I called Maggie next, pulling on my shoes as the phone rang against my ear.

"Hi, Kath. What's up?" she said when she answered.

"I was wondering if you know where Liam is," I said. If I was going to stop what Wren had planned, it would help to have support for her. "Is he working or is he in town?"

"He was working. I'm waiting for him now. He's meeting Alex Scott over at the tents later for a walk-through, but we're going to get some supper first."

"Mags, could you and Liam meet me at Eric's?" I asked.

"Something's going on," she said.

I explained what I'd figured out, hoping that somehow in telling her I'd find a flaw in my logic. I didn't.

"Good goddess," she said softly. "I'll make sure Liam's there."

"Thanks," I said.

"Kath, if Wren didn't kill Mike, who did?"

I sighed. "That's the problem," I said. "I still don't know."

I ended the call and stood there, staring at the phone. I couldn't leave Marcus in the dark on this.

All I got was his voice mail. I tried his house. Same thing. I left another message.

Hercules hadn't moved the entire time I'd been on the phone. "I have to go," I told him.

Wren thought she'd killed someone and she couldn't live with that.

I couldn't do nothing.

I couldn't do *nothing*.

21

Elizabeth and Wren were sitting at one of the tables in the window at Eric's Place. Elizabeth saw me coming up the sidewalk and waved. I stepped inside the restaurant and walked over to them.

"Hi, Kathleen," she said. "Are you by yourself? Would you like to join us?"

"Thank you. I would," I said. I grabbed a chair from a nearby empty table. Claire came over with coffee. I added cream and sugar and folded my fingers around the cup.

"Wren's leaving in the morning," Elizabeth said.

"I'm sorry," I said. I was. I was sorry that so many things hurt her and sorry that I was about to add to them.

"There're some things I have to do," Wren said, tucking a strand of her fine blond hair behind her ear. "And it's just too sad here right now." She looked even thinner, somehow, than the last time I'd seen her, with dark smudges like bruises under her eyes.

"And it must have been hard pretending you felt bad because Mike Glazer was dead when really you didn't," I said. "At least at first."

She swallowed, and a little color came into her pale face. "I do feel bad," she said. She set her fork down and dropped her hands into her lap.

Elizabeth leaned forward, a frown creasing her forehead. "What are you talking about?" she asked.

Maggie and Liam came in then. She nodded at me and caught Liam's sleeve, and they walked over to us.

Liam looked at Wren and frowned. "Is something wrong?" he asked.

"It's all right," Wren said in her soft voice.

"No, it isn't," Elizabeth said. I could see Harrison in the way she held herself and the assurance in her voice. She turned to me. "I think you should go sit somewhere else, Kathleen."

I kept my eyes on Wren. "I know that you hated Mike. I know you wanted him dead," I said. "And I know why. But you didn't kill him. You just knocked him out. So . . . so I think you should stay here." I looked back over my shoulder. Eric was at the counter. He raised his eyebrows at me. I gave my head a little shake and he nodded.

Liam held up both hands. "Hold on," he said. "Everyone knows Wren didn't have anything to do with Glazer's death. She didn't knock him out. She wasn't even in town that night. She had a flat tire out on the highway. I stopped to help her." He shrugged. "Anyway, he died of a heart attack or something like it. So this doesn't even matter."

"Mike Glazer didn't die from a heart attack," I said. I kept watching Wren. Her left hand was covering her right one in her lap. That bottom hand was tightly clenched in a fist.

Elizabeth stood up and grabbed her purse from the back of her chair. "Let's go, Wren," she said. She glared at me. "You're crazy."

"No, she isn't," Harry Taylor said behind me. I hadn't even noticed him come in. He must have broken every speed limit driving down from Wild Rose Bluff.

"You don't know what she's saying, Harry. It's all crazy," she said.

He stuffed his hands in the pockets of his denim jacket. "You have time to listen."

Liam turned to Harry. He gestured at me. "It is crazy," he said. "Kathleen thinks Wren hit Glazer over the head or something. I already told her Wren was miles away from here."

Maggie touched his arm and smiled. "Liam, loyalty is one of your very best qualities," she said. "But you need to stop talking right now, because you aren't helping."

"You found out the truth about how Mike's brother, Gavin, died, didn't you?" I asked Wren. "You found out that Mike was partially responsible for the death of the man you thought of as your stepfather."

Out of the corner of my eye, I saw a tiny muscle in Liam's cheek begin to twitch.

Elizabeth was still standing. "That's ridiculous," she said. "Why would she say what a great guy he was if she thought he had something to do with that?"

"Because you didn't want anyone to know how much you hated him, did you?" I said gently.

Wren gave her head a tiny shake, the movement almost imperceptible. "No, I didn't."

Elizabeth stiffened and swallowed a couple of times before she could speak. "Why?" The one word came out in a whisper.

Wren turned from me to look at her friend. "Because I didn't want anyone to know I killed him," she said.

Liam ducked his head and stared at the floor. Maggie pressed her lips together. Harry moved around the table and put his arm around his sister's shoulders. She stood there rigidly, but she didn't shrug him off.

"Except you didn't," I said.

"Yes, I did," Wren repeated, pushing back the strand of hair that had fallen in her face again.

I leaned forward and laid my hand on her arm. "I know you think you did. But you didn't. *You didn't.* Tell me what happened."

"I read my mother's journals," she said. "The first week I got here after classes ended. They were in this old leather trunk. It was out in a storage unit she had. I just picked out random ones and started reading. One of them was from the time when Gavin died.

"Some people were saying that Mike had bought beer that night and that he'd kept telling Gavin that my mother had him whipped." She swiped at a tear that had started to slide down her face. "My mother . . . confronted Mike, the morning of the . . . the funeral. She found out the stories were true. That was . . . that was why she never had anything to do with any of that family again."

"What did you do?" I asked.

"I decided I was going to drive to Chicago and confront him. I didn't even get out of town before my crappy car broke down. It took a while before I had the money to get it fixed."

Out of the corner of my eye, I could see that Elizabeth was listening, although she was looking down at the floor.

"Then I found out he was here, in Mayville Heights," Wren continued. "I couldn't believe it, but I saw him crossing the street and it just seemed like a sign, you know?"

I nodded. "Why did you wait a day and a half to go see him?"

She folded one arm across her middle as though she were hugging herself. "I didn't," she said. "Not exactly. I went to the St. James—that's where he was staying—the first night Mike got here. I don't know what I planned to do. I was just so angry. I watched him in the bar and I realized that hurting him wasn't going to make anything different. So I just left."

"But you couldn't let the chance to talk to him go by," I said.

Wren nodded. "I thought about it all the next day. I couldn't let him just go without telling him what he did to me, to my family, either. I waited for everyone to leave Wednesday night and then I confronted him."

Her face tightened in anger. "He didn't recognize

me, and when I told him who I was and why I was there, he tried to . . . to make excuses." She was breathing hard. "I was so . . . so angry."

The hand still resting in her lap was squeezed so tightly into a fist, I thought the skin pulled white over her knuckles would split open. "There was . . . a metal table just inside the tent. I think he was using it for a desk, and I kicked it or maybe I shoved it. I don't know. He had this leather briefcase on top, and when I hit the table it fell off. When Mike went to grab it, the table knocked him off balance."

She stopped to swallow and get her breath. "He went backward and he hit his head—on the ground, I think. I . . . I . . . waited for him to move . . . to get up, but he didn't and . . . and I just ran." She brushed another tear away. "I killed him. It was an accident, but I killed him just the same. I panicked. I used a rock to put a nail in my tire so it would go flat. I drove up onto the highway because I knew there was a good chance Liam would drive by and see me."

"You didn't kill Mike, Wren," I said. She turned her head. I leaned sideways so she had to look at me again and put a hand over hers. "I swear you didn't kill him. He didn't die from a head injury. He was suffocated with one of the backdrops for the booths. Whatever you were going to do . . . don't. Please, please, please don't." I swallowed, but I couldn't seem to get the lump in my throat to move.

Marcus was standing quietly off to the side. I'd seen him come in a couple of minutes before, and now I turned to look at him. "Could you please tell her?" I said.

His shoulders were rigid and his expression unreadable. For a moment I wasn't sure he was going to answer my question. Then he gave an almost imperceptible nod. "Mike Glazer didn't die from a head injury," he said.

22

Elizabeth pushed her way around the table and wrapped Wren in a hug. Wren looked stunned. She was crying and shaking at the same time.

"Ms. Magnusson, I do need to hear the whole story," Marcus said. "Officially." He looked at me.

Harry stepped forward. "We'll come over to the police station," he said. "Soon as I line up a lawyer. You understand, Detective. No offense."

Marcus nodded. "Of course."

"Thank you, Kathleen," Harry said quietly as he moved past me. He put one hand on Elizabeth's back and steered both young women over to another table.

"I'll need to talk to you too," Marcus said to Liam, "but that can wait until morning."

"I'll be there," Liam said. He looked at me. "She really was going to . . . hurt herself, wasn't she?"

I nodded. "She told you, didn't she? That Mike had been partly responsible for what happened to his brother? It's what you were arguing about the night he died."

He swallowed before he answered. "Yes."

"You were afraid she might be a suspect. That's why you lied about what time you'd found her with the flat tire."

"I knew it would hurt a lot of people if the truth came out," Liam said, swiping a hand over his chin. "Especially Wren. I was friends with her brother. I've known her since she was a little kid." He looked over to where Wren was sitting with Elizabeth's arm still around her shoulders. "I had no idea she would . . ." He shook his head and looked at me again. "Thank you, Kathleen."

Maggie gave me a hug. "You done for the night?" she whispered.

"I'm not sure," I said softly.

"Call me if you need me," she said before letting go. She touched Liam's arm. "Let's get something to go." They started for the counter and Claire met them partway.

I'd been watching Marcus out of the corner of my eye, but now I turned and looked at him directly. "Thank you," I said.

He stared at me for a long moment. "We need to talk, later," he said.

I could tell by the cool tone to his voice and the rigid way he was standing that he was angry. But I knew once he understood that Wren really had been planning to kill herself, he'd also understand why I hadn't waited for him to call me back.

"I know," I said. "I'll be home."

He nodded and left.

Eric came around the counter and walked over to me. He had a take-out cup in one hand and a paper bag in the other. He held them out to me.

"What's this?" I asked.

"Coffee and cinnamon rolls," he said. "On the house."

"Thank you," I said. "I'm sorry about all this."

Eric smiled. "I figure you had a good reason." He inclined his head toward the street. "Everything okay between you and the detective?"

"I think so," I said.

Eric glanced over his shoulder. "I have to get back to work," he said.

I held up the coffee. "Thanks again."

Eric nodded and walked back to the counter. I headed for the truck.

Hercules was waiting in the porch. The moment I opened the door, he meowed. "It's all right," I told him. I set the coffee and cinnamon rolls next to him on the bench and scooped him into a hug. I had a kind of giddy, unsettled energy. "Wren's going to be just fine."

He licked my chin and then squirmed to be set down so he could investigate the bag. "Cinnamon rolls," I said, waggling my eyebrows. There was a loud meow from the other side of the porch door. I reached over and opened it, and Owen came in. He looked from me to his brother and licked his whiskers.

"How did you know?" I asked.

His nose twitched.

"You did not smell cinnamon rolls from out in the yard," I told him. I grabbed the bag off the bench before Hercules managed to poke a hole in it with his paw.

Once I was settled at the table with the cats at my feet, I brought them up-to-date on what had happened with Wren and Mike Glazer the night he died.

"She gave the table a shove." I mimed the motion. "Mike tried to grab his briefcase and he was off balance when the table hit him. He went backward and was knocked out for a minute. He was probably still groggy when whoever killed him showed up."

Owen's head snapped up as though he'd had the same realization I'd just had.

"Where did the briefcase go?" I said. I pictured the inside of the tent, working my way around it in my head. There had been no leather briefcase on the grass, no briefcase on the table. I looked at Owen. "Did you see it?" His golden eyes met mine and he gave a sharp meow.

No.

"The killer must have taken it," I said. "But why?"

Owen didn't have an answer for that question. But it seemed Hercules did. He jumped onto the chair opposite me and poked at my laptop with one paw.

I remembered that I hadn't read Lise's e-mail, so I pulled the computer closer and turned it on. "Chairs are for people," I said to Hercules.

He gave me a blank look. Both cats thought they were people.

"People with two legs," I added. "And you're sitting on my sweater."

He jumped down, making complaining noises low in his throat. Then he launched himself onto my lap, a glint of triumph in his eyes.

There was an e-mail from my sister, Sara, in my in-box too, but I opened Lise's message first. She'd found out quite a lot in just a couple of days.

According to Lise's information, Alex and Chris Scott wouldn't have been able to push Mike out of the business that easily. He apparently had a deal that entitled him to major compensation if they let him go before the fourth full year of his contract—more than a million dollars.

"People have killed for less," I said to Hercules. "And that would explain why Mike's briefcase disappeared." It also explained the way Mike Glazer had been killed. Holding something over someone's face until they stopped breathing would take strength—it would also take a lot of anger.

"Both Scott brothers were at that fund-raising dinner in Minneapolis," I said to Herc. "And yes, it is a very nice coincidence that they happened to be just an hour away when their partner was killed. But how could they be there and here at the same time?"

Hercules touched the screen with his paw as though he were pointing to Sara's e-mail.

"Okay, I'll read Sara's e-mail," I said. "I don't have any other ideas."

Sara had sent some of the photos from the video shoot. My favorite image was the guys looking like clean-cut members of a boy band in white shirts with the sleeves pushed back, vests, loosened skinny ties and not a sign of piercings, tattoos or even stubble. The shot of them in their ruffled pirate shirts was pretty funny, too. I remembered what she'd said about seeing way more of the guys than she'd ever wanted to: *Best way to cover up all their ink was to airbrush. It did a great job, but none of those guys were on my list of men I wanted to see without their shirts.*

Hercules cocked his head to one side. His whiskers twitched as though he were waiting for me to make the connection. And just like that, I figured it out.

I closed my e-mail and used a search engine to bring up all the photos I could find from the dinner in Minneapolis. I checked each one carefully. It wasn't what I was seeing on the screen that told me who had killed Mike Glazer; it was what I wasn't seeing.

There were no images of Alex and Christopher Scott together. In the dozens and dozens of pictures from that night, not once had the brothers been photographed together. Because both of them hadn't been there.

It was a pretty outrageous plan, Christopher covering up his tattoo and pretending to be Alex for part of the evening. On the other hand, they were identical twins and it couldn't have been the first time they had impersonated each other.

"They planned it," I said to Hercules. I thought about the frosting spatula belonging to Georgia Tepper that had been shoved down into the dirt by the edge of the tent. "Do you think that making it look like Georgia was involved somehow was part of the plan too?"

He narrowed his eyes and considered the question. Marcus had said the company Georgia's former father-in-law worked for was a longtime client of Legacy Tours. Had Alex Scott recognized Georgia and figured she'd be a good person to frame? My stomach turned over at the thought.

"Maggie said that Liam and Alex were going to do a walk-through of the tents before tomorrow's tasting and art show," I said. "What if he's going to plant some other piece of so-called evidence to implicate Georgia?"

Owen meowed loudly. He was already on his way to the living room.

I stood up and set Hercules down. "We have to call Maggie and see if she and Liam can stall Alex until I can get in touch with Marcus."

I called Marcus's cell phone first, hoping I'd get him and not his voice mail, but I didn't. He must have still been talking to Wren. I left a short message and then I tried Maggie. She didn't answer at her apartment, and when I tried her cell, I got that voice mail too.

"Where is everybody?" I asked, pulling a hand back through my hair. Owen and Hercules didn't seem to have any more idea than I did.

I couldn't stop thinking about Georgia, saying maybe it was time for her and her little girl to move on. If any more "evidence" turned up, I felt certain she'd bolt. She'd leave Mayville Heights, where she had a good life, and run. She wouldn't wait to see how things worked out. I'd already seen that in her eyes.

I looked down at the two furry faces staring up at me. "Marcus would say I don't know anything," I said. "Not for sure." So why did I feel so certain? I had no real proof the Scott brothers had killed Mike. I had no proof that Georgia would go on the run again. Still, I knew I was right. I was as certain about my instincts as Marcus always was about his facts.

"Marcus said being a police officer is part of who he is," I said to the boys. "This is who I am. He'll understand that."

I got up, grabbed my purse and my keys and stepped into my shoes. Owen and Hercules were right behind me. They followed me out into the porch, and I decided to let them come with me. It wasn't any crazier than anything else I was about to do.

I opened the driver's-side door of the truck and lifted Hercules onto the seat. Owen jumped up on his own. I got in, started the engine and looked over at them sitting quietly beside me with what seemed to me to be a fierce look of determination on both of their furry faces. I was about to confront a potential murderer with just a couple of small cats for backup.

I looked at the house through the windshield. I could have gone back inside and waited for Marcus to call me. I could have gone down to the police station and waited for him.

But I didn't.

23

Maggie's bug was angled nose-in at the curb along the boardwalk, in front of the two tents. There was no sign of her or Liam. Or Alex Scott.

"Stay here," I told the cats. I got out of the truck, locked the door and headed for the nearest tent, where I could see lights inside.

Larry Taylor had finished rigging the lighting, so the inside of the tent was as bright as day. The booths were all in place, following an S-shaped curve. Maggie was about a quarter of the way down the line, just past Sweet Things, which was Georgia's booth. Alex Scott was with her. There was no sign of Liam. This wasn't how I'd wanted things to go.

Maggie smiled when she saw me. "Hi," she said. "What are you doing here?"

I shrugged, hoping I didn't look as anxious as I felt. "I knew there was a lot to get done tonight. I just came to see if you needed any help."

"Thanks," she said. "You've met Alex, haven't you?"

"A couple of times, but not officially," I said. I walked over to them and held out my hand. "Hi, Alex. I'm Kathleen Paulson," I said.

"It's nice to see you again," he said. He was wearing jeans, a dove gray shirt and a dark blue jacket. He turned to Maggie. "Kathleen gave me directions at the library and she suggested the little café down the street." His gaze moved back to me and he gave me a practiced smile. "The food was excellent, by the way. Thank you."

He was handsome and charming, but I knew that was just the outside man. If you peeled off the manners and the expensive clothes, underneath there was something dark and slimy.

"You're welcome," I said. I glanced around the tent. "Where's Liam?"

"There was something Marcus needed him to take care of," Maggie said. "It couldn't wait, so I offered to meet Alex and show him around."

Maybe I was wrong. Maybe Alex wasn't going to plant something to throw suspicion on Georgia. Or maybe he hadn't had a chance with Maggie right beside him. Maybe I could walk around with the two of them and everything would be fine.

I took a few steps backward and gestured at the Sweet Things booth. "Maggie, who did the sign for Sweet Things?" I asked. "It's wonderful."

It actually was. The artist had created a stylized line drawing of a cupcake with a cherry on top, the bottom edge of the cupcake turning into the words "Sweet Things," written in pink script.

"Ruby did that," Maggie said. "She did the signs we're going to use outside and over at the art show too."

"Ruby is the artist with the rainbow-sherbet-colored hair, isn't she?" Alex asked. When he smiled, I noticed it didn't go as far as his eyes.

"That's right," Mags said. The smile she gave Alex was much warmer. "Guess what? Alex is going to take four dozen of Georgia's cupcakes with him for a meeting tomorrow morning in Minneapolis."

"That's wonderful," I said.

I moved closer to the front of the kiosk, eyeing the pale varnished wood and the area around it while I pretended to look at Ruby's work. *You're just being paranoid*, I told myself. Then I saw it: a tiny corner of cream-colored paper. It looked as though a business card had been slipped in between a side support and the flat front counter of the booth.

I swallowed, hoping no reaction showed on my face. All I had to do was keep an eye on the booth and wait to hear from Marcus.

Maggie came to stand beside me. She pointed up at the sign. "See how Ruby has the letters coming out of the line of the cupcake? For outside, she did an outline of Wild Rose Bluff, which turns into the words 'A Taste of Mayville Heights,' and then into a wild rose."

"I can't wait to see it," I said.

I was about to suggest that she finish showing Alex around when suddenly she frowned and leaned forward. "Wait a second. What's that?" She was pointing at that little corner of card stock. "I thought Burtis said all the booths had been cleaned."

As an artist, Maggie was incredibly observant. This time I wished she hadn't been.

"I think it's just a bit of cardboard," I said. "Burtis probably had cardboard and plastic around all of these booths to keep them from getting banged up when they're not being used."

Before I could say anything else, she leaned over, caught the edge of the card with a nail—it was a business card—and pulled it free. She looked at me, giving her head a little shake. "How the heck did that get there?" she said. She studied the heavy off-white card stock. "I wonder who Victor Wyler is."

Alex shrugged. "Probably the last person who rented the tent and the booths." He looked around. "Maggie, I think everything is fine. I appreciate you coming to let me look things over, but you have a lot to do. I'm just going to go. Tell Liam I'll see him tomorrow."

"Are you sure?" Maggie asked.

He nodded. "It looks fantastic. I need to head back to Minneapolis anyway. I have that meeting in the morning. I should be here before lunch tomorrow, though."

He'd ordered four dozen of Georgia's cupcakes to take to that meeting. Was he going to plant something at her house, too? I couldn't take the chance.

"Victor Wyler is Georgia's father-in-law," I said. "Former father-in-law, actually."

Maggie looked from the card to me. "He is?"

"She probably just dropped it, then," Alex said, pulling his keys from the pocket of his jacket.

In a moment, he was going to be past me and I wouldn't be able to stop him from leaving. I pressed my hand against my leg, hoping he wouldn't see the tiny tremble in my fingers.

"She didn't drop it," I said. "You put it there."

"Sorry," he said. "I don't know anyone by the name of—what was it? Wyler?" He didn't seem the least bit uncomfortable. He gave Maggie that polite, practiced smile. "I'll see you tomorrow."

I didn't want to do the big melodramatic moment, like we were playing a game of Clue—the killer was Mr. Scott in the tent with the curtain—but I couldn't think of any other way to keep him from going. And suddenly it seemed like a very bad idea to let him leave.

"Did you plan on killing Mike from the beginning?" I asked. "Or were you hoping somehow that you could convince him to just go away quietly?"

"Excuse me?" Alex said. He had just the right amount of incredulous anger in his expression.

Maggie's eyes shifted between the two of us. "Kathleen, what's going on?" she asked. I noticed she had carefully slipped the business card into the pocket of her jeans.

I took a step close to Alex, effectively blocking his way. I wondered if he could hear my heart pounding in my chest. "Mike was ruining your business, wasn't he? Oh, you were making money, but not in the way you wanted to."

"My business isn't any of your business," he said.

"I wondered why on earth you'd ever agreed to that

juicy contract in the first place," I said. "But you had to, didn't you? That's the problem when you make a deal with the devil. He gets to dictate the terms."

He switched his keys from one hand to the other. "I don't mean to offend you, Ms. Paulson," he said. "But I think you need some professional help."

"Your brother wrote the bar exam for you."

His hand tightened around the ring of keys. If I hadn't been watching for the movement, I would have missed it.

He gave me a cool smile. "Clearly, research is one of your strengths. You obviously know I didn't pass the bar on my first try—or my second—but I did pass eventually. Myself."

I kept going as though he hadn't spoken. "I don't know how Mike figured it out, or what he had for proof, but you paid him off and you thought that would be the end of things. And then Mike needed a job. He blackmailed you." I wrapped my hand around the cell phone in my pocket, wishing Marcus would call, or even better, show up.

"Mike Glazer was my friend as well as my partner," Alex said. "And there was nothing to blackmail me about. I'm offended that you'd even suggest he'd do something like that." His voice was just a little bit less controlled.

Maggie touched my arm. "Are you serious?" she said. "You think he killed Mike?"

"He did kill Mike," I said. I didn't look at her. I kept my eyes on Alex. "I'm guessing you didn't set out to make Georgia Tepper the fall guy," I continued. "I think that was just a happy little coincidence of Georgia being in the wrong place at the wrong time."

He shook his head and moved to push past me. I stepped in front of him. "Somewhere there's going to be a receipt for that airbrush makeup kit you bought," I said with a confidence I didn't feel. "The police are going to figure out that there isn't a single photo of you and your brother together at that benefit. And they will find Mike Glazer's briefcase. They might have to search every garbage can and Dumpster between Mayville Heights and Minneapolis, but they will find it."

Just like that, the charming businessman was gone, his face all tight, angry lines. He grabbed my upper arm, fingers digging painfully into the skin. "Stop talking!" he said in a rough-edged voice.

Maggie sucked in a breath.

I swallowed and bit the inside of my cheek so I wouldn't give away how much he was hurting me. "What did he do?" I asked, working to keep any shakiness out of my voice. "I know you didn't plan to hurt him."

"I didn't," he said. He swiped his free hand over the back of his neck. The veneer of the polished businessman had all peeled away.

"What happened?"

"He had some kind of crisis of conscience." He exhaled loudly. "He said he wanted to be a man of integrity." Alex laughed, and the sound was harsh against the soft wall of the tent. "He didn't know a damn thing about integrity."

So something Wren had said to Mike had gotten

through to him. I didn't say that, though. "So tell that to the police," I said. "Everyone in town knows the kind of person Mike Glazer was."

"I don't think so," he said. He pulled on my arm, twisting it up behind my back at an unnatural angle.

I clenched my teeth. It felt as though my shoulder were going to come right out of its socket. Out of the corner of my eye, I saw a blur of black-and-white fur as a yowling Hercules seemed to come from nowhere to land in a crouch on the counter of the Sweet Things booth. His fur was on end and his ears were flat against his head.

Alex swore. "Where the hell did that thing come from?" he said. The cat was enough of a distraction that I managed to wrench my arm free.

He raised his hand and a voice behind us said, "Don't do that, Mr. Scott."

Marcus.

Alex hesitated, and without warning, Maggie's hand shot out and locked on to his arm at the elbow. She smiled, but there was no warmth in her expression. "It would be a good idea to listen to Detective Gordon," she said. "I could break your arm if I have to. I don't want to, but I can." Hercules shook himself and straightened up, watching Maggie intently.

Marcus walked over to us. "You can let go," he said to Mags.

She nodded and released Alex's arm, wiping her hand on her jeans.

Marcus looked at me. "You all right?" he asked.

I nodded. "He killed Mike Glazer," I said.

Marcus nodded. "I know."

He knew? How did he know?

After that, things seemed to happen in a blur of activity. Alex Scott was taken away in a police car, more police officers arrived and we were herded out onto the walkway.

"Are you all right?" Maggie asked. She touched my shoulder and I winced. "Okay, obviously you're not."

"No, I'm all right," I said. I had my good arm wrapped around Hercules. It had gotten colder now that the sun was down, but holding the little black-and-white cat was like having a portable heater. Maggie was already pulling out her cell phone. "What are you doing?" I said.

"Calling Roma." She shrugged. "I know you won't go to the emergency room, and since you're stubborn as a mule, it seems appropriate to get her to take a look at that shoulder."

I made a face at her, and she gave me a smile as she put the phone to her ear and took a couple of steps away from me. Roma had first aid training, so it wasn't really that outlandish an idea to call her.

Hercules put a paw gently on my shoulder. "I'm okay," I said. He narrowed his eyes at me. "I am, really."

I stroked his fur with one finger. "You were supposed to stay in the truck." He looked all around as though he had suddenly lost the ability to hear me. I bent down and kissed the top of his furry head. "Thank you," I whispered.

Maggie closed her phone and walked back to me.

"Roma is going to meet us at your house in a little while." She gestured at Hercules. "How did he end up here?"

"They like to ride in the truck. I didn't see him jump out when I got out." She frowned, but I figured it was more believable than "He walked through the closed truck door because that happens to be his superpower."

Maggie looked over at the tent. "Why did Alex kill Mike?"

"He couldn't pass the bar exam. Christopher, on the other hand, aced it the first time. They were identical twins. I think eventually they came up with the idea that Christopher would take Alex's place."

"And somehow Mike found out."

I nodded. "It looks that way." Herc twisted in my arm so he could look over my shoulder.

"And he was blackmailing them."

"And taking kickbacks from some of the businesses they dealt with."

"Do you think Mike did have a change of heart?"

"I do. I think Wren's words got to him."

Maggie pushed a stray curl off her forehead. She glanced over at the sidewalk. Liam was there, talking to a police officer. She pointed in his direction. "I'm just going to go talk to Liam for a minute, and then I'm going to find Marcus and see if we can leave."

"Okay," I said. She headed for the sidewalk, and at the same time Marcus came out of the tent. He stared at me for a long moment and then walked across the grass to me.

"Is your shoulder all right?" he asked.

"I think so," I said.

"Someone should take a look at it."

"Maggie's already taken care of that."

"Everything that happened at Eric's wasn't enough for you?" he said.

I realized then how very angry he was. "I tried to call you," I said. "I did call you. You were talking to Wren and then Liam." I stopped and looked away for a moment. "When Maggie said that Alex wanted to do a walk-through of the setup tonight, I figured there was a pretty good chance he was going to plant something to make it look like Georgia had killed Mike. She's been running and hiding for the past three years, trying to stay away from her ex-in-laws. I was afraid she'd bolt again—or even worse, that they'd find her and start harassing her again. What did you want me to do?"

I'd expected him to say "Nothing," but instead he just looked at me. "Trust me," he said.

"I do trust you."

He looked past me, over my shoulder. I waited, and his eyes came back to my face. "No, you don't, Kathleen." He gestured at Hercules. "I almost think you trust those cats more than you trust me." He held up a finger before I could speak. "Did you think you were the only one who was suspicious of Alex Scott and his brother? I was working a lot of the same information, and in time, I probably would have gotten to the same place. But I have to play by the rules."

He stared up at the darkening sky for a moment. "The award that Alex got the night of that fund-raising dinner? The only fingerprints that were on it were Christopher's."

"I'm sorry," I whispered. I could barely get the words out, and my heart was pounding in the hollow at the base of my throat.

Marcus looked down at me. "Twice, twice tonight you went rushing in to fix things because you thought I was too incompetent to do my job."

Suddenly there was a lump in my throat and the burn of unshed tears in my eyes. "I don't think you're incompetent," I whispered. "I just . . . It was complicated."

His lips were pulled into a tight line. "Just once, Kathleen, just once it would be nice if you had a little faith in me."

Maggie was on her way back to us. "You can go," Marcus said. He didn't look at me, and his voice was as cold as winter ice in the lake. He turned and walked away, and I felt the tears start to slide down my face.

24

Maggie moved her car into her parking spot behind River Arts and drove my truck home. She didn't ask what had happened between Marcus and me; she just squeezed my hand, pulled a Kleenex out of her pocket and handed it to me.

Owen sat in the middle of the truck's bench seat, sending me concerned looks every few minutes. Hercules sat on my lap, his head against my chest in sympathy.

Maggie waylaid Roma in the driveway, and she must have told her something had happened with Marcus, because Roma kept her questions solely about my shoulder. "I'm sorry, Kathleen," she said. "That needs to be seen by a real doctor." I was too upset to argue.

The two of them drove me to the ER, which was miraculously quiet for a Sunday night. The doctor who examined my shoulder decided I probably had some strained tendons and ligaments. He put my arm in a sling, gave me some painkillers and told me to ice and rest the arm.

"Why don't I stay with you?" Maggie said when Roma pulled into the driveway.

I forced myself to give her a small smile. "I appreciate that, but if you really want to do something for me, go help Liam let everyone know what's happened. And would you call Abigail and get her to check on Georgia? Please? That would make me feel better."

She and Roma exchanged looks.

"I'm all right, really," I said. "I'm just going to take a couple of these pills and go to bed."

"Okay," Maggie said.

"If you need anything, you call me," Roma warned.

"I will," I said.

Maggie walked me to the back door and gave me a hug. "He won't stay mad forever," she whispered.

I let myself into the kitchen. Both cats were waiting. I kicked off my shoes and knelt beside them. Owen immediately began sniffing the sling. Hercules climbed up on my lap and licked my chin. I wasn't going to sit around on the floor, crying. I was going to fix things with Marcus. I was going to keep apologizing until he listened.

His cell phone went to voice mail. I wasn't surprised. There was no answer at his house. I heard something clatter to the floor in the kitchen. I went out to find Owen and Hercules with my truck keys between them. "You're not exactly subtle," I said, bending to pick up the key ring. "Then again, if I see him in person, maybe I can get him to listen."

Owen meowed loudly. I looked at Hercules, and after what seemed to be a moment's hesitation, he gave a soft meow as well. I knew it was a bad idea to be driving one-handed, but I was past caring.

The cats followed me out to the truck, and there didn't seem to be any reason not to let them come. This time Owen looked out the passenger window while Herc sat beside me and stared out the windshield.

Marcus wasn't down by the tents. He wasn't at the police station, either. We drove all over the downtown, but there was no sign of him or his car. I ground my teeth together against the gnawing pain in my shoulder and drove out to his little house. It was in darkness and there was no SUV in the driveway.

I tried his cell again and his home phone. Voice mail, both times.

"He doesn't want to talk to me." Hercules leaned against my side, and Owen walked across the front seat to rub his furry cheek against my good hand. "Let's go home," I said.

I pulled into the driveway, turned off the truck and pulled the key out of the ignition. "I ruined everything with Marcus," I said. I sucked in a breath. "It's over, and maybe it never really got started."

I walked around the side of the house with the cats trailing me. I didn't see the chair until I almost fell over it. It was sitting on the path in front of the back stairs.

My rocking chair.

It wasn't in pieces anymore. It was all there, every

joint strong and tight, with a new leather back and seat. It was back together, every single piece.

The chair looked wonderful. Absolutely wonderful.

But not nearly as wonderful as the long-legged detective who was sitting on my back step.

ABOUT THE AUTHOR

Sofie Kelly is an author and mixed-media artist who lives on the East Coast with her husband and daughter. In her spare time she practices Wu-style tai chi and likes to prowl around thrift stores. And she admits to having a small crush on Matt Lauer.

CONNECT ONLINE

www.sofiekelly.com